continued ...

Midnight Alley

"A fast-paced, page-turning read packed with wonderful characters and surprising plot twists. Rachel Caine is an engaging writer; readers will be completely absorbed in this chilling story, unable to put it down until the last page. . . . For fans of vampire books, this is one that shouldn't be missed!"
—Flamingnet

"Weaves a web of dangerous temptation, dark deceit, and loving friendships. The nonstop vampire action and delightfully sweet relationships will captivate readers and leave them craving more."
—Darque Reviews

The Dead Girls' Dance

"It was hard to put this down for even the slightest break . . . forget what happens to the kid with the scar and glasses, I want to know what happens next in Morganville. If you love to read about characters with whom you can get deeply involved, Rachel Caine is so far a one hundred percent sure bet to satisfy that need. I love her Weather Warden stories, and her vampires are even better."
—The Eternal Night

"Throw in a mix of vamps and ghosts, and it can't get any better than *Dead Girls' Dance*."
—Dark Angel Reviews

Glass Houses

THE MORGANVILLE VAMPIRES NOVELS

CARPE CORPUS

THE MORGANVILLE VAMPIRES, BOOK SIX

RACHEL CAINE

nal
jam
books

NAL Jam
Published by New American Library, a division of
Penguin Group (USA) Inc., 375 Hudson Street,
New York, New York 10014, USA
Penguin Group (Canada), 90 Eglinton Avenue East, Suite 700, Toronto,
Ontario M4P 2Y3, Canada (a division of Pearson Penguin Canada Inc.)
Penguin Books Ltd., 80 Strand, London WC2R 0RL, England
Penguin Ireland, 25 St. Stephen's Green, Dublin 2,
Ireland (a division of Penguin Books Ltd.)
Penguin Group (Australia), 250 Camberwell Road, Camberwell, Victoria 3124,
Australia (a division of Pearson Australia Group Pty. Ltd.)
Penguin Books India Pvt. Ltd., 11 Community Centre, Panchsheel Park,
New Delhi - 110 017, India
Penguin Group (NZ), 67 Apollo Drive, Rosedale, North Shore 0632,
New Zealand (a division of Pearson New Zealand Ltd.)
Penguin Books (South Africa) (Pty.) Ltd., 24 Sturdee Avenue,
Rosebank, Johannesburg 2196, South Africa

Penguin Books Ltd., Registered Offices:
80 Strand, London WC2R 0RL, England

First published by NAL Jam, an imprint of New American Library,
a division of Penguin Group (USA) Inc.

First Printing, June 2009
10 9 8 7 6 5 4

ACKNOWLEDGMENTS

There were many people who helped me out with technical review, including:

Amie
Jenn Clack
Stephanie Hill
Alan Balthrop
Loa Ledbetter
CJ
Minde Briscoe
Trisha
Joann Casper
Lisa Lapkovitch
Bethany
Virginia
Sharon Sams

Also, a special note for someone I left out of the dedication for *Feast of Fools* even though I promised to put her in:

Sarah Magilnick

Sarah, I'm very sorry for leaving you out. It was completely my fault.

1

"Happy birthday, honey!"

In the glow of the seventeen candles on Claire's birthday cake, her mother looked feverishly happy, wearing the kind of forced smile that was way too common around the Danvers house these days.

It was way too common all over Morganville, Texas. People smiled because they had to, or else.

Now it was Claire's turn to suck it up and fake it.

"Thanks, Mom," she said, and stretched her lips into something that didn't really feel like a smile at all. She rose from her chair at the kitchen table to blow out the candles. All seventeen of the flames guttered and went out at her first puff. *I wish* . . .

She didn't dare wish for *anything*, and that, more than anything else, made frustration and anger and grief roll over her in a hot, sticky wave. This wasn't the birthday she'd been planning for the past six months, since she'd arrived in Morganville. She'd been counting on a party at her home, with her friends. Michael would have played his guitar, and she could almost see that lost, wonderful smile he had when he was deep in the music. Eve, cheerfully and defiantly Goth, would have baked some outrageous and probably inedible cake in the shape of a bat, with licorice icing and black candles. And Shane . . .

Shane would have . . .

Claire couldn't think about Shane, because it made

her breath lock up in her throat, made her eyes burn with tears. She missed him. No, that was wrong . . . *missed him* was too mild. She *needed* him. But Shane was locked up in a cage in the center of town, along with his father, the idiot vampire hunter.

She still couldn't quite get her head around the fact that Morganville—a normal, dusty Texas town in the middle of nowhere—was run by vampires. But she could believe *that* more easily than the idea that Frank Collins was somehow going to make it all better.

After all, she'd met the man.

Bishop—the new master vampire of Morganville—was planning something splashy in the way of executions for Frank and Shane, which apparently was the old-school standard for getting rid of humans with ideas of grandeur. Nobody had bothered to fill her in on the details, and she guessed she should be grateful for that. It would certainly be medievally awful.

The worst thing about that, for Claire, was that there seemed to be nothing she could do to stop it. *Nothing.* What was the use of being a main evil minion if you couldn't even enjoy it—or save your own friends?

Evil minion. Claire didn't like to think of herself that way, but Eve had flung it at her the last time they'd spoken.

And of course, as always, Eve was right.

A slice of birthday cake—vanilla, with vanilla frosting and little pastel sprinkles (and the exact opposite of what Eve would have baked)—landed in front of her, on her mom's second-best china. Mom had made the cake from scratch, even the frosting; she didn't believe in ready-made anything. It'd be delicious, but Claire already knew that she wouldn't care. Eve's fantasy cake would have tasted awful, left her teeth and tongue black, and Claire would have loved every bite.

Claire picked up her fork, blinked back her tears, and dug into her birthday treat. She mumbled, "Wonderful,

Mom!" around a mouthful of cake that tasted like air and sadness.

Her dad seated himself at the table and accepted a slice, too. "Happy birthday, Claire. Got any plans for the rest of the day?"

She'd had plans. All kinds of plans. She'd imagined this party a million times, and in every single version, it had ended with her and Shane alone.

Well, she was alone. So was he.

They just weren't alone *together*.

Claire swallowed and kept her gaze down on the plate. She was about to say the honest truth: *no*. She didn't have any plans. But the thought of being stuck here all day with her parents, with their frightened eyes and joyless smiles, was too much for her. "Yeah," she said. "I'm ... supposed to go to the lab. Myrnin wants me."

Myrnin was her boss—her *vampire* boss—and she hated him. She hadn't always hated him, but he'd betrayed her one time too many, and the last time had been a doozy: he'd turned her and Michael and Shane over to their worst enemy, just because it was easier for him than being loyal to them when things got tough.

She could practically hear Shane's voice, heavy on the irony: *Well, he's a vampire. What did you expect?*

Something better, she guessed. And maybe that made her an idiot, because, hey, vampire, and Myrnin had never been big on sanity anyway. She would have refused to work for him after that ... only she couldn't refuse anything Bishop ordered her to do directly. Magic. Claire didn't believe in magic—that was, as far as she was concerned, just science that hadn't been fully investigated yet—but this felt uncomfortably close to meeting the standard definition.

She didn't like to think of that moment when she became—as Eve had so clearly put it—the pawn of evil, because she was afraid, down in the sickest depths of her nightmares, that she'd made the wrong choice. As she reached for her glass of Coke, her long-sleeved shirt slipped back on her forearm to reveal what Bishop had done to her—blue ink, like some tribal biker tattoo, only this ink *moved*. Watching it slowly revolve and writhe under her skin made her sick.

No such thing as magic. No such thing.

Claire tugged her sleeve back down to hide it—not from her parents; they couldn't see anything wrong with her arm at all. It was something only she could see, and the vampires. She thought that it had gotten a little lighter since the day that Bishop had forced it on her, but maybe that was just wishful thinking. *If it fades out enough, maybe it'll stop working.* Stop forcing her to obey him when he gave her orders.

She had no way of knowing whether it was getting weaker, one way or the other, unless she was willing to risk openly defying Bishop. That was slightly less healthy than swimming in a shark tank, smeared with fish oil and wearing a big Eat Me sign.

She'd ransacked Myrnin's library, looking for any hint of what Bishop had done to her, and how to get rid of it, but if the information was there, he'd hidden it away too well for her to find. *For your own good*, he'd probably have said, but she wouldn't believe him. Not anymore. Myrnin did only what was good for him, and no one else.

At least she could define what the tattoo had done to her—it had taken away her will to say no to Mr. Bishop. *It's not magic*, she told herself for the thousandth time today. *It's not magic because there's no such thing as magic. Everything has an explanation. We just may not understand it yet, but this tattoo thing has rules and laws, and there's got to be a way to make it go away.*

Claire again tugged down the sleeve over the tattoo, and her fingers skimmed over the gold bracelet she still wore. Amelie's bracelet, with the symbol on it of the former vampire ruler of Morganville. Before Mr. Bishop had arrived, it had been a mark of Protection . . . it meant she owed Amelie taxes, usually in the form of money, services, and donated blood, and in return Amelie—and the other vampires—would play nice. It was sort of like the Mafia, with fangs. And it hadn't always worked, but it had been a lot better than walking around Morganville as a free lunch.

Now, though, the bracelet wasn't such an asset. She hadn't seen or heard from Amelie in weeks, and all of Amelie's allies seemed to be MIA. The most prominent vampires in Morganville were in hiding, or maybe even dead . . . or else they were under Bishop's control, and they had no real will of their own. Seemed like that was happening more and more as time went along. Bishop had decided it was more trouble to kill the opposition than to convert them.

Just like he'd converted her, although she was pretty much the only human he'd bothered to put directly under his thumb. He didn't have a very high opinion of people, generally.

Claire finished her cake, and then dutifully opened the birthday presents her parents brought to the table. Dad's package—wrapped by Mom, from the neat hospital corners on it—contained a nice silver necklace with a delicate little heart on it. Mom's package revealed a dress—Claire never wore dresses—in a color and cut that Claire was sure would be drastically unflattering on her smallish frame.

But she kissed them both and thanked them, promised to try the dress on later, and modeled the necklace for her dad when her mom buzzed off to the kitchen to put away the rest of the cake. She put it on over the cross necklace Shane had given her.

"Here," Dad said, trying to be helpful. "I'll get that other one off."

"No!" She slapped a hand over Shane's necklace and backed away, eyes wide, and Dad looked hurt and baffled. "Sorry. I . . . I never take this one off. It . . . was a gift."

He understood then. "Oh. From that boy?"

She nodded, and tears prickled at her eyes again, burning hot. Dad opened his arms and held her tight for a moment, then whispered, "It'll be okay, honey. Don't cry."

"No, it won't," she said miserably. "Not if we don't *make* it okay, Dad. Don't you understand that? We have to *do* something!"

He pushed her back to arm's length and studied her with tired, faded eyes. He hadn't been in good health for a while, and every time she saw him, Claire worried a little more. *Why couldn't they leave my parents out of this? Why did they drag them here, into the middle of this?*

Things had been fine before—well, maybe not fine, but stable. When she'd come to attend college at Texas Prairie University, she'd had to leave the crazy-dangerous dorm to find some kind of safety, and she'd ended up rooming at the Glass House, with Eve and Shane and Michael. Mom and Dad had remained safely far away, out of town.

Or they had, until Amelie had decided that luring them here would help control Claire better. Now they were Morganville residents. Trapped.

Just like Claire herself.

"We tried to leave, honey. I packed your mom up the other night and headed out, but our car died at the city limits." His smile looked frail and broken around the edges. "I don't think Mr. Bishop wanted us to leave."

Claire was a little bit relieved that at least they'd tried, but only for a second—then she decided that she was a lot more horrified. "*Dad!* Please don't try that again. If the vampires catch you outside the city limits—" Nobody left Morganville without permission; there were all kinds of safeguards to prevent it, but the fact that the vampires were ruthless about tracking people down was enough to deter most.

"I know." He put his warm hands on either side of her

face, and looked at her with so much love that it broke her heart. "Claire, you think you're ready to take on the world, but you're not. I don't want you in the middle of all this. You're just too *young*."

She gave him a sad smile. "It's too late for that. Besides, Dad, I'm not a kid anymore—I'm seventeen. Got the candles on the cake to prove it and everything."

He kissed her forehead. "I know. But you'll always be five years old to me, crying about a skinned knee."

"That's embarrassing."

"I felt the same way when my parents said it to me." He watched as she fiddled with Shane's cross necklace. "You're going to the lab?"

"What? Oh, yeah."

He knew she was lying, she could tell, and for a moment, she was sure he'd call her on it. But instead he said, "Please just tell me you're not going out today to try to save your boyfriend. Again."

She put her hands over his. "Dad. Don't try to tell me I'm too young. I know what I feel about Shane."

"I'm not trying to do that at all," her father said. "I'm trying to tell you that right now, being in love with *any* boy in this town is dangerous. Being in love with *that* boy is suicidal. I wouldn't be thrilled under normal circumstances, and this is isn't even close to normal."

No kidding. "I won't do anything stupid," she promised. She wasn't sure she could actually keep that particular vow, though. She'd happily do something stupid if it gave her a single moment with Shane. "Dad, I need to go. Thanks for the necklace."

He stared at her so hard that she thought for a second he'd lock her in her room or something. Not that she couldn't find a way out, of course, but she didn't want to make him feel any worse than she had to.

He finally sighed and shook his head. "You're welcome, honey. Happy birthday. Be careful."

She stood for a moment, watching him play with his

piece of birthday cake. He didn't seem hungry. He was losing weight, and he looked older than he had just a year ago. He caught her look. "Claire. I'm *fine*. Don't make that face."

"What face?"

Innocence wasn't going to work on him. "The my-dad's-sick-and-I-feel-guilty-for-leaving face."

"Oh, that one." She tried for a smile. "Sorry."

In the kitchen, her mom was buzzing around like a bee on espresso. As Claire put the plates in the sink, her mother chattered a mile a minute—about the dress, and how she just knew Claire would look perfect in it, and they really should make plans to go out to a nice restaurant this week and celebrate in style. Then she went on about her new friends at the Card Club, where they played bridge and some kind of gin rummy and sometimes, daringly, Texas Hold 'Em. She talked about everything but what was all around them.

Morganville looked like a normal town, but it wasn't. Casual travelers came and went, and never knew a thing; even most of the college students stayed strictly on campus and put in their time without learning a thing about what was *really* going on—Texas Prairie University made sure it was a world unto itself. For people who lived here, the real residents, Morganville was a prison camp, and they were all inmates, and they were all too afraid to talk about it out in the open. Claire listened with her patience stretching thin as plastic wrap, ready to rip, and finally interrupted long enough to get in a hasty, "Thanks," and, "Be back soon; love you, Mom."

Her mother stopped and squeezed her eyes shut. "Claire," she said in an entirely different tone—a genuine one. "I don't want you to go out today. I'd like you to stay home, please."

Claire paused in the doorway. "I can't, Mom," she said. "I'm not going to be a bystander in all this. If you want to be, I understand, but that's not how you raised me."

Claire's mom broke a plate. Just smashed it against

the side of the sink into a dozen sharp-edged pieces that skittered all over the counter and floor.

And then she just stood there, shoulders shaking.

"It's okay," Claire said, and quickly picked up the broken pieces from the floor, then swept the rest off the counter. "Mom—*it's okay*. I'm not afraid."

Her mom laughed. It was a brittle, hysterical little laugh, and it scared Claire down to her shoes. "You're not? Well, I am, Claire. I'm as afraid as I've ever been in my life. *Don't go.* Not today. Please stay home."

Claire stood there for a few seconds, took a deep breath, and dumped the broken china in the trash.

"I'm sorry, but I really need to do this," she said. "Mom—"

"Then go." Her mother turned back to the sink and picked up another plate, which she dipped into soapy water and began to scrub with special viciousness, as if she intended to wash the pink roses right off the china.

Claire escaped back to her room, put the dress in her closet, and grabbed up her battered backpack from the corner. As she was leaving, she caught sight of a photograph taped to her mirror. Their Glass House formal picture—Shane, Eve, herself, and Michael, caught mid-laugh. It was the only photo she had of all of them together. She was glad it was such a happy one, even if it was overexposed and a little out of focus. Stupid cell phone cameras.

On impulse, she grabbed the photo and stuck it in her backpack.

The rest of her room was like a time warp—Mom had kept all her things from high school and junior high, all her stuffed animals and posters and candy-colored diaries. Her Pokémon cards and her science kits. Her glow-in-the-dark stick-on stars and planets on the ceiling. All her certificates and medals and awards.

It felt so far away now, like it belonged to someone else. Someone who wasn't facing a shiny future as an evil minion, and trapped in Morganville forever.

Except for her parents, the photograph was really the only thing in this whole house that she'd miss if she never came back.

And that was, unexpectedly, kind of sad.

Claire stood in the doorway for a long moment, looking at her past, and then she closed the door and walked away to whatever the future held.

2

Morganville didn't look all that different now from when Claire had first come to town, and she found that really, really odd. After all, when the evil overlords took over, you'd think it would have made some kind of visible difference, at least.

But instead, life still went on—people went to work, to school, rented videos, and drank in bars. The only real difference was that nobody roamed around alone after dark. Not even the vampires, as far as she knew. The dark was Mr. Bishop's hunting time.

Even that wasn't as much of a change as you'd think, though. Sensible people in Morganville had *never* gone out after dark if they could help it. Instincts, if nothing else.

Claire checked her watch. Eleven a.m.—and she really didn't have to go to the lab. In fact, the lab was the last place she wanted to be today. She didn't want to see her supposed boss Myrnin, or hear his rambling crazy talk, or have to endure his questions about why she was so angry with him. He knew why she was angry. He wasn't *that* crazy.

Her dad had been right on the money. She intended to spend the day trying to help Shane.

First step: see the mayor of Morganville—Richard Morrell.

Claire didn't have a car, but Morganville wasn't all that big, really, and she liked walking. The weather was still good—a little cool even during the day now, but crisp instead of chilly. It was what passed for winter in west Texas, at least until the snowstorms. They'd had a few days of fall, which meant the leaves were a sickly yellow around the edges instead of dark green. She'd heard that fall was a beautiful season in other parts of the country and the world, but around here, it was more or less a half hour between blazing summer and freezing winter.

As she walked, people noticed her. She didn't like that, and she wasn't used to it; Claire had always been one of the Great Anonymous Geek Army, except when it came to a science fair or winning some kind of academic award. She'd never stood out physically—too short, too thin, too small—and it felt weird to have people focus on her and nod, or just plain stare.

Word had gotten around that she was Bishop's errand girl. He'd never made her *do* anything, really, but he made her carry his orders.

And bad things happened. Making her do it, while she was still wearing Amelie's bracelet, was Bishop's idea of a joke.

All the staring made the walk feel longer than it really was.

As she jogged up the steps to Richard's replacement office—the old one having been mostly trashed by a tornado at City Hall—she wondered if the town had appointed Richard as mayor just so they didn't have to change any of the signs. His father—the original Mayor Morrell, one of those Texas good ol' boys with a wide smile and small, hard eyes—had died during the storm, and now his son occupied a battered old storefront with a paper sign in the window that read, MAYOR RICHARD MORRELL, TEMPORARY OFFICES.

She would be willing to bet that he wasn't very happy in his new job. There was a lot of that going around.

A bell tinkled when Claire opened the door, and her eyes adjusted slowly to the dimness inside. She supposed he kept the lights low out of courtesy to vampire visitors—same reason he'd had the big glass windows in front blacked out. But it made the small, dingy room feel like a cave to her—a cave with bad wallpaper and cheap, thin carpeting.

Richard's assistant looked up and smiled as Claire shut the door. "Hey, Claire," she said. Nora Harris was a handsome lady of about fifty, neatly dressed in dark suits most of the time, and had a voice like warm chocolate butter sauce. "You here to see the mayor, honey?"

Claire nodded and looked around the room. She wasn't the only person who'd come by today; there were three older men seated in the waiting area, and one geeky-looking kid still working off his baby fat, wearing a T-shirt from Morganville High with their mascot on it—a snake, fangs exposed. He looked up at her, eyes wide, and pretty obviously scared, and she smiled slightly to calm him down. It felt weird, being the person other people were scared to see coming.

None of the adults looked at her directly, but she could feel them studying her out of the corners of their eyes.

"He's got a full house today, Claire," Nora continued, and nodded toward the waiting area. "I'll let him know you're here. We'll try to work you in."

"She can go ahead of me," one of the men said. The others looked at him, and he shrugged. "Don't hurt none to be nice."

But it wasn't being nice; Claire knew that. It was simple self-interest, sucking up to the girl who acted as Bishop's go-between to the human community. She was *important* now. She hated every minute of that.

"I won't be long," she said. He didn't meet her gaze at all.

Nora gestured her toward the closed door at the back. "I'll let him know you're coming. Mr. Golder, you'll be next as soon as she's done."

Mr. Golder, who'd given up his place for Claire, nodded

back. He was a sun-weathered man, skin like old boots, with eyes the color of dirty ice. Claire didn't know him, but he smiled at her as she passed. It looked forced.

She didn't smile back. She didn't have the heart to pretend.

Claire knocked hesitantly on the closed door as she eased it open, peeking around the edge like she was afraid to catch Richard doing something . . . well, non-mayorly. But he was just sitting behind his desk, reading a file folder full of papers.

"Claire." He closed the file and sat back in his old leather chair, which creaked and groaned. "How are you holding up?" He stood up to offer her his hand, which she shook, and then they both sat down. She'd gotten so used to seeing Richard in a neatly pressed police uniform that it still felt odd to see him in a suit—a nice pin-striped one today, in gray, with a blue tie. He wasn't that old—not even thirty, she'd guess—but he carried himself like somebody twice his age.

They had that in common, she guessed. She didn't feel seventeen these days, either.

"I'm okay," she said, which was a lie. "Hanging in there. I came to—"

"I know what you're going to ask," Richard said. "The answer's still no, Claire." He sounded sorry about it, but firm.

Claire swallowed hard. She hadn't expected to get a no right off the bat. Richard usually heard her out. "Five minutes," she said. "Please. Haven't I earned it?"

"Definitely. But it's not my call. If you want permission to see Shane, you have to go to Bishop." Richard's eyes were kind, but unyielding. "I'm doing all I can to keep him alive and safe. I want you to know that."

"I know you are, and I'm grateful. Really." Her heart sank. Somehow, she'd had her hopes up, even though she'd known it wouldn't work out, today of all days. She studied her hands in her lap. "How is he doing?"

"Shane?" Richard laughed softly. "How do you expect him to be? Pissed off. Angry at the world. Hating every minute of this, especially since he's stuck in there with nobody but his father for company."

"But you've seen him?"

"I've dropped in," Richard said. "Official duties. So far, Bishop hasn't seen fit to yank my chain and make me stop touring the cells, but if I try to get you in . . ."

"I understand." She did, but Claire still felt heartsick. "Does he ask—"

"Shane asks about you every day," Richard said very quietly. "Every single day. I think that boy might really love you. And I never thought I'd be saying that about Shane Collins."

Her fingers were trembling now, a fine vibration that made her clench them into fists to make it stop. "It's my birthday." She had no idea why she said that, but it seemed to make sense at the time. It seemed *important.* Looking up, she saw she'd surprised him with that, and he was temporarily at a loss for words.

"Offering congratulations doesn't seem too appropriate," he said. "So. You're seventeen, right? That's old enough to know when you're in over your head. Claire, just go home. Spend the day with your parents, maybe see your friends. Take care of yourself."

"No. I want to see Shane," she said.

He shook his head. "I really don't think that's a very good idea."

He meant well; she knew that. He came around the desk and put his hand on her shoulder, a kind of half hug, and guided her back out the door.

I'm not giving up. She thought it, but she didn't say it, because she knew he wouldn't approve.

"Go home," he said, and nodded to the man whose appointment Claire had taken. "Mr. Golder? Come on in. This is about your taxes, right?"

"Getting too damn expensive to live in this town," Mr. Golder growled. "I ain't got that much blood to give, you know."

Claire hoisted her backpack and went out to try something else that might get her in to see Shane.

Of course, it was something a lot more dangerous.

She tried to talk herself out of it, but in the end, Claire went to the last place she wanted to go—to Founder's Square, the vampire part of town. In broad daylight, it seemed deserted; regular people didn't venture here anymore, not even when the sun was blazing overhead, although it was a public park. There were some police patrolling on foot, and sometimes she could believe there were shapes flitting through the shadows under the trees, or in the dark spaces of the large, spacious buildings that faced the parklike square.

Those weren't people, though. Not technically.

Claire trudged down the white, smooth sidewalks, head down, feeling the sun beat on her. She watched the grimy, round tips of her red lace-up sneakers. It was almost hypnotic after a while.

She came to a stop as the tips of her shoes bumped into the first of a wide expanse of marble stairs. She looked up—and up—at the largest building on the square: big columns, lots of steps, one of those imposing Greek temple styles. This was the vampire equivalent of City Hall, and inside . . .

"Just go on already," she muttered to herself, and hitched her backpack to a more comfortable position as she climbed the steps.

Claire felt two things as the edge of the roof's shadow fell over her—relief, from getting out of the sun, and claustrophobia. Her footsteps slowed, and for a second she wanted to turn around and take Richard's advice—just go home. Stay with her parents. Be safe.

Pretend everything was normal, like her mom did.

The big, shiny wooden doors ahead of her swung open, and a vampire stood there, well out of the direct glare of sunlight, watching her with the nastiest smile she'd ever seen. Ysandre, Bishop's token sex-kitten vamp, was beautiful, and she knew it. She posed like a Victoria's Secret model, as if at any moment an unexpected photo shoot might begin.

Just now, she was wearing a skintight pair of low-rise blue jeans, a tight black crop top that showed acres of alabaster skin, and a pair of black low-heeled sandals. Skank-vamp casual day wear. She smoothed waves of shiny hair back from her face and continued to beam an evil smile from lips painted with Hooker Red #5.

"Well," she said low in her throat, sweet as grits and poisoned molasses, "look what the cat dragged in. Come on, little Claire. Y'all are letting all the dark out."

Claire had hoped that Ysandre was dead, once and for all; she'd thought that was pretty much inevitable, since the last time she'd seen her Ysandre had been in Amelie's hands, and Amelie hadn't been in a forgiving kind of mood.

But here she was, without a mark on her. Something had gone really wrong for Ysandre to still be alive, but Claire had no real way of finding out what. Ysandre might tell her, but it would probably be a lie.

Claire, lacking any other real choice, came inside. She stayed as far away from the skank as she could, careful not to meet the Vampire Stare of Doom. She wasn't sure that Ysandre had the authority to hurt her, but it didn't seem smart to take chances.

"You come to talk to Mr. Bishop?" Ysandre asked. "Or just to moon around after that wretched boy of yours?"

"Bishop," Claire said. "Not that it's any of your business, unless you're just a glorified secretary with fangs."

Ysandre hissed out a laugh as she locked the doors behind them. "Well, you're growing a pair, Bite-size. Fine, you skip off and see our lord and master. Maybe I'll see him later, too, and tell him you'd be better at your job if you didn't talk so much. Or at all."

It was hard to turn her back on Ysandre, but Claire did it. She heard the vampire's hissing chuckle, and the skin on the back of her neck crawled.

There was a touch of ice there, and Claire flinched and whirled to see her trailing pale, cold fingers in the air where the back of Claire's neck had been.

"Where'd you learn to be a vampire?" Claire demanded, angry because she was scared and hating it. "The movies? Because you're one big, walking, stupid cliché, and you know what? *Not impressed.*"

They stared at each other. Ysandre's smile was wicked and awful, and Claire didn't know what to do, other than stare right back.

Ysandre finally laughed softly and melted into the shadows.

Gone.

Claire took a deep breath and went on her way—a way she knew all too well. It led down a hushed, carpeted hallway into a big, circular atrium armored in marble, with a dome overhead, and then off to the left, down another hallway.

Bishop always knew when she was coming.

He stared right at her as she entered the room. There was something really unsettling about the way he watched the door, waiting for her. As bad as his stare was, though, his smile was worse. It was full of satisfaction, and ownership.

He was holding a book open in his hand. She recognized it, and a chill went down her spine. Plain leather cover with the embossed symbol of the Founder on it. That book had nearly gotten her killed the first few weeks she'd been in Morganville, and that had been well before she'd had any idea of its power.

It was a handwritten account, written mostly in Myrnin's code, with all his alchemical methods. All the secrets of Morganville, which he'd documented for Amelie. It had details even Claire didn't know about the town. About Ada. About *everything.*

It also contained jotted-down notes for what she could think of only as magic spells, like the one that had embedded the tattoo in her arm. She had no idea what else was in it, because Myrnin himself couldn't remember, but Bishop had wanted that book very, very badly. It was the most important thing in Morganville to him—in fact, Claire suspected it was why he'd come here in the first place.

He snapped the book closed and slipped it into the inside pocket of his jacket, where a religious person might keep a copy of the Bible handy.

The room he'd taken over for his own was a big, carpeted office, with a small, fancy sofa and chairs at one end of it, and a desk at the other. Bishop never sat at the desk. He was always standing, and today was no different. Three other vampires sat in visitors' chairs—Myrnin, Michael Glass, and a vamp Claire didn't recognize . . . she wasn't even sure whether it was a man or a woman, actually. The bone structure of the pale face looked female, but the haircut wasn't, and the hands and arms looked too angular.

Claire focused on the stranger to avoid looking at Michael. Her friend—and he *was* still her friend; he couldn't help being in this situation any more than she could—wouldn't meet her eyes. He was angry and ashamed, and she wished she could help him. She wanted to tell him, *It's not your fault,* but he wouldn't believe that.

Still, it was true. Michael didn't have a magic tattoo on his arm; instead, he had Bishop's fang marks in his neck, which worked just as well for the life-challenged. She could still see the livid shadow of the scars on his pale skin.

Bishop's bite was like a brand of ownership.

"Claire," Bishop said. He didn't sound pleased. "Did I summon you for some reason I've forgotten?"

Claire's heart jumped as if he'd used a cattle prod. She willed herself not to flinch. "No, sir," she said, and kept her voice low and respectful. "I came to ask a favor."

Bishop—who was wearing a plain black suit today, with a white shirt that had seen brighter days—picked a piece of lint from his sleeve. "Then the answer is no, because I don't grant favors. Anything else?"

Claire wet her lips and tried again. "It's a small thing—I want to see Shane, sir. Just for a few—"

"I said *no*, as I have half a hundred times already," Bishop said, and she felt his anger crackle through the room. Michael and the strange vamp both looked up at her, eyes luminously threatening—Michael against his will, she was sure. Myrnin—dressed in some ratty assortment of Goodwill-reject pants and a frock coat from a costume shop, plus several layers of cheap, tacky Mardi Gras beads—just seemed bored. He yawned, showing lethally sharp fangs.

Bishop glared at her. "I am very tired of you making this request, Claire."

"Then maybe you should say yes and get it over with."

He snapped his fingers. Michael got to his feet, pulled there like a puppet on a string. His eyes were desperate, but there seemed to be nothing he could do about it. "Michael. Shane is your friend, as I recall."

"Yes."

" 'Yes, *my lord Bishop*.' "

Claire saw Michael's throat bob as he swallowed what must have been a huge chunk of anger. "Yes," he said. "My lord Bishop."

"Good. Fetch him here. Oh, and bring some kind of covering for the floor. We'll just remove this irritation once and for all."

Claire blurted out, "No!" She took a step forward, and Bishop's stare locked tight onto her, forcing her to stop. "Please! I didn't mean . . . Don't hurt him! You can't hurt him! Michael, don't! Don't do this!"

"I can't help it, Claire," he said. "You know that."

She did. Michael walked away toward the door. She could see it all happening, nightmarishly real—Michael bringing Shane back here, forcing him to his knees, and Bishop . . . Bishop . . .

"I'm sorry," Claire said, and took a deep, trembling breath. "I won't ask again. Ever. I swear."

The old man raised his thick gray eyebrows. "Exactly my point. I remove the boy, and I remove any risk that you won't keep your word to me."

"Oh, don't be so harsh, old man," Myrnin said, and rolled his eyes. "She's a teenager in love. Let the girl have her moment. It'll hurt her more, in the end. Parting is such sweet sorrow, according to the bards. I wouldn't know, myself. I never parted anyone." He mimed ripping someone in half, then got an odd expression on his face. "Well. Just the one time, really. Doesn't count."

Claire forgot to breathe. She hadn't expected Myrnin, of all of them, to speak up, even if his support had been more crazy than useful. But he'd given Bishop pause, and she kept very still, letting him think it over.

Bishop gestured, and Michael paused on his way to the door. "Wait, Michael," Bishop said. "Claire. I have a task for you to do, if you want to keep the boy alive another day."

Claire felt a trembling sickness take hold inside. This wasn't the first time, but she always assumed—had to!— that it would be the *last* time. "What kind of task?"

"Delivery." Bishop walked to the desk and flipped open a carved wooden box. Inside was a small pile of paper scrolls, all tied up with red ribbon and dribbled with wax seals. He picked one seemingly at random to give her.

"What is it?"

"You know what it is."

She did. It was a death warrant; she'd seen way too many of them. "I can't—"

"I can order you to take it. If I do, I won't feel obliged to offer you any *favors*. This is the best deal you are going to get, little Claire: Shane's life for the simple delivery of a message," Bishop said. "And if you won't do it, I will send someone else, Shane dies, and you have a most terrible day."

She swallowed. "Why give me the chance at all? It's not like you to bargain."

Bishop showed his teeth, but not his fangs—those were kept out of sight, but that didn't make him any less dangerous. "Because I want you to understand your role in Morganville, Claire. You belong to me. I could order you to do it, with a simple application of will. Instead, I am allowing you to *choose* to do it."

Claire turned the scroll in her fingers and looked down at it. There was a name on the outside of it, written in old-fashioned black calligraphy. *Detective Joe Hess.*

She looked up, startled. "You can't—"

"Think very carefully about the next thing you say," Bishop interrupted. "If it involves telling me what I can or can't do in my own town, they will be your last words, I promise you."

Claire shut her mouth. Bishop smiled.

"Better," he said. "If you choose to do so, go deliver my message. When you come back, I'll allow you to see the boy, just this once. See how well we can get along if we try?"

The scroll felt heavy in Claire's hand, even though it was just paper and wax.

She finally nodded.

"Then go," Bishop said. "Sooner started, sooner done, sooner in the arms of the one you love. There's a good girl."

Michael was looking at her. She didn't dare meet his eyes; she was afraid that she'd see anger there, and betrayal, and disappointment. It was one thing to be forced to be the devil's foot soldier.

It was another thing to choose to do it.

Claire walked quickly out of the room.

By the time she hit the marble steps and the warm sun, she was running.

3

Detective Joe Hess.

Claire turned the scroll over and over in sweaty fingers as she walked, wondering what would happen if she just tossed it down a storm drain. Well, obviously, Bishop would be *pissed*. And probably homicidal, not that he wasn't mostly that all the time. Besides, what she was carrying might not be anything bad. Right? Maybe it just *looked* like a death warrant. Maybe it was a decree that Friday was ice cream day or something.

A car cruised past her, and she sensed the driver staring at her, then speeding up. *Nothing to see here but a sad, stupid evil pawn*, she thought bitterly. *Move along.*

The police station was in City Hall as well, and the entire building was being renovated, with work crews ripping out twisted metal and breaking down stone to put in new braces and bricks. The side that held the jail and the police headquarters area hadn't been much damaged, and Claire headed for the big, high counter that was manned by the desk sergeant.

"Detective Joe Hess," she said. "Please."

The policeman barely glanced up at her. "Sign in; state your name and business."

She reached for the clipboard and pen and carefully wrote her name. "Claire Danvers. I have a delivery from Mr. Bishop."

There were other things going on in the main reception area—a couple of drunks handcuffed to a huge wooden bench, some lawyers getting a cup of coffee from a big silver pot near the back.

Everything stopped. Even the drunks.

The desk sergeant looked up, and she saw a weary anger in his eyes before he put on a blank, hard expression. "Have a seat," he said. "I'll see if he's here."

He turned away and picked up a phone. Claire didn't watch him make the call. She was too lost in her own misery. She stared down at the writing on the scroll and wished she knew what was inside—but then, it might make it worse if she did know. *I'm only a messenger.*

Yeah, that was going to make her sleep nights.

The desk sergeant spoke quietly and hung up, but he didn't come back to the counter. Avoiding her, she assumed; she was getting used to that. The good people avoided her, the bad people sucked up to her. It was depressing.

Her tattoo itched. She rubbed the cloth of her shirt over it, and watched the reinforced door that led into the rest of the police station.

Detective Hess came out just about a minute later. He was smiling when he saw her, and that hurt. Badly. He'd been one of the first adults to really be helpful to her in Morganville—he and his partner, Detective Lowe, had gone out of their way for her not just once, but several times. And now she was doing *this* to him.

She felt sick as she rose to her feet.

"Claire. Always a pleasure," he said, and it sounded like he actually meant it. "This way."

The desk sergeant held out a badge as she passed. She clipped it on her shirt and followed Joe Hess into a big, plain open area. His desk was near the back of the room, next to a matching one that had his partner's nameplate on the edge. Nothing fancy. Nobody had a lot of personal stuff on their desks. She supposed that maybe it wasn't a good idea to have breakables, if you interviewed angry people all day.

She settled into a chair next to his desk, and he took a seat, leaned forward, and rested his elbows on his knees. He had a kind face, and he wasn't trying to intimidate her. In fact, she had the impression he was trying to make it easy on her.

"How are you holding up?" he asked her, which was the same thing Richard Morrell had said. She wondered if she looked that damaged. Probably.

Claire swallowed and looked down at her hands, and the scroll held in her right one. She slowly stretched it out toward him. "I'm sorry," she said. "Sir, I'm . . . so sorry." She wanted to explain to him, but there really didn't seem to be much to excuse it at the moment. She was here. She was doing what Bishop wanted her to do.

This time, she'd chosen to do it.

No excuse for that.

"Don't blame yourself," Detective Hess said, and plucked the scroll from her fingers. "Claire, none of this is your fault. You understand that, right? You're not to blame for Bishop, or anything else that's screwed up around here. You did your best."

"Wasn't good enough, was it?"

He watched her for another long second, then shook his head and snapped the seals on the scroll. "If anybody failed, it was Amelie," he said. "We just have to figure out how to survive now. We're in uncharted territory."

He unrolled the scroll. His hands were steady and his expression carefully still. He didn't want to scare her, she realized. He didn't want her to feel guilty.

Detective Hess read the contents of the paper, then let it roll up again into a loose curl. He set it on his desk, on top of a leaning tower of file folders.

She had to ask. "What is it?"

"Nothing you need to worry about," he said, which couldn't have been true. "You did your job, Claire. Go on, now. And promise me . . ." He hesitated, then sat back in his chair and opened a file folder so he could look busy. "Promise me you won't do anything stupid."

She couldn't promise that. She had the feeling she'd already been stupid three or four times since breakfast.

But she nodded, because it was really all she could do for him.

He gave her a distracted smile. "Sorry. Busy around here," he said. That was a lie; there was almost nobody in the room. He tapped a pencil on the open file. "I've got court this morning. You go on now. I'll see you soon."

"Joe—"

"Go, Claire. Thank you."

He was going to protect her; she could see that. Protect her from the consequences of what she'd done.

She couldn't think how she would ever really pay him back for that.

As she walked out, she felt him watching her, but when she glanced back, he was concentrating on his folder again.

"Hey, Claire? Happy birthday."

She *would not* cry.

"Thanks," she whispered, and choked on the word as she opened the door and escaped from whatever awful thing she'd just brought to his desk.

It was nearly one o'clock when she made it back to Bishop's office—not so much because it was a long trip as because she had to stop, sit, and cry out her distress in private, then make sure she'd scrubbed away any traces before she headed back. Ysandre would be all over it if she didn't.

And Bishop.

Claire thought she did a good job of looking calm as Ysandre waved her back to the office. Bishop was just where he'd been, although the third vampire, the stranger, was gone.

Michael was still there.

Myrnin was trying to build an elaborate abstract structure out of paper clips and binder clips, which was one of his less crazy ways to pass the time.

"The prodigal child returns," Bishop said. "And how did Detective Hess take the news?"

"Fine." Claire wasn't going to give him anything, but even that seemed to amuse him. He leaned on the corner of his desk and crossed his arms, staring at her with a faint, weird smile.

"He didn't tell you, did he?"

"I didn't ask."

"What a civilized place Morganville is." Bishop made that into an insult. "Very well, you've done your duty. I suppose I'll have to keep my half of the bargain." He glanced at Myrnin. "She's your pet. Clean up after her."

Myrnin gave Bishop a lazy salute. "As my master commands." He stood with that unconscious vampire grace that made Claire feel heavy, stupid, and slow, and his bright black eyes locked with hers for a long moment. If he was trying to tell her something, she had no idea what it was. "Out, girl. Master Bishop has important work to do here."

What? she wondered. *Working on his evil laugh? Interviewing backup minions?*

Myrnin crossed the room and closed ice-cold fingers around her arm. She pulled in a breath for a gasp, but he didn't give her time to react; she was yanked along with him down the hall, moving at a stumbling run.

She looked back at Michael mutely, but he couldn't help her. He was just as trapped as she was.

Myrnin stopped only when there were two closed doors, and about a mile of hallway, between them and Mr. Bishop.

"Let go of me!" Claire spat, and tried to yank free. Myrnin looked down at her arm, where his pale fingers were still wrapped around it, and raised his eyebrows as if he couldn't quite figure out what his hand was doing. Claire yanked again. "Myrnin, *let go*!"

He did, and stepped back. She thought he looked disappointed for a flicker of a second, and then his loony smile was firmly in place. "Will you be a good little girl, then?" She glared at him. "Ah. Probably not. All right, then, on your head be it, Claire, and let's do our best to keep your head attached to the rest of you. Come. I'll take you to your boy, since evidently our mutual benefactor is in a giving sort of mood."

He turned, and the skirts of his frock coat flared. He was wearing flip-flops again, and his feet were dirty, though he didn't smell too bad in general. The layers of cheap metallic beads clicked and rattled as he walked, and the slap of his shoes made him just about the noisiest vampire Claire had ever heard.

"Are you taking your medicine?" she asked. Myrnin sent her a glance over his shoulder, and once again, she didn't know what that look meant at all. "Is that a no?"

"I thought you hated me," he said. "If you do, you shouldn't really care, should you?"

He had a point. Claire shut up and hurried along as he walked down a long, curved hallway to a big wooden door. There was a vampire guard on the door, a man who'd probably been Asian in his regular life, but was now the color of old ivory. He wore his hair long, braided in the back, and he wasn't much taller than Claire.

Myrnin exchanged some Chinese-sounding words with the other vampire—who, like Michael, sported Bishop's fang marks in his neck—and the vampire unlocked the door and swung it open.

This was as far as Claire had ever been able to get before. She felt a wave of heat race through her, and then she shivered. Now that she was here, actually walking through the door, she felt faintly sick with anticipation. *If they've hurt him* . . . And it had been so long. What if he didn't even want to see her at all?

Another locked door, another guard, and then they were inside a plain stone hallway with barred cells on the left side. No windows. No light except for blazing fluorescent fixtures far overhead. The first cell was empty. The second held two humans, but neither one was Shane.

Claire tried not to look too closely. She was afraid she might know them.

The third cell had two small cots, one on each side of the tiny room, and a toilet and sink in the middle. Nothing else. It was almost painfully neat. There was an old man with straggly gray hair asleep on one of the beds, and it took Claire a few seconds to realize that he was Frank Collins, Shane's dad. She was used to seeing him awake, and it surprised her to see him so ... fragile. So helpless and old.

Shane was sitting cross-legged on the other bed. He looked up from the book he was reading, and jerked his head to get the hair out of his eyes. The guarded, closed look on his face reminded Claire of his father, but it shattered when Shane saw her.

He dropped the book, surged to his feet, and was at the bars in about one second flat. His hands curled around the iron, and his eyes glittered wildly until he squeezed them shut.

When he opened them again, he'd gotten himself under control. Mostly.

"Hey," Shane said, as calmly as if they'd just run into each other in the hallway at the Glass House, their strange little minifraternity. As if whole months hadn't gone by since they'd been parted. "Imagine seeing you around here. Happy birthday to you, and all."

Claire felt tears burn in her eyes, but she blinked them back and put on a brave smile. "Thanks," she said. "What'd you get me?"

"Um ... a shiny diamond." Shane looked around and shrugged. "Must have left it somewhere. You know how it is, out all night partying, you get baked and forget where you left your stuff...."

She stepped forward and wrapped her hands around his. She felt tremors race through him, and Shane sighed, closed his eyes, and rested his forehead against the bars. "Yeah," he whispered. "Shutting up now. Good idea."

She pressed her forehead against his, and then her lips, and it was hot and sweet and desperate, and the feelings that exploded inside her made her shake in re-action. Shane let go of the bars and reached through to run his fingers through her soft, short hair, and the kiss deepened, darkened, took on a touch of yearning that made Claire's heart pound.

When their lips finally parted, they didn't pull away from each other. Claire threaded her arms through the bars and around his neck, and his hands moved down to her waist.

"I hate kissing you through prison bars," Shane said. "I'm all for restraint, but self-restraint is so much more fun."

Claire had almost forgotten that Myrnin was still there, so his soft chuckle made her flinch. "There speaks a young man with little practical experience," he said, yawned, and draped himself over a bench on the far side of the wall. He propped his chin up on the heel of one hand. "Enjoy that innocence while you can."

Shane held on to her, and his dark eyes stared into hers. *Ignore him,* they seemed to say. *Stay with me.*

She did.

"I'm trying to get you out," she whispered. "I really am."

"Yeah, well . . . it's no big deal, Claire. Don't get yourself in trouble. Wait, I forgot who I'm talking to. What kind of trouble are you in today, anyway?"

"I'm not. Don't worry."

"I've got nothing to do but worry, mostly about you." Shane was looking very serious now, and he tilted her head up to force her to meet his eyes again. "Claire. What's he got you doing?"

"You're worried about *me*?" She laughed, just a little, and it sounded panicked. "You're the one in a cage."

"Kind of used to that, you know. Claire, tell me. Please."

"I . . . I can't." That wasn't true. She *could*. She just

desperately didn't want to. She didn't want Shane to know any of it. "How's your father holding up?"

Shane's eyebrows rose just a little. "Dad? Yeah, well. He's okay. He's just . . . you know."

And that, Claire realized, was what she was afraid of—that Shane had forgiven his father for all his crazy stunts. That the Collins boys were together again, united in their hatred of Morganville in general.

That Shane was back in the vampire-slayer fold. If that happened Bishop would *never* let him out of his cell.

Shane read it in her face. "Not like that," he said, and shook his head. "It's pretty close quarters in here. We have to get along, or we'd kill each other. We decided to get along, that's all."

"Yeah," said a deep, scratchy voice from the other bunk. "It's been one big, sloppy bucket of joy, getting to know my son. I'm all teary-eyed and sentimental."

Shane rolled his eyes. "Shut up, Frank."

"That any way to talk to your old man?" Frank rolled over, and Claire saw the hard gleam of his eyes. "What's your collaborator girl doing here? Still running errands for the vampires?"

"Dad, Christ, will you *shut up*?"

"This is the two of you getting along?" Claire whispered.

"You see any broken bones?"

"Good point." This was not how she'd imagined this moment going, except for the kissing. Then again, the kissing was better than she'd dared believe was possible. "Shane—"

"Shhhh," he whispered, and pressed his lips to her forehead. "How's Michael?" She didn't want to talk about Michael, so she just shook her head. Shane swallowed hard. "He's not . . . dead?"

"Define *dead* around here," Claire said. "No, he's okay. He's just . . . you know. Not himself."

"Bishop's?" She nodded. He closed his eyes in pain. "What about Eve?"

"She's working. I haven't seen her in a couple of weeks." Eve, like everyone else in Morganville, treated Claire like a traitor these days, and Claire honestly couldn't blame her. "She's really busted up about Michael. And you, of course."

"No doubt," Shane said softly. He seemed to hesitate for a heartbeat. "Have you heard anything about me and my dad? What Bishop has planned for us?"

Claire shook her head. Even if she knew—and she didn't, in detail—she wouldn't have told him. "Let's not talk about it. Shane—I've missed you so much—"

He kissed her again, and the world melted into a wonderful spinning blend of heat and bells, and it was only when she finally, regretfully pulled back that she heard Myrnin's mocking, steady clapping.

"Love conquers all," he said. "How quaint."

Claire turned on him, feeling fury erupt like a volcano in her guts. *"Shut up!"*

He didn't even bother to glance at her, just leaned back against the wall and smiled. "You want to know what he's got planned for you, Shane? Do you really?"

"Myrnin, don't!"

Shane reached through the bars and grabbed Claire's shoulders, turning her back to face him. "It doesn't matter," he said. "*This* matters, right now. Claire, we're going to get out of this. We're going to live through it. Both of us. Say it with me."

"Both of us," she repeated. "We're going to live."

Myrnin's cold hand closed around her wrist, and he dragged her away from the bars. The last thing she let go of was Shane's hand.

"Hey!" Shane yelled, as Claire fought, lost, and was pulled through the door. "Claire! We've going to live! Say it! *We're going to live!*"

Myrnin slammed the door. "Theatrical, isn't he? Come on, girl. We have work to do."

She tried to shake him off. "I'm not going anywhere with you, you traitor!"

Myrnin didn't give her a choice; he half dragged, half marched her away from the first vampire guard, then the second, and then pulled her into an empty, quiet room off the long hallway. He shut the door with a wicked boom and whirled to face her.

Claire grabbed the first thing that came to hand—it happened to be a heavy candlestick—and swung it at his head. He ducked, rushed in, and effortlessly took it away from her. "Girl. *Claire!*" He shook her into stillness. His eyes were wide and very dark. Not at all crazy. "If you want the boy to live, you'll stop fighting me. It's not productive."

"What, I should just stand here and let you bite me? Not happening!" She tried to pull away, but he was as solid as a granite statue. Her bones would break before his grip did.

"Why on earth would I bite you?" Myrnin asked, very reasonably. "I don't work for Bishop, Claire. I never have. I thought you certainly had enough brains to understand that."

Claire blinked again. "Are you trying to tell me that *you're still on our side*?"

"Define *our*, my dear."

"The side of . . ." Well, he was right. It was a little tough to define. "You know. Us!"

Myrnin actually laughed, let go, and stuffed his hands casually into the pockets of his frock coat. "Us, indeed. I understand you might be skeptical. You have reason. Perhaps I should allow someone else to convince you— Ah. Right on time."

She wouldn't have believed him, not for a second, except that a section of the wall opened, there was a flash of white-hot light, and a woman stepped through, followed by a long line of people.

The woman was Amelie, vampire queen of Morganville—though she didn't look anything like the perfect pale princess that Claire had always seen. Amelie had on black pants, a black zip-up hoodie, and *running shoes*.

So wrong.

And behind her was the frickin' vampire *army,* led by Oliver, all in black, looking scarier than Claire could remember ever seeing him—he usually at least tried to look nondangerous, but today, he obviously didn't care. He wore his graying hair tied back in a ponytail, and it pulled his face into an unsmiling mask.

He crossed his arms and looked at Myrnin and Claire like they were something slimy he'd found on his coffee shop floor.

"Myrnin," Amelie said, and nodded graciously. He nodded back, like they were passing on the street. Like it was just a normal day. "Why did you involve the girl?"

"Oh, I had to. She's been quite difficult," he said. "Which helped convince Bishop that I am, indeed, his creature. But I think it's best if you leave her behind for now, and me as well. We have more work to do here, work that can't be done in hiding."

Claire opened her mouth, then closed it without thinking of a single coherent question to ask. Oliver dismissed both of them with a shake of his head and signaled his vampire shock troops to fan out around the room on either side of the door to the hallway.

Amelie lingered, a trace of a frown on her face. "Will you protect her, Myrnin? I was loath to let you lead her this far into the maze; I should hate to think you'd abandon her on a whim. I do owe her Protection." Her pale gray eyes bored into his, colder than steel in winter. "Be careful what you say. I will hold you to your answer."

"I'll defend the girl with my last breath," he promised, and clasped his hand dramatically to the chest of his ragged frock coat. "Oh, wait. That doesn't mean much, does it, since I gasped that last breath before the Magna Carta was dry on the page? I mean, of course I'll look after her, with whatever is left of my life."

"I'm not joking, jester."

He suddenly looked completely sober. "And I'm not

laughing, my lady. I'll protect her. You have my word on it."

Claire's head was spinning. She looked from Myrnin to Amelie to Oliver, and finally thought of a decent question to ask. "Why are you *here*?"

"They're here to rescue your boyfriend," Myrnin said. "Happy birthday, my dear."

Amelie sent him a sharp, imperious look. "Don't lie to the girl, Myrnin. It's not seemly."

Myrnin sobered and bowed his head very slightly. Claire could still see a manic smile trembling on his lips.

Amelie transferred her steady gray gaze to Claire. "Myrnin has been helping us gain entry to the building. There are things we are doing to retake Morganville, but it is a process that will take some time. Do you understand?"

It hit Claire a little late. "You're . . . you're *not* here to rescue Shane?"

"Of course not," Oliver said scornfully. "Don't be stupid. What possible strategic value does your boyfriend hold for us?"

Claire bit her lip on an instinctive argument and forced herself to *think*. It wasn't easy; all she wanted to do was scream at him. "All right," she finally said. "I'm going to *make* him strategically valuable to you. How's that?"

Myrnin slowly raised his head. He had a warning look on his face, which she ignored completely.

"If you don't rescue Shane *and his father*, I'm not going to help keep Myrnin on track, and I'll destroy the maintenance drugs and the serum we were working on. I'm guessing you still want to avoid getting on the crazy train, right?" Because that was where all the vampires were headed, even Oliver and Amelie.

When she'd first come to Morganville, she'd thought they were immortal and perfect, but in many ways, that was all just a front. The reason there were no other vampires out there in the world—or very few, anyway—was that over the years, their numbers had gradually declined, and their ability to make other vampires had slipped away. It was a kind of disease, something nasty and progressive, although they'd been in denial about it for a very long time.

Amelie had created Morganville to be their last, best hope of survival. But the disease hadn't gotten better; it had gotten worse, and seemed to be affecting them faster and faster these days. Claire had learned to pick up the subtle signs by now, and they were already visible—tremors in the pale hands, sometimes up the arms. Soon, it'd be worse. They were all terrified of it. They had good reason to be.

Myrnin had developed a maintenance drug, but they needed a cure. Badly. And with Myrnin slipping fast, Claire was the key to getting that done.

There was a profound silence in the room, and for a second, Claire's angry resolve faltered. Then she saw the look in Oliver's eyes. *Oh no you don't*, she thought. *Don't you look smug.*

"We do this my way," Claire said, "or I'll destroy all the work and let you all die."

"Claire," Myrnin murmured. He sounded horrified. Good. She was glad. "You can't mean that."

"I *do* mean it. All your work, all your research. If you let Bishop kill Shane, none of it matters to me anyway." She was scared to say this, but in a way, it was a relief. "It's not all about you and your stupid ancient feuds. There are living people in this town. We have *lives*. We *matter*!" She'd let the lid off her simmering, terrified anger, and now it was boiling all over the place. She whirled on Myrnin. "*You! You gave us to him! You turned on us when we needed you*! And *you*"—Amelie, this time—"*you didn't even care. Where have you been*? I thought you were different; I thought you wanted to help—but you're just like the rest of them; you're just—"

"Claire." Just the one word, but from Amelie that was all it took to stop Claire in her tracks. "What else could I do? Bishop turned enough of my followers that any action I would take would have been against my own people. It would have been a fight to the death, and that fight would have destroyed everyone you or I love. I had to withdraw and allow him to think he had triumphed. Myrnin did what he could to protect you and all your friends, while we found another way."

Claire snorted out a bitter little laugh. "Sure he did."

"You're all alive, I believe, unlike most who've crossed Bishop throughout his life. You might think on how unlikely that is, so long after he should have lost interest and torn you and my town apart." Amelie's face was as hard as carved marble. "My father has no interest in *administering*. Only in destroying. Myrnin has been persuading him to at least try to keep Morganville alive, and putting himself at constant risk to do so."

Claire didn't want to believe it, but when she actually thought about it, she remembered how often Bishop had ordered people killed, and how often Myrnin—or Myrnin and Michael!—had managed to distract him from carrying it out. "Michael," Claire said slowly. "You turned Michael back, didn't you? He's not really Bishop's anymore."

Amelie and Oliver exchanged looks, and Oliver shrugged very slightly. "She is a quick study," he said. "I never said otherwise. Unless the boy's a bad actor."

"If he were a bad actor, he'd be long dead by now," Amelie said. "Claire—you must not treat Michael any differently. For his life's sake, you must not. Now, I need you to go with Myrnin. The serum you've cultured from Bishop's blood is of vital importance to us now; we need to treat all those we can reach, and we must have enough of a supply to do the job. I rely upon you for that, Claire."

"Why should I help you at all?" Claire asked, and felt a tremor of pure chill along the back of her neck when

Amelie's gray eyes sharpened their focus on her. "You haven't promised me anything. I want you to swear you'll get Shane and his father out of there alive."

Oliver growled, and from her peripheral vision she saw the ivory flash of his fangs. "You're going to permit this puppy to bark at you?"

"What I do is my affair, Oliver." Amelie let a long, long moment pass before she said, "Very well, Claire, you have my word that we will retrieve Shane and his father before they are executed. What else?"

Claire hadn't really been prepared to win that argument. She blinked, searched for another demand, and came up with nothing in particular.

Then she did. "I . . . want you to promise me that when this is over, you're going to change things in Morganville."

Amelie looked, for a moment, perplexed. "Change things? What sort of things?"

"No more hunting humans," she said. "No more owning people. You'll make everybody equal around here."

"You're speaking of things you don't understand. These things are required for us to survive in relative security. I won't put my people at further risk, nor leave them at the whims and mercies of yours. I've seen too many centuries of death and destruction." Amelie shook her head. "No, if that is your price, then it's too high for me to pay, Claire. Do as you will, but I won't betray all we've built here to accommodate your sentimental idea of modern life."

Claire had been raised to be kind, to agree, to *help*, and for just a second, locked in a stare with the Founder of Morganville, she wanted to give up.

The only thing that stopped her was imagining what Shane would have said, if he'd been standing in her place.

"No," she said, and felt her heart flutter madly in panic. Her whole body was shaking, pleading for her to run, avoid the confrontation. "You hear what you're saying, right? You want to save your people at the cost of human lives. I won't agree to that; I *can't*. Deal's off. I'm not helping you anymore. And the first chance I get, I tell Bishop about Myrnin, too."

Amelie turned on her hard and fast, and before she knew what was happening Claire felt a cold hand around her throat, and she was smashed up against the wall. Claire screamed and slammed her eyes shut, but not fast enough to block out the rage on Amelie's face, or the wicked-sharp white fangs and staring eyes.

She felt Amelie's cool breath on her throat, and heard Myrnin murmur something under his breath, something in a language she couldn't understand. He sounded horrified.

Amelie's hard, cold hands let go of her throat. Instead, they fastened around Claire's shoulders and shook her. Claire's skull bounced off of brick, and she winced and saw stars. "*Open your eyes!*" Amelie barked. Claire did, blinking away confusion. "I have *never* met such a vexing, foolish human being in my entire life. There are *eight hundred vampires* in the world, Claire. In the *world*. Fewer each day. We are hunted, we are sick, we are *dying*. There are billions of you! I *will not* put you *first*!" That last was a raw, furious hiss, and it sparked something terrible in Amelie's eyes, something out of control and hungry. "I *will* save my people!"

Behind her, another vampire stepped out of the shadows and said, very quietly, "Amelie. None of this is Claire's fault. You know that. And she's right. It's the same thing I told you fifty years ago. You got mad then, too, as I recall."

The vampire taking Claire's side was Sam Glass, Michael's grandfather; he still looked college-age, even after all these years. He was probably the only one of the nonbreathing who could have stepped in on Claire's behalf—or would have.

He touched Amelie's shoulder.

She turned on him, but he wrapped her in his arms,

and for a second, one second, Amelie let herself be held before she pushed him away and stalked to the far corner of the room, agitation in every movement. "Oh, just get her out," she said. "Myrnin, get her *out*. Now! Before I do something I regret. Or possibly, which I don't."

Claire could hardly breathe, much less protest. Myrnin took her hand in his and yanked, hard. She brushed by Oliver, whose eyes were flaring in hunting-vampire colors, and felt a low-decibel growl fill the room.

Myrnin shoved her toward what looked like a blank wall, and for an instant of panic Claire thought she was going to hit it face-first . . . and then she felt the telltale tingle of one of Myrnin's stable wormhole portals, his alchemical travel network that led to some of the most dangerous places in Morganville. The wall dissolved in a swirl of mist, and Claire had the feeling of helplessly falling into the dark, with no idea of where she'd land. It seemed to last forever, but then she was stumbling out . . . into her *home*.

4

The Glass House was pretty much as she'd last left it, when she'd packed her pitifully few belongings and moved in with her parents after they'd been brought to Morganville. The house seemed quiet, lonely, somehow sad and colorless. That was just its mood. Shane's things were still strewn around—a new game console that he'd only just gotten hooked up, games piled in the corners along with his Wii controllers, his ratty old black sweatshirt crumpled on the corner of the couch. Claire walked to it, sat down, and pulled it into her lap like a pet, then held it up to her face and breathed.

I'm home. It felt wonderful and sad and horrible, all at the same time.

Holding Shane's shirt was like having him holding her, just for a moment.

When she looked up, Myrnin was watching her. "What?" she demanded. He shrugged and turned away. "Why did you bring me here?"

"I had to bring you somewhere," Myrnin said. "I thought perhaps you would enjoy this more than, say, the sewage treatment plant."

Michael's guitar lay in its case on the floor near the bookcases. Some of Eve's magazines still littered the coffee table, edges curling up from neglect more than use.

It still smelled so *familiar*, and Claire felt the loss of Shane, of her friends, hit her hard once again.

"Is Eve here?" she asked him, but Myrnin didn't answer.

Eve did, from the kitchen doorway. "Where else would I be?" she asked. She leaned against the doorjamb and crossed her arms, staring at them. "What are you doing in my house, freaks?"

"Hey, it's my house, too!" Claire knew she sounded defensive, but she couldn't help it. From the very first time they'd met, Eve had been on her side—always in her corner, always believing her. Believing *in* her, which was even more important.

It hurt that all that had changed now.

Eve's face was a rice-powder mask, aggressively marked up with black lipstick and way too much eyeliner. Her black hair was pulled back into a severe ponytail, and she was wearing a skintight black knit shirt with a red skull on the front, and oversize cargo pants with loads of pockets and chains. Heavy combat-style boots.

Eve was ready to kick ass, and she wouldn't bother to take names while she was at it.

"I'm serious," Eve said. "I'm giving you about five seconds to get out of my house. And take your pet leech with you before I play a game of Pin the Stake in the Vamp."

Claire held Shane's sweatshirt in her arms for comfort. "Aren't you going to at least ask how they are?"

Eve stared at her with eyes like burned black holes. "I've got sources," she said. "My boyfriend's still evil. Your boyfriend's still in jail. You're still sucking up to the Dark Lord of Mordor. By the way, I'm going to start calling you Gollum, you little creep."

"Eve, wait. It's not like that—"

"Actually, it is exactly like that," Myrnin said. "We should go, Claire. Now."

He tried to take her hand; she shook him off and moved closer to Eve, who straightened from her slouch and slipped one hand into a pocket on her cargo pants. "I'm not screwing around, Claire. *Get out of my house!*"

"I *live here*!"

"No, you *used to* live here!" That came out of Eve's blackened lips in a raw, vicious snarl. "This is still Michael's house, and no matter what's happened to him, I'm going to defend it, do you understand? I'm not letting you—"

"Michael's not evil," Claire blurted out desperately. "He's working for Amelie."

Eve stopped, lips parted, eyes wide.

"Claire," Myrnin warned softly from behind her. "Secrets are best kept cold."

"Not from her." Claire tried again, desperate to see some of that anger leave her friend. "Michael's working for Amelie. He's not on Bishop's side. He'd want me to tell you that. He never left us, Eve. He never left *you.*"

Silence. Dead, cold silence, and in it, Claire could hear Eve's breathing. Nothing else.

Eve took her hand out of her pocket. She was holding a knife.

"So this is Bishop's latest game? Taunt the loser? See how crazy you can make me? Because honestly, that's not much of a challenge—I'm pretty crazy already." Her dark eyes sparkled with tears. "Runs in my family, I guess."

"Claire isn't lying to you," Myrnin said, and stepped around Claire to block any threatening moves Eve might make. "Do you have to be so full of—"

Eve lunged at him. Myrnin didn't seem to move at all, but suddenly he had her from behind, arms pinned, and the knife was spinning on the floor and skidding to bump into Claire's feet. Eve didn't even have time to scream. Once he had her, she wasn't able to, because his hand was across her mouth, muffling any sounds.

Myrnin's eyes sparked an unholy color of red, and he brushed his lips against Eve's pale neck. "—so full of useless bravado?" he finished, in exactly the same tone as before. "She didn't lie to you. She's an awful liar, when it comes down to it. That's what makes her so terrifyingly useful to us—we always know where we stand with little Claire. Now play *nicely,* make-believe dead girl. Or I will fulfill your darkest wishes."

He shoved Eve away, toward Claire, who kicked the knife far out of anybody's reach. Eve whirled, evidently (and understandably) finding Myrnin more of a threat. Under the rice-powder makeup, her face was flushed, her eyes shining with fear.

Myrnin circled like a hyena. He grinned like one, too.

"Call him off," Eve said. "Claire, *call him off!*"

"Myrnin, leave Eve alone. Please?" Which was about the closest Claire dared come to telling Myrnin to do anything, especially when he had that particular glow in his eyes. He was enjoying this. "I need to talk to her, and I can't do that if you're scaring the crap out of her. Please."

He paced a few more steps, and she saw him get control of himself with a real physical effort. He sat down in a chair at the dining table and put his dirty feet up. "Fine," he said, and crossed his arms. "Talk. I'll just wait, shall I? Because *my* mission to save this town is of no importance whatsoever next to your *girl talk.*"

Claire rolled her eyes. "Oh, shut *up,* you medieval drama queen." Now that he was sitting down and the glow was gone from his eyes, she could say it, and he could acknowledge it with a snort and a roll of his shoulders. "Eve, I tried to call. I tried to come by and see you." She was talking to her friend now, and Eve was staring right at her, not at Myrnin, as if Claire were the actual threat in the room. "Eve?"

"I heard you."

"And?"

"And I'm thinking," she said. "Because you've been awfully chummy with Fang-Daddy Bishop. You're his little pet, scurrying around all over town, delivering his little love notes. Right?"

Claire couldn't really dispute that. "Not like I had a choice," she said. "Believe me, I'd rather not be in the middle of this, but he knew I belonged to Amelie. I was just another thing to take away from her, that's all. He likes making her squirm by using me."

Eve thawed just a tiny bit. "Sucks to be the object lesson."

"You have no idea."

"He hasn't, you know . . . ?" Eve mimed the fang thing, just in case Claire thought she meant something else. Then she looked worried about that, too.

"He's not interested in me at all," Claire assured her. "I'm just some pawn for him to move around on the chessboard. And besides, Myrnin looks after me." Myrnin waved his hand in the air, halfway between a dismissal and a prince's lazy wave of acknowledgment. "He won't let Bishop hurt me." Well . . . not much. If he was paying attention. "How about you?"

"It's been quiet," Eve said, and looked away for a moment. "My brother's been coming around to check on me."

"Jason?" Wow, that was not the most comforting thing Claire could think of. "Tell me you're kidding."

"No, he's . . . I think he finally has his head on straight. He seems . . . different. Besides, I need somebody on my side, and he's the only one still around."

"Jason is the one who *sold us out* at the feast; do you remember that? He kicked this whole thing off! Talk about me being Bishop's favorite—at least I didn't choose it!" Not until today, anyway.

Eve sent her a fierce glare. "Jason's still my brother. Hey, I wish he wasn't, but it's not like I got to pick my family!"

"You sound like Shane talking about his dad."

"Did you just come here to insult me, or do you have a *point*? Because if you don't, I need to get to work." Eve pushed away from the doorway and snatched up a patent-leather backpack and a set of keys, which she rattled impatiently. "That's Latin for *get the hell out*, by the way. I'd think a college girl like you would know that."

Myrnin slowly sat up, eyes going wider. "I'm sorry, little pale creature—did you just give us an order?"

"Not so much you as her, but yeah, if you want to take it that way. Sure, you knockoff Lestat. Get the hell out of my house." Eve waited expectantly, but nothing happened. "Damn, that really doesn't work anymore, does it?"

"Not since the owner of the house turned vampire," Myrnin said, and stood up in that eerie way he had, as if gravity had just been canceled in his neighborhood. "Please feel free to try to make me leave. I'd quite enjoy it."

"Myrnin." Claire sighed. "Eve. We're not enemies, okay? Stop poking at each other."

That got her stares from both of them. Not nice ones.

"We're just ... passing through," Claire said, and felt a surge of real regret. "On our way to ... Where are we going?"

"Somewhere remote," Myrnin said. "And I don't intend to tell your angry little friend about it in any case. Finish your babble. It's time to go."

As if it was his idea, and they weren't getting tossed out. Claire couldn't resist rolling her eyes.

She caught Eve doing the same thing, and they shared sudden, sheepish grins.

"Sorry," Claire murmured. "Honest, Eve. I miss you."

"Yeah," Eve said. "Miss you, too, freak. Wish I didn't, sometimes, but there you go."

Claire wasn't sure which of them moved first, but it really didn't matter; they both put their arms out, and the hug felt warm and good and real. Eve kissed her quickly on the cheek, then let go and hurried out, hiding her tears. "I'm leaving!" she shouted back, and disappeared into the hallway. "That means you should, too!" The front door slammed.

As Myrnin opened the portal in the wall, Claire grabbed up Shane's sweatshirt and pulled it on over her clothes. It was huge on her. She rolled up the sleeves, and couldn't resist lifting the neck to smell it one more time.

Myrnin smirked. "There is no drama so great as that of a teenage girl," he said.

"Except yours."

"Did no one ever teach you to respect your elders?" He grabbed her by the shoulder and pushed her through the portal. "Mind the gap. Oh, and you have black lipstick on your cheek."

They came out in a dim, damp basement—a generic sort of place, full of molding boxes. "You take me to the nicest places," Claire said, and sneezed. Myrnin shoved boxes out of his way without bothering to answer, uncovering a set of iron steps that looked to be more rust than actual iron. Claire followed him up, testing every tread carefully along the way. The whole thing seemed ready to collapse, but they made it to the top, which featured . . . a locked door.

Myrnin patted his pockets, sighed, and punched the lock with his fist. It shattered. The door sagged open, and he bowed to her like an old-school gentleman. Which he was, she supposed, on his good days.

"Where are we?"

"Morganville High School."

Claire hadn't ever set foot in the place. She'd started her senior year at the age of fifteen, courtesy of her mutant freak-smart brain, but as they stepped out into the hallway, she felt like she'd traveled back in time. Only a year, actually, which made it especially weird.

Scarred, polished linoleum floors. Industrial green walls. Battered rows of lockers stretching the length of the hallway, most secured with dial locks. Butcher-paper posters and banners advertising the Drama Club's production of *Annie Get Your Gun* and the band bake sale. The place smelled like industrial cleaners, sweat, and stress.

Claire paused to stare at the oversize painted mascot on the cinder-block wall at the end of the hallway.

"What?" Myrnin asked impatiently.

"Seriously. You guys have no sense of subtlety, do you?" It was the same image the boy at Richard Morrell's office had worn on his T-shirt: a menacing viper lunging, with fangs displayed. *Cute.*

"I have no idea what you mean. Come on. We have very little time before classes let out—"

A loud bell clattered, and all up and down the hallway, doors banged open, releasing floods of young people Claire's own age, or close to it. Myrnin grabbed Claire's arm and yanked her onward, fast.

School. It was surreal how normal it all seemed—like nobody could handle the truth, so they just kept on with all the surface lies, and in that sense, Morganville High was just like the rest of the town. All the chatter seemed falsely bright, and kids walked in thick groups, seeking comfort and protection.

They all avoided Myrnin and Claire, although *everybody* looked at them. She heard people talking. *Great. I'm famous in high school, finally.*

Another quick left turn led through a set of double doors, and the noise of feet, talk, and locker doors slamming faded behind them into velvety silence. Myrnin prodded her onward. More classrooms, but these were dark and empty.

"They don't use this part of the building?" Claire asked.

"No need for it," Myrnin said. "It was built with a plan that the human population of Morganville would grow. It hasn't."

"Can't imagine why," Claire muttered. "Such a great place to live and all. You'd think there'd be people just dying to get in. Operative word, dying."

He didn't bother to debate it. There was another door at the end of the hall, and this one had a shiny silver dead-bolt lock on it.

Myrnin knocked.

After a long moment of silence, the dead bolt was pulled back with a metallic *clank*, and the door swung open.

"Dr. Mills?" Claire was surprised. She hadn't heard much about Dr. Mills, ER doctor and their sometime lab assistant, for weeks. He'd dropped out of sight, along with his family. She'd tried to find out what had happened to him, but she'd been afraid it would be bad news. Sometimes, it was just better not to know.

"Claire," he said, and stepped back to let her and Myrnin inside the room. He closed and locked the door before turning a tired smile in her direction. "How are you, kid?"

"Um, fine, I guess. I was worried—"

"I know." Dr. Mills was middle-aged and kind of average in every way, except his mind, which was—even by Claire's standards—pretty sharp. "Mr. Bishop got word that I was doing research on vampire blood. He wanted it stopped—it's not in his best interest for anyone to get better right now, if you know what I mean. We had to move quickly. Myrnin relocated us." He nodded warily to Myrnin, who gave him a courtly sort of wave of ac-. knowledgment.

"Your family, too?"

"My wife and kids are in the next room," he said. "It's not what you might call comfortable, but it's safe enough. We can use the gym showers at night. There's food in the cafeteria, books in the library. It's about the best safe haven we could have." Dr. Mills looked at Claire closely, and frowned. "You look tired."

"Probably," she said. "So . . . this is the new lab?"

"Seems like we always have a new one, don't we? At least this one has most of what we need." He gestured around vaguely. The room had clearly been intended to be a science classroom; it had the big granite-topped tables, equipped with sinks and built-in gas taps. At the back of the room were rows and rows of neat shelves filled with glassware and all kinds of bottled and labeled ingredients. One thing about Morganville—the town really did invest in education. "I've made some unexpected progress."

"Meaning?" Myrnin turned to look at him, suddenly not at all fey and weird.

"You know I've been trying to trace the origins of the disease?"

"The origins are not as important as developing an effective and consistent palliative treatment, not to mention mass producing the cure," Myrnin said. "As I've told you before. Loudly."

Dr. Mills looked at Claire for support, and she cleared her throat. "I think we can do both," she said. "I mean, it's important to know where something came from, too."

"That's the thing," Dr. Mills said. "It didn't seem to come from *anywhere*. There weren't any other vampire diseases; everything I tested within the medium of their blood went down without a fight, from colds and flu to cancer. Granted, I can't get my hands on some of the top-level contagious viruses, but I don't see anything in common between this disease and any other, except one."

Myrnin forgot his objections and came closer. "Which one?"

"Alzheimer's disease. It's a progressive degenerative disease of—"

Myrnin gestured sharply. "I know what it is. You said it had things in common."

"The progress of the disease is similar, yes, but here's the thing: Bishop's blood contains antibodies. It's the *only* blood that contains antibodies. That means that there is a cure, and Bishop took it, because he contracted the disease and recovered."

Myrnin turned slowly and raised his eyebrows at Claire. It was a mild expression, but the look in his eyes was fierce. "Interpret, please."

"Bishop might have done this on purpose," she said. "Right, Dr. Mills? He might have developed this disease and deliberately spread it—used the cure only for himself. But why would he do that?"

"I have no idea."

Myrnin stalked away, moving in jerky, agitated strides; when a lab stool got in his way, he picked it up and smashed it into junk against the wall without so much as pausing. "Because he wants control," he said. "And revenge. It's perfect. He can once again decide who lives, who dies—he had that power once, until we took it from him. We thought he was destroyed. We were *sure.*"

"You and Amelie," Claire said. There was a long, ugly history behind all this—she didn't understand it and didn't really want to, but she knew that at some point, maybe hundreds of years ago, Amelie had tried to kill Mr. Bishop once and for all. "But you failed. And this is his way of hitting you back. Hitting you all back at once."

Myrnin stopped, facing a blank corner for a moment without replying. Then he slowly walked back toward them and took a seat on one of the lab stools that hadn't been destroyed, flipping back the tails of his frock coat as he sat. "So it is deliberate, this bane."

"Apparently," Claire said. "And now he's got you where he wants you."

Myrnin smiled. "Not quite." He gestured around the lab. "We do have weapons."

Most of the granite-topped tables had metal pans spread with drying reddish crystals. Claire nodded toward them with a frown. "I thought we were going with the liquid version of that stuff?" *That stuff* being the maintenance drug that she and Myrnin had developed—or at least refined to the point of being useful—that acted to keep the vampire disease's worst effects at bay. It wasn't a cure; it helped, but it had diminishing returns, at best.

"We were," Dr. Mills said. "But it takes longer to distill the liquid form than it does to manufacture the crystals, and we need to medicate more and more of the vampires—so here we are. Two prongs of attack."

"What about the cure?" He didn't look happy, and Claire's heart shrank down to a small, tight knot in her chest. "What's wrong?"

"Unfortunately, the sample of Bishop's blood we had degraded quickly," he said. "I was able to culture a small amount of serum out of it, but I'm going to need more of the base to really develop enough to matter."

"How much more of his blood do you need?"

"Pints," he said apologetically. "I know. Believe me, I know what you're thinking."

Claire was thinking of exactly how stupidly suicidal it would be to try to get *drops* of Bishop's blood, never mind pints. Myrnin had managed it once, but she doubted even he could pull it off twice without being staked and sunbathed to death. But she wasn't willing to give up, either. "We'd have to drug him," she said.

Myrnin looked up from fiddling with glassware on the table. "How? He's not one of those partial to human food and drink. And I doubt any of us could get close enough to give him a shot large enough to matter."

Claire pulled in a deep breath as it occurred to her in a cold and blinding flash. "We have to drug him through what it is he *does* drink."

"From everything I've heard about Bishop, he doesn't drink from blood bags," Dr. Mills said. "He only feeds from live victims."

Claire nodded. "I know." She felt sick saying it, so sick she almost couldn't speak at all. "But it's the only way to get to him—if you really want to end this."

The two men looked at her—one older than her, the other infinitely older—and for just a moment, they had the same expression on their faces: as if they'd never seen her before.

Myrnin said thoughtfully, "It's an idea. I'll have to give it some thought. The problem is that loading blood with sufficient poison to affect Bishop will certainly kill a human subject."

Poison. She'd been thinking of some kind of knockout drug—but that wouldn't work, she realized. Doses big enough to affect a vampire would be poison to humans in their bloodstream. "Does he always drink from humans?"

Myrnin flinched. She knew why; she knew Myrnin had drained a couple of vampire assistants he'd had, which was strictly against the rules. He'd done it accidentally, kind of, when he was crazy. "Not . . . always," he said, very quietly. "There are times—but he'd have to be greatly angered."

"Yeah, like that's a trick," Claire said. "Would it kill a vampire to put that amount of poison in his bloodstream?"

"The drugs would not necessarily kill a vampire," Myrnin said. "Bishop draining him certainly would."

The silence stretched. Myrnin looked down at his dirty feet in those ridiculous flip-flops. In the other room, Claire heard a child singing her ABCs, and then a woman's quiet voice hushing her.

"Myrnin," Claire said. "It doesn't have to be you."

Myrnin raised his head and fixed his gaze on hers.

"Of course it doesn't," he said. "But it will have to be someone you know. Someone you might perhaps like. Of all the people in Morganville, Claire, I never expected you to turn so cold to that possibility."

She shivered deep inside from the disappointment in his voice, and fisted her hands in the folds of Shane's oversize sweatshirt. "I'm not cold," she said. "I'm desperate. And so are you."

"Yes," Myrnin said. "That's unfortunately quite true."

He turned away, clasped his hands behind his back, and began to pace the far end of the room, turn after turn, head down.

Dr. Mills cleared his throat. "If you have some time, I

need help bottling the serum I do have. There's enough for maybe twenty vampires—thirty if I stretch it. No more."

"Okay," Claire said, and followed him to the other side of the room, where a beaker and tiny bottles waited. She poured and handed him bottles to place the needle-permeable caps on with a metal crimper. The serum was milky and slightly pink. "How long does it take to work?"

"About forty-eight hours, according to my tests," he said. "I need to give it to Myrnin; he's the worst case we have who isn't already confined in a cell."

"He won't let you," Claire said. "He thinks he needs to be crazy so that Bishop can't sense that he's still working for Amelie."

Dr. Mills frowned at her. "Is that true?"

"I think he needs to be crazy," she said. "Just probably not for the reason he says."

Myrnin refused the shot. Of course. But he took pocketfuls of the medicine and disposable syringes, and escorted Claire back out of the lab. She heard the lock snap shut behind them.

"Are Dr. Mills and his family safe in there?" she asked. Myrnin didn't answer. "Are they?"

"As safe as anyone is in Morganville," he said, which really wasn't an answer. He stopped and leaned against a wall and closed his eyes. "Claire. I'm afraid. . . ."

"What?"

He shook his head. "I'm just afraid. And that's rare. That's so very rare."

He sounded lost and uncertain, the way he sometimes did when the disease began to take hold—but this was different. This was the real Myrnin, not the confused one. And it made Claire afraid, too.

She reached out and took his hand. It felt like a real person's hand, just cold. His fingers tightened on hers, briefly, and then released.

"I believe that it's time for you to learn some things," he said. "Come."

He pushed off from the wall, and led her at a brisk walk toward the portal, flip-flops snapping with urgency.

5

Myrnin's actual lab was a deserted wreck.

Whether it was Bishop's goons, vandals, or just Myrnin being crazy, there was even more destruction now than the last time Claire had seen the place. Virtually all the glass had been shattered; it covered the floor in a deadly glitter. Tables had been overturned and splintered. Books had been ripped to shreds, with the leather and cloth covers gutted and empty, tossed on piles of trash.

The whole place smelled foul with spilled chemicals and molding paper.

Myrnin said nothing as they descended the steps into the mess, but on the last step, he paused and sat down—more like *fell* down, actually. Claire wasn't sure what to do, so she waited.

"You okay?" she finally asked. He slowly shook his head.

"I've lived here a long time," Myrnin said. "Mostly by choice, as it happens; I've always preferred a lab to a palace, which Amelie never really understood, although she humored me. I know it's only a place, only things. I didn't expect to feel so much . . . loss." He was silent again for a moment, and then sighed. "I shall have to rebuild again. But it will be a bother."

"But . . . not right now, right?" Because the last thing Claire wanted to do was get a broom and a dump truck to pick up all that broken glass when the fate of Morganville was riding on their staying focused.

"Of course not." He leaped up and—to her shock—walked across the broken glass. *In flip-flops*. Not even pausing when the glass got ankle-deep. Claire looked down at her own shoes—high-top sneakers—and sighed. Then she very carefully followed him, shoving a path through the glass as she went while Myrnin heedlessly crunched his way through.

"You're hurting yourself!" she called.

"Good," he shot back. "Life is pain, child. Ah! Excellent." He crouched down, brushed a clear spot on the floor, and picked up something that looked like a mouse skeleton. He examined it curiously for a few seconds, then tossed it over his shoulder. Claire ducked as it sailed past. "They didn't find it."

"Find what?"

"The entrance," he said. "To the machine."

"What machine?"

Myrnin smiled his best, looniest smile at her, and punched his fist down into the bare floor, which buckled and groaned. He punched again, and again—and an entire six-foot section of the floor just *collapsed* into a big black hole. "I covered it over," he said. "Clever, yes? It used to be a trapdoor, but that seemed just a bit too easy."

Claire realized her mouth was gaping open. "We could have fallen right through that," she said.

"Don't be overly dramatic. I calculated your weight. You were perfectly safe, so long as you weren't carrying anything too heavy." Myrnin waved at her to join him, but before she got halfway there, he jumped down into the hole and disappeared.

"Perfect." She sighed. When she finally reached the edge, she peered down, but it was pitch-black ... and then there was the sound of a scratch, and a flame came to life, glowing on Myrnin's face a dozen feet down. He lit an oil lamp and set it aside. "Where are the stairs?"

"There aren't any," he said. "Jump."

"I can't!"

"I'll catch you. Jump."

That was a level of trust she really never wanted to have with Myrnin, but ... there was no sign of mania in him, and he watched her with steady concentration.

"If you don't catch me, I'm totally killing you. You know that, right?"

He raised a skeptical eyebrow, but didn't dispute that. "Jump!"

She did, squealing as she fell—and then she landed in his strong, cold arms, and at close range, his eyes were wide and dark and almost—*almost*—human.

"See?" he murmured. "Not so bad as all that, was it?"

"Yeah, it was great. You can put me down now."

"What? Oh. Yes." He let her slide to the ground, and picked up the oil lamp. "This way."

"Where are we?" Because it looked like wide, industrial tunnels, obviously pretty old. Original construction, probably.

"Catacombs," he said. "Or drainage tunnels? I forget how we originally planned it. Doesn't matter; it's all been sealed off for ages. Mind the dead man, my dear."

She looked down and saw that she was standing not on some random sticks, but on *bones*. Bones in a tattered, ancient shirt and trousers. And there was a white skull staring at her from nearby, too. Claire screamed and jumped aside. "What the *hell*, Myrnin?"

"Unwanted visitor," he said. "It happens. Oh, don't worry; I didn't kill him. I didn't have to—there are plenty of safeguards in place. Now come on, stop acting like you've never seen a dead man before. I told you, this is important."

"Who was he?"

"What does it matter? He's dust, child. And we are not, as yet, although at this rate we certainly may be before we get where we're going. Come on!"

She didn't want to, but she wanted to stay inside the

circle of the lamplight. Dark places in Morganville really were full of things that could eat you. She joined Myrnin, breathless, as he marched down an endlessly long tunnel that seemed to appear ten feet ahead and disappear ten feet behind them.

And suddenly, the roof disappeared, and there was a cave. A big one.

"Hold this," Myrnin said, and passed her the lamp. She juggled it, careful to avoid hot glass and metal, and Myrnin opened a rusty cabinet on the wall of the tunnel and pulled down an enormous lever.

The lamp became completely redundant as bright lights began to shine, snapping on one by one in a circle around the huge cavern. The beams glittered off a tangled mass of glass and metal, and as Claire blinked, things came into focus.

"What is that?"

"My difference engine," Myrnin said. "The latest version, at least. I built the core of it three hundred years ago, but I've added to and embroidered on it over the years. Oh, I know what you're thinking—this isn't Babbage's design, that limited and stupid thing. No, this is half art, half artifice. With a good dash of genius, if I might say so."

It looked like a huge pipe organ, with rows and rows of thin metal plates all moving and clacking together in vertical columns. The whole thing hissed with steam. In and around that were spaghetti tangles of cables, tubes, and—in some cases—colorful duct tape. There were three huge glass squares, too thick to be monitors, and in the middle was a giant keyboard with every key the size of Claire's entire hand. Only instead of letters on it, there were symbols. Some of them—many of them—she knew from her studies with Myrnin about alchemy. Some of them were vampire symbols. A few were just . . . blank, like maybe there'd been something on them once, but it had worn completely off.

Myrnin patted the dirty metal flank of the beast affectionately. It let out a hiss from several holes in the tubing. "This is Ada. She's what drives Morganville," Myrnin said. "And I want you to learn how to use her."

Claire stared at it, then at him, then at the machine once again. "You're kidding."

And the machine said, "No. He's not. Unfortunately."

Claire had seen a lot of weird stuff since moving to Morganville, but a living, steam-operated Frankenstein of a computer, built out of wood and scraps?

That was just too much.

She sat down suddenly on the hard rocks, gasping for breath, and rested her head on her trembling palms. Distantly, she heard the computer—that was what it was, right?—ask, "Did you break another one, Myrnin?" and Myrnin answered, "You are not to speak until spoken to, Ada. How many times do I have to tell you?"

Claire honestly didn't even know how to start to deal with this. She just sat, struggling to keep herself from freaking out totally, and Myrnin finally flopped down next to her. He reclined, with his arms folded behind his head, staring straight up.

"What do you want to know?" he asked.

"I don't," she said, and wiped trickles of tears from her face. "I don't want to know *anything* anymore. I think I'm going crazy."

"Well, it's always a possibility." He shrugged. "Ada is a living mind inside an artificial form. A brilliant woman— a former assistant of mine, actually. This preserved the best parts of her. I have never regretted taking the steps to integrate technology and humanity."

"Well, of course you wouldn't. I have," Ada said, from nowhere in particular. Claire shuddered. There was something not quite right about that voice, as if it was coming out of some old, cheap AM radio speakers that had been blown out a few times. "Tell your new friend the truth, Myrnin. It's the least you can do."

He closed his eyes. "Ada was dying because I had a lapse."

"In other words," the computer said acidly, "he killed me. And then he trapped me inside this box. Forever. The fact that he doesn't regret it only proves how far from human he is."

"You are *not* trapped in the box forever," Myrnin said, "as you well know. But I still need you, so you will simply have to stop your endless wailing and get on with things. If you want an escape, research your way out."

"Or you'll what?"

Myrnin's eyes snapped open, and he bared his fangs—not that he could bite the *computer*. It was just a reaction of frustration, Claire thought. "Or I'll disconnect your puzzle sets," he said, "and you can read the works of Bulwer-Lytton for entertainment for the next twenty years before I take pity on you."

Ada was notably silent in response to that, and Myrnin folded up his fangs and smiled. "Now," he said to Claire, "let me explain Ada. She is the life force that powers the town, of course; without her, we could not operate the portals, and we could not maintain the invisible fields that ensure Morganville residents stay put, and suffer memory loss if they manage to make their way out of town. The drawback is that Ada is a living being, and living beings have . . . moods. Feelings. She has been known to grow fond of people, and to sometimes interfere. Such as with your friend Michael."

"Michael?" Claire blinked, intrigued despite everything. She didn't *want* to know more. . . . Oh, hell, yes she did. She really did. "What do you mean?"

"I mean that Ada interceded to keep Michael alive, because she could. Ada's presence is most felt in the Founder Houses, which are closely linked to her; she can, with enough of an effort, manifest in them, or anywhere there is a portal, for short periods of time. In Michael's case, she chose to save his life by storing him in the matrix of the Glass House rather than allowing him to die when Oliver attempted, and failed, to turn him into a vampire."

"She didn't just save him, she *saved* him," Claire said. "Like a computer saving a crashed file."

"I suppose, if you want to put it in mundane terms." Myrnin yawned. "I told her to let him go. She ignored me. She does that."

"Frequently," Ada's disembodied voice said. "And with great satisfaction. So. You are the girl from the Glass House. Myrnin's new pet."

"I . . ." Claire wasn't sure how to respond to that, so she settled for a quick shrug. "I guess."

"You've done well," Ada said. "You work the portals without much understanding of how they function or how to create them, but I suppose that most modern children couldn't begin to construct the toys with which they play."

Claire's cell phone suddenly rang, its cheerful electronic tone startling in the silence. She jumped, flailed, and fished it out of her pocket, only to have it immediately go dark.

"Did you do that?" she asked.

"Do what?" Ada asked, but there was a dark, amused edge to the words. "Oh, do forgive. I've got little enough to occupy me down here in the *dungeon*. In my *box*."

"Ada." Myrnin sighed. "I brought her here so you could explain to her how to maintain your functions, not to have her listen to your endlessly inventive complaints."

Ada said nothing. Nothing at all. In the silence, Claire heard the steady whir and click of gears turning, and the hiss of steam—but Ada stayed quiet.

"She's pouting," Myrnin said, and heaved himself up to a sitting position. "Don't worry, my dear. You can trust Claire. Here, let me introduce you properly."

Myrnin's idea of a proper introduction was to grab Claire by the arm and haul her over in front of the machine. Before she could yell at him to let go, he slipped back a metal cover and pushed her hand down on a metal plate . . . and something pierced her palm, lightning fast, like a snakebite. Claire tried to snatch her hand back, but something—some *force*—held it in place.

She could feel blood trickling out of the hot, aching wound. "Let go!" she yelled, and kicked the machine in fury. "Hey! *Hey!*"

Ada giggled. It was a weirdly metallic sound; up close, she really didn't sound human at all, more like parts grinding together inside.

The force holding Claire's hand in place suddenly let go, and she stumbled back, clutching her burning hand to her chest and trying—without much success—to stop herself from gasping for breath. She was afraid to look, but she forced herself to open her left hand.

There was a small puncture wound in the middle of her palm, a red circle about the size of a pencil point; there was a whiter circle all around it, like a target. As Claire watched, the white faded.

Blood trickled out of the hole in her skin in fat red drops. Claire looked at Myrnin, who was standing a few feet away; he was gazing at her hand with fascination.

Ewwwwww.

Claire made a fist, willing the bleeding to stop. "What the hell was *that*?"

"That?" Myrnin didn't seem to be able to take his gaze off of her fist. "Oh, it's simple enough. Ada needed to know who you were. She'll know you now, and she'll follow your orders."

Ada made a sound suspiciously like a strangled cough.

"That doesn't explain why she *bit me!*" Claire said.

Myrnin blinked. "Blood is the fuel that drives the engine, my dear. As with us all. Ada requires regular infusions of blood to operate."

"You never heard of *plugging her in*? My God, Myrnin, you made a vampire computer?"

"I ..." He seemed honestly unsure how to answer that, and finally gave up. "She requires about a pint of blood each month—not refrigerated blood; it should be warmed to at least room temperature, preferably to body temperature, of course. I generally feed her close to the beginning of the month, though she can, in a pinch, go weeks without nourishment. Oh, and do feed her at night. Blood is less effective when offered under the influence of the sun. We do work according to hermetic rules here, you know."

"You're insane," Claire said. She backed up against a wall and stood there staring at him. "Seriously. *Insane.*"

He didn't pay any attention to her at all. "You also need to recalibrate her once on each solstice day, winter and summer, to accommodate the shifting influences of sun and moon. You do remember the hermetic symbology I taught you, don't you? Well, the formula is quite simple. I've noted it down for you, here." Myrnin patted his jacket pockets, and finally came up with a much-scratched-out, torn scrap of grimy paper, which he offered to Claire.

She didn't take it. "This is crazy," she said again, as if it was really important that he understand it. Myrnin slowly raised his eyebrows. "You built a vampire computer. Out of *wood.* And *glass.* You're not ... This isn't ..."

He patted her gently on the shoulder. "This is Morganville, dear Claire. You should know by now that it would not be what you expect." With a sudden burst of energy, Myrnin took Claire's unwilling hand, slapped the paper into it, and bounced to his feet. "Ada!"

"What?" The computer sounded surly. Hurt. *She's not even real,* Claire told herself. *Yeah. She's not real, and she drinks blood. She just drank* mine.

"You will accept all commands from Claire Danvers as my own. Do you understand me?"

"All too clearly." Ada sighed. "Very well. I shall record her essence for future reference."

Myrnin turned back to Claire and folded her hand over the scrap of paper. His fingernails were filthy and sharp, and she shuddered at how cold his touch was. "Please," he said. "You must keep this safe. It's the only record of the sequence. I made it to remind myself, in case ... when I forgot. If you get the sequence wrong, you could risk killing her. Or worse."

Claire shuddered. "What could be worse than her being here at all?"

"Turning her against us," Myrnin said. "And believe me, dear, you wouldn't want that to happen."

6

By the time they made their way out of Ada's cavern, it was night—full, dark night.

Which was a problem.

"We can't walk," she told Myrnin, for about the eleven hundredth time. "It's not safe out there. You really don't get it!"

"Of course I get it," he said. "There are vampires a-roaming the dark. Very frightening. I'm quaking in my beach sandals. Come on; buck up, girl. I'll protect you." And then he leered like a total freak show, which made Claire feel not so much reassured. She didn't trust him. He was starting to get that jittery, manic edge she dreaded, and he kept insisting that he couldn't take the serum yet—or even the maintenance drug, the red crystals that Claire kept in a bottle in her backpack.

Past a certain point, Myrnin was crazy enough that he thought he was normal. That was when things got really, really dangerous around him.

"We could take the portal," Claire said. Myrnin, halfway up the stairs, didn't so much as pause.

"No, we can't," he said. "Not from this node. I've shut it down. I don't want anyone else coming here anymore. They'll ruin my work."

Claire took a look around at the wreckage—the smashed glass, the shredded books, the broken furniture. In her view, there wasn't anything *left* for vandals to destroy, and even if there was, sealing up the portal wouldn't stop them; it would only inconvenience her (and Myrnin) from getting here.

Only ... maybe that was what he intended. "What about the entrance to the cave?" she asked. He snapped his fingers as if he'd forgotten all about it.

"Excellent point."

Myrnin dragged the largest, heaviest table over, top down, and covered up with it the hole he'd made in the floor. Then he took handfuls of broken glass and mounded it up on all sides.

"What if they move the table?" she asked.

"Then they'll find Ada, and my countermeasures will likely eat them," he said happily. "Speaking of that, I really must find some lunch. Not you, dear."

Claire would have been happier if he'd had some magical way to repair it, but she supposed that would have to do. It looked like the bad guys had been through this place a dozen times already, anyway; they probably wouldn't be back and in the mood to redecorate.

Claire unzipped her backpack. At the bottom, rattling around loose, were two sharpened wooden stakes. She took one out and slipped it into her pocket. It wouldn't kill a vampire by itself, but it would paralyze one until it was removed ... and it would weaken one enough to die by other means.

If trouble came—even if it was Myrnin himself—she'd settle for slowing it down long enough for her to run for her life.

Myrnin artistically sprinkled some more broken glass. "There," Myrnin said, and backed off to the stairs again. "What do you think?"

"Fabulous." She sighed. "Brilliant job of camouflage."

"Normally, I'd add a corpse," he said, "just to keep people at bay. But that might be good enough."

"Yeah, that's ... good enough," she said. "Can we go now?" Before he decided to go with the corpse idea.

As she followed Myrnin out of the wreck of a shack

that covered the entrance to his lair, he took the time
to carefully close and padlock the door. Which was really ridiculous, because Claire could have kicked right
through the rotten old boards, and she wasn't exactly
She-Hulk.

Claire pulled her phone out and flipped it open, scroll-
ing for Eve's number.

Myrnin batted it right out of her hand, straight up
into the air like a jump ball, and caught it with ease. He
grinned smugly, all sharp teeth at crazy angles, and put
the phone in his jacket pocket. "Now, now," he chided
her. "Where's your sense of adventure?"

"Off on a beach somewhere with your sanity? We
can't do this. You know what happens out on the streets
at night."

"I can't help that. I need some air, and besides, walking is very healthy for humans, you know." With that,
Myrnin dismissed her and started walking down the nar-
row alley into the dark. Claire gaped for a second, then
hurried after him, because the being-left-behind option
didn't seem all that fantastic a choice. On her right, over
the high wooden fence, she saw the looming dark bulk
of the Day House. It was deserted these days. Gramma
Day had moved out, temporarily, and her daughter had
gone into hiding—probably for good, considering that
she'd thrown in her lot with the antivampire forces in
town, and that had not gone well for anybody.

Claire slowed for a second, staring at the unlit windows
of the house. She could have sworn that in the cold starlight she'd seen one of those white lace curtains move.
"Myrnin," she said. "Is there somebody in there?"

"Very likely." He didn't slow down. "People are hiding
out in dozens of places all over Morganville, waiting."

"Waiting for what?"

"God to descend from on high and save them? Who
knows?"

From the other side of the fence, Claire heard a faint,
breathless giggle. She came to a stop, staring at Myrnin,

who paused and looked at the fence, shook his head, and shrugged. He moved on.

But Claire was convinced that whatever was on the Day side of the fence was pacing them now, and when they got to the end of the row . . . *Bad. That will be bad.*

"Myrnin, maybe we should call somebody. You know, get a cab. Or Eve, we could call Eve—"

Myrnin turned on her.

It happened fast, so *fast*, and she barely had time to gasp and duck as he came at her, a white blur in the starlight. There was a sense of hard impact, of falling, and then everything went a little soft around the edges.

Myrnin was stretched out on top of her, and as the world stopped wobbling, she realized she was flat on her back on the ground. "Get off!" she yelped, and battered at his chest with both fists. "Off!"

He put his cold hand over her mouth and lifted a single finger of his other hand to his lips. She couldn't see his face in the shadows, but she saw the gesture, and it made the panic in her shift directions from *oh my God, Myrnin's going to bite me* to *oh my God, Myrnin's trying to save me.*

Myrnin dipped his head low, so low he was well within critical vein range, and she heard him whisper, "Don't move. Stay here."

Then he was gone, just like that. As noisy as he could be at times, he could also be as silent as a shadow when he wanted.

Claire raised her head just a little to look around, but she saw nothing. Just the alley, the fence, the sky overhead with wispy clouds moving across the stars.

And Myrnin's flip-flops, which he'd left behind, lying sad and abandoned on the ground.

There was a sudden, enraged shriek from the other side of the fence, and something crashed against the wood with enough force to splinter heavy boards. Claire rolled to her feet, heart pounding, and gripped the stake in her hand hard. *Funny, I didn't think to use it on*

Myrnin. . . . Maybe she'd known, deep down, that he was acting to protect her.

She hoped so. She hoped it wasn't that she couldn't see the threat in him anymore, because that would eventually get her killed.

Whatever was happening on the other side of the fence, it was bad. It sounded like tigers fighting, and as she backed up from the snarls and howls and sounds of bodies slamming around, the boards of the fence broke again, and a white hand—not Myrnin's, this was a woman's—clawed the air.

Reaching for Claire.

"I've changed my mind," Myrnin called. He sounded eerily normal. "Do go on and run, Claire. I'll catch up. This may take a few moments."

She didn't wait. She grabbed up her fallen backpack and ran for the exit of the alley, where it dumped out into the cul-de-sac next to the Day House.

A vampire car was parked there, door open, engine idling. Nobody around.

Claire hesitated, then looked inside. In the glow of the instrument panel, she couldn't see much: dark upholstery, mainly. She didn't think there was anybody inside, although it was tough to see into the back. She ducked into the cabin and flipped on the overhead light, then bounced back on her heels with the stake held in her most threatening way possible. (Which, she had to admit, probably wasn't very intimidating at all.)

Luckily, nothing lunged at her from the backseat.

Claire threw herself behind the wheel, dumped her backpack on the floorboard of the passenger side, and slammed the door. She leaned on the horn, a long blast, and yelled, "Myrnin! Come on!"

It was a risk. There was every possibility that whoever won that fight back there, it wouldn't be Myrnin opening the car door, but she had to try. He'd taken on another vampire—more than one, she thought—to save her life.

The least she could do was give him fair warning that she was about to speed away and leave him behind.

It was impossible to see through the dark tinting on the windshield and windows. Claire counted to ten, slowly and deliberately, and got to a whispered *seven* before there was a casual knock on the passenger window. She yelped, fumbled, and found the switch that rolled down the glass.

Myrnin leaned in and smiled at her. "Fair lady, may I ride with you in your carriage?"

"God—get in!" He looked ... messy. Messier than usual, anyway; his coat was shredded in places, he had bloodless scratches on his face, and his eyes were still glowing a dull, muddy red. As he slid into the passenger seat, she caught a sharp scent from him—fresh vampire blood. In the dashboard glow, she saw traces of it around his mouth and smeared on his hands. "Who was it?"

"No idea," Myrnin said, and yawned. His fangs flashed lazily. "Someone Bishop set to spy on me, no doubt. She won't be reporting back. Sadly, her companion was too fast for me. And too frightened."

He was so casual about it. Claire, freaked, made sure all the doors were locked and the windows rolled up, and then realized that they were sitting in an idling car, and she couldn't see a thing ahead of her. Of course. It was a standard-issue vampire-edition sedan. Not meant for humans at all.

Myrnin sighed. "Please, allow me."

"Do you have the faintest idea of how to drive a car?"

"I am a very fast learner."

In fact, he wasn't.

Myrnin dropped Claire off at her parents' house well before dawn, tossed her cell phone out of the car to her, and drove off still bumping into curbs and running over mailboxes with cheerful abandon. He seemed to enjoy driving. That terrified her, but he was officially the Morganville police's problem, not hers.

The weight of the day crashed in on her as she unlocked the front door, and all she wanted to do was crawl onto the sofa in the living room and go to sleep, but she smelled like dirt, old bones, and other things she didn't really want to think about. *Shower.* Mom and Dad were in bed, she guessed; their door was shut at the top of the stairs. She tiptoed past it to the far end of the hall, dumped her backpack on the bed, and pulled an old thin cotton nightgown from a drawer before heading to the bathroom.

Déjà vu struck her as she locked the door and turned on the water. Mom and Dad's Founder House was the same layout as the Glass House—which still felt more like home, even though she'd been in both houses for about the same amount of time. Even the countertops and flooring were the same. Only the Mom-approved shower curtain and bath towels were different. *I want to go back.* Claire sat down on the toilet seat and let the sadness well up inside. *I want to go back to my friends. I want to see Shane. I want all this to stop.*

Not that any genie was going to pop in and grant her wishes, unfortunately. And crying didn't make anything easier, in the end.

After the long, hot shower, she felt a little better—cleaner, anyway, and pleasantly tired. Claire used the dryer on her hair until it was a tousled mop—it was getting longer now, and brushed her shoulders when she combed it out. Her eyes looked a little haunted. She needed sleep, and about a month with nobody trying to kill her. After that, she could deal with all the chaos again. Probably.

She touched the delicate cross Shane had given her, and thought about him trapped in a cage halfway across town. Amelie had made her a promise, but it had been significantly light on specifics and timing; she also hadn't really promised to set Shane free, only to keep him from being executed.

Claire was still thinking about that when she turned on the lights in her bedroom and found Michael sitting on the bed.

"Hey!" she blurted, and grabbed a fluffy pink robe from the back of her door to cover herself up, suddenly aware of just how thin her nightgown really was. "What are you *doing*?" After the first surge of embarrassment, though, she felt an equally strong wave of delight. She hadn't seen Michael—not on his own, away from Bishop—since that horrible day when everything had gone so wrong for all of them.

As she struggled into her robe, he stood up, holding out both hands in a very Michael-ish sort of attempt at calming her down. "Wait! I'm not who you think I am. I'm not here to hurt you, Claire. Please believe me—"

Oh. He thought she still believed he was Bishop's little pet. "Yeah, you're working for Amelie, not evil anymore, I get it. That doesn't mean you can show up without warning when I'm in my nightgown!"

Michael gave her a smile of utter relief and lowered his hands. He looked a million miles tall to her just then, and when he opened his arms, she just about flew into his embrace. She came nearly up to his chin. He was a vampire, so there was no sense of warmth from his body, but there was comfort, real and strong. Michael was his own person. Always.

There was genuine love in him. She could feel it.

"Hey, kid," he said, and hugged her with care, well aware of his strength. "You doing okay?"

"I'm okay, and man, I wish everybody would stop asking me," she said, and pulled back to look at him. "What are you doing here?"

Michael's face took on hard lines, and he sat down on the bed again. Claire climbed up next to him, feeling her happiness bleed away. She picked up a pillow and hugged it absently. She needed something to hold.

"Bishop sent me out to run one of his errands," he said. "He still thinks I'm one of his good little soldiers.

At least, I hope he does. This is probably his idea of a test."

"Sent you out to do what?"

"You don't want to know." Clearly, something that Michael hated. His blue eyes were shadowed, and he didn't seem to want to look at her directly. "Things are getting too dangerous for you to be in the middle of this. Promise me you won't come back to Bishop. Not even if he uses that tattoo to call for you. Just stay away from him. Handcuff yourself to a railing if you have to, but don't go back."

"But—"

"Claire." He took her hand and squeezed it. "Trust me. Please. You have to stay here. Stay safe."

She nodded mutely, suddenly more afraid than she'd been all night. "You know something. You heard something."

"It's not that simple," Michael said. "It's more of a feeling. Bishop's getting bored, and when he gets bored with something . . . he breaks it."

"You mean me?"

"I mean Morganville," he said. "I mean everything. Everybody. You're just an easy, obvious target."

Claire swallowed hard. "But you . . . you're okay, right?"

"Yeah." He sighed and ran a hand through his curling blond hair. "I'd better be. Not much of a choice anymore. Don't worry about me—if I need to get out, I will. I'm just trying to stay with it as long as I can."

Claire hated the sadness in him, and the anger, and she wished she could say something to make him feel better. Anything.

Wait—there was something. "I saw Eve."

That got an immediate response from him—his head jerked up, and his blue eyes widened. "How is she?" There was so much emotion behind the question it made Claire shiver.

"She's good," Claire said, which wasn't exactly true. "She's, uh, kind of pissed, actually. I had to tell her. About you being not really evil."

Michael sighed and closed his eyes for a moment. "I'm not sure that was a good idea."

"It will be if you go see her tonight and tell her ... well, whatever. Oh, but watch out. She's gone all Buffy with the stakes and things."

"Sounds like what she'd do, all right." Michael was smiling now, happier than she'd seen him in months. "Maybe I'll try to see her. Thank you."

"You're welcome." She wasn't sure how much more to say, but she was tired of not telling the truth. "She really loves you, you know. She always has."

He sat for a few seconds in silence, then shook his head. "I'd better let you rest," he said. "Remember what I said. Stay here. Don't go back to Bishop."

"Aye-aye, Captain." She mock-saluted him. "Hey. I missed you, Fang Boy."

"You've been hanging around Eve too much."

"Not nearly enough. Not recently, anyway." And she was sad about that.

"I know," he said, and kissed the back of her hand. "We'll fix it. Get some sleep."

"Night," she said, and watched him walk toward the door. "Hey. How'd you get in?"

He wiggled his fingers at her in a spooky oogie-boogie pantomime. "I'm a *vampire*. I have *secret powers*," he said with a full-on fake Transylvanian accent, which he dropped to say, "Actually, your mom let me in."

"Seriously? *My* mom? Let *you* in my room? In the middle of the night?"

He shrugged. "Moms like me."

He gave her a full-on Hollywood grin, and slipped out the door.

Claire got under the covers and, for the first time all night, felt like it was safe to sleep.

In the morning—not *too* early—Claire found cereal and juice waiting for her downstairs, along with a note from her mother that she'd gone shopping, and that she

hoped Claire would stay home today. It was the same
sort of note Mom left every day. At least, the "hope you
stay home" part.

Claire intended to, this time. She intended to right up
until she looked at her calendar, and realized what day
it was, and that it was circled in red with multicolored
exclamation points all around it.

"Oh, *crap*!" she muttered, and pawed through her
backpack, hauling out textbooks, notebooks, her much-
abused laptop, floods of colored markers, and assorted
change. She found the purple notebook, the one she
kept for important test dates.

Today was the final exam for her physics class. Fifty
percent of her grade, and no makeup tests for anything
less than life support.

It's only a test. Michael said—

It wasn't only a test; it was her most important final
exam. And if she didn't show up for it, she'd automatically fail a class she had no business not acing. Besides,
Michael had said not to hang around *Bishop*—he hadn't
said anything about going to classes. That was normal
life.

She needed normal right now.

After the cereal and juice, Claire packed her backpack
and set out in the cool morning for Texas Prairie University. It was a short walk from pretty much anywhere in
Morganville; from her parents' house, the route took her
down four residential blocks, then into Morganville's so-
called business district, about six square blocks of stores.
Walking in daylight showed just how much Morganville
had changed since Mr. Bishop had shown up: burned-
out houses on every block, with few attempts to clear
them away or rebuild. Abandoned houses, doors hanging open and windows broken. Once she got into the business district, half the stores were shut, either temporarily
or permanently. Oliver's coffee shop, Common Grounds,
was shuttered and quiet, with a Closed sign in the dark
window.

Everywhere, there was a feeling that the town was holding its breath, closing its eyes, trying to wish away its problems. The few people Claire saw trying to go about their normal lives seemed either jumpy and distracted, or as if they were putting on some false smile and happy face. It was creepy, and she felt a little bit relieved when she passed the gates of the university—open, like it was a regular sort of day—and fell in with the crowds of young people moving around the campus. TPU wasn't a huge school, but it sprawled over a fairly large area, with lots of park spaces and quads. She usually would have made a stop at the University Center for a mocha, but there wasn't time. Instead, she headed for the science building, navigating the crowds piling into Chem 101 and Intro to Geology. The physics classes were held toward the end of the hallway, and they were a lot less well attended. TPU wasn't exactly MIT on the plains; most students just wanted to get their core courses and transfer out to better schools. Most of them never had a single clue about the true nature of Morganville, because they didn't get off campus all that much—TPU prided itself on its student services.

Of course, there were also local students, destined to stay in Morganville their entire lives. Until a few months ago, she could have identified those people at a glance, because they'd be wearing identification bracelets with odd symbols on them to identify the vampire they owed their allegiance to—their Protector. Only that system had mostly broken down after Bishop's arrival. The vampires were no longer Protectors; most were out-and-out predators. No more blood banks, at least for those loyal to Bishop; they were all about hunting.

Hunting people.

So far, Bishop had seen the wisdom of keeping his hunting parties out of the TPU campus; after all, the kids here helped fund the town and keep the economy running. Most of them stayed on campus, where they had everything they needed except for the occasional trip to a store or a bar, so they didn't know much—and couldn't care less—about Morganville. Morganville didn't offer much in the way of entertainment, when you came right down to it. Even the shops were boring.

If he started allowing his vampires to hunt students, it would get very, very bad. Claire couldn't even imagine how the fragile system Morganville was built on could survive an exposure like that—the press would show up. The government. Not even Amelie could keep control under those kinds of conditions, and Bishop wouldn't even bother to try.

Looking around, all Claire could think about was how precarious it was—and how oblivious everybody was to the tipping point.

Claire slid into her usual seat in her physics class, two minutes early. There were only about ten other people attending now; they'd started out with about twenty, but plenty had dropped out, and of those who were left, she thought she was the only one with a solid A. As in most of her classes, nobody made eye contact. Unless you had friends when you came to TPU, you weren't likely to make them casually.

Claire's professor didn't put in an appearance, but his teaching assistant did, a twenty-two-year-old Morganville native named Sanaj, who handed out sealed tests but told the students not to open them yet. Claire tapped her pen impatiently on the test, waiting for time. She expected this to be over fast—after all, she'd mastered most of the basics of this class in the first two weeks. If she was fast enough, she might be able to grab a coffee, say hello to Eve, and get the scoop on whether Michael had dropped in for a visit. She was dying to hear all about it.

The door at the bottom of the lecture hall opened, and in strolled Monica Morrell.

Claire hadn't seen her archenemy much lately, but that had mostly been good luck on her part. Monica had been highly visible—first at her dad's funeral, then taking her role as Morganville's First Sister as a blanket excuse for any kind of crazy behavior she wanted to try. Most people in town looked worn, tired, and worried, including Monica's own brother, the mayor; not Monica, though. She looked like she was deeply enjoying herself these days. She'd gone through a bad patch for a while, after losing her status as Oliver's best girl, but disgrace was something that never seemed to stick, not to her.

Monica walked slowly. She was the center of attention and loving every minute of it. She'd gone off blond again; Claire thought the new color suited her better anyway, but she doubted it would last. Monica changed her hair the way she changed her makeup—according to mood and trend.

Currently, though, she'd let her hair grow out, long and lustrous, and it was a dark, bouncy brown. Her makeup was—of course—perfect, on a perfect face flawed only by the nasty arrogance that showed in her smile. Claire was wearing blue jeans and a camp shirt over a red tee; Monica was dressed in a flirty little dress, something more suited to Hollywood than Morganville, and some impressively tall shoes in magenta that Claire was sure had come mail-order—no store in town would have carried those. In short, she looked glossy, perfect, and utterly in command of herself and everything around her.

Behind her trailed her perpetual wingmen, Gina and Jennifer. They looked good, but never as good as Monica. That was how the whole thing worked: the backup singers never took center stage.

Sanaj paused at the top of the terraced classroom in handing out the last couple of tests to look down at Monica and her groupies. "Miss?" he asked. "Can I help you?"

"Doubt it." Monica sniffed. "I'm not here for you." Her eyes focused on Claire, and she smiled. She made a little come-here motion.

Claire calmly sent her back a middle finger. Monica pouted, an effect greatly enhanced by her shiny pink lip gloss. "Don't be that way, Claire," she said. "It'd be a shame if something happened to these nice people."

The TA looked honestly shocked and offended. "Excuse me; are you threatening my students?"

Monica rolled her eyes. "Look, idiot, just sit down and shut up. This doesn't concern you. If you think it does, I'll call up my new friend. Maybe you know him?" She pulled out a tiny bejeweled phone and held it at eye level, ready to dial. "Mr. Bishop?"

Sanaj handed out the last two tests in silence and looked at Claire apologetically. "Perhaps you should talk with your friend outside," he said. "So as not to disturb the other students."

"But I'm taking the test!"

Monica began to slowly dial a number. Sanaj grew pale, watching her—he was clearly one of those who knew the score. "No," he said, and grabbed Claire's test from her desk. "I'm sorry. You can take the test once you're finished with them. Please go."

"But—"

"Go now!"

The other students had their heads down, though they were shooting Claire looks that were sympathetic, scared, or angry. Nobody tried to stand up for her.

Claire put her pen down, looked Sanaj in the eyes, and said, "Save my test. I'm coming back."

He nodded and turned away.

She walked down to meet Monica on the stage.

"Well, that was easy," Monica said, and flipped her phone closed. "Hey, loser. How goes the war? Oh, yeah, you lost."

"What do you want?" Claire was determined to get it over with, fast. She wasn't interested in fighting, or sparring, or even sarcasming. Monica smiled at her and put her phone in her tiny little purse.

"Walk with me," she said. "Let's find out."

Claire resisted making an Eve-style joke about Monica's gaudy shoes, and silently followed Monica out of the classroom. Gina and Jennifer brought up the rear guard.

Outside, the hallway was mostly deserted, except for a few students hurrying late to classes. Monica led the way around the corner to a break area with well-used chairs and study tables. She took a seat, showing off her perfectly waxed legs.

She looked like a queen on a throne. Instead of standing in front of her like some criminal waiting to be judged, Claire moved to a chair off to the side and flopped down. Monica's smile curdled. "Fine," Claire said. "You've got me. What now? The beatings will continue until my attitude improves?"

"Cut the crap," Monica said. "I'm not in the mood. What did you do to my brother?"

"Your . . ." Claire sat up slowly. "Richard? What happened to Richard?"

"Like you don't know? Please. He's *missing*. He disappeared right after he talked to you—went out the door and never came back. I know it's something you said to him. Tell me what you talked about." Her eyes narrowed at Claire's silence. "Don't make me say *please*."

Claire tried to stand up. Gina, positioned behind her, pushed down on her shoulders and held her in the chair.

Jennifer moved in from the side and took out a folding knife.

"Tell me," Monica said, "or I promise you, this is going to get ugly. And so will you."

Claire felt a nasty, cold burst of fear. Sure, she could scream the place down, but this was *Morganville*. She wasn't sure anybody would come. And besides, Monica—who'd had a brief, shining period as the town pariah—had turned back into her usual glossy, predatory self again. Bishop had interviewed her and found her amusing. Claire figured he thought lots of nasty, stinging things were amusing, too. But he'd given her his official seal of approval and sent her out with a new sense of entitlement, which

Monica had promptly translated into a mandate to hurt everyone who'd kicked her when she was down.

Some of those people were no longer around at all, which put Claire among the lucky ones.

"I went to Richard to ask him for a favor," Claire said as calmly as she could. "He tried to help, but he couldn't. So I left. The end. As far as I know, he was having a normal day; I didn't see anything or anybody weird hanging around. That's all I know."

"What kind of favor did you ask him for?" Monica asked. Out of the corner of her eye, Claire saw the glitter of the knife as it turned in Jennifer's fingers. "Let me guess. Loser boyfriend rescue favor?"

Claire didn't answer. There really wasn't any good way to go with that. Monica smiled, but it wasn't a comforting kind of smile.

"So my brother turned you down when you wanted him to use his influence to spring your skanky boyfriend, and you made him disappear," she said. "Nice. I guess you figure the next mayor might be a bigger idiot and let you have what you want."

Claire took a deep breath. "Why would I think that? Since apparently running Morganville is a family business, and you'd be next in line. Oh, I see your point. You're definitely the bigger idiot."

"Ooh, she is just *begging* for it," Gina said, and pressed cruelly hard down on Claire's shoulders. "Cut her, Jen. Give her something to think about."

"I'm serious! Why would I think a new mayor would help me any more than Richard? Look, I *like* your brother. I like him a lot more than I like you. Why would I do anything to hurt him? Am I likely to get anybody *more* likely to help me?"

Monica didn't move. She didn't say anything. Jennifer took her silence for encouragement, and put the edge of the knife on Claire's cheek.

It felt hot. Claire stopped breathing.

"You're sure," Monica said. "You don't know what happened to my brother."

Now she could breathe, because Monica hadn't nodded a go-ahead on the cutting. "No. But maybe I could find out. If you don't piss me off."

The pressure of the knife went away. Claire kept watching Monica, which was where the real threat was coming from.

"Why would you help me?" Monica asked, which was a pretty reasonable question.

"Not helping you. I'm looking to help Richard. I *like* Richard."

Monica nodded. "You do that. I'm going to give you a day. If I don't hear from Richard, or he doesn't show up alive and well, then you're the next one who disappears. And I promise you, they'll never find the body."

"If I had a nickel for every time somebody said that to me around this town . . ." Claire said, and Monica's lips quirked into something that was *almost* a smile. "Come on; you know it's true. Morganville. Come for the education, stay for the terrifying drama."

"Try being born here," Monica said.

"I know. Not easy." Claire looked up at Gina, who was still holding her down; Gina exchanged looks with Monica, then shrugged and let go. Claire flexed her shoulders. She'd probably have aches later, if not bruises. "How's your mom holding up?"

"She's . . . not, exactly. It's been hard." Monica actually thawed a little. Not that they would ever like each other, Claire thought; Monica was a bully, and a bitch, and she would always feel entitled to more than anyone around her. But there were moments when Monica was just a girl only a little older than Claire—someone who'd already lost her dad, was losing her mom, and was afraid of losing her brother.

Then she surprised Claire by asking, "Your parents okay?"

"I don't know if *okay* is the right word for it, but they're safe. For now, anyway." Claire picked up her backpack. "Mind if I go finish my test now?"

Monica raised one eyebrow. "You *want* to take the test? Seriously? I was giving you an excuse, you know. They'd let you make it up. You could probably just buy the answers." She said that as if she really couldn't imagine wanting to take any test, ever.

"I like tests," Claire said. "If I didn't, why would I still be in Morganville?"

Monica smiled this time. "Wow. Good point. It is kind of pass/fail."

Test turned in (and still ahead of everyone else), Claire headed for the University Center. Specifically, she headed for the coffee bar, which was where Eve put in her slave-wage hours pulling espresso shots for the college crowd. There was more of a line than usual; with Common Grounds being "closed for renovations" (according to the sign), more students were settling for the local fare than usual. Behind the hissing machines, Eve worked with silent concentration, barely looking up as she delivered each order, but when she said, "Mocha," and slid it across, Claire touched her on the hand.

"Hey," she said.

Eve looked up, startled, and blinked for a second, as if she had trouble remembering who Claire was, and why she was standing in front of her interrupting the flow of work.

Then she yelled, "Tim! Taking five!"

"No, you're not!" Tim, who was working the register, yelled back. "Do *not* take that apron off. Eve!"

Too late. Eve's apron hit the counter, and she ducked under the barrier to join Claire on the other side. Tim sighed and motioned one of the other register clerks to cover the espresso station as they walked away.

"One of these days, he's going to fire you for that," Claire said.

"Not today. Too busy. And he'll forget by tomorrow. Tim's kind of like a goldfish. Three-second memory." Eve looked relaxed. In fact, despite the fact that she was typically Gothed up in red and black, with clown-white makeup and bloodred lipstick, Eve looked almost . . . content. "Thanks."

Claire sipped the mocha, which was actually pretty good. "For what?"

"You know what."

"Don't, actually."

Eve's smile turned wicked around the edges. "Michael came by."

"Oh?" Claire dumped her backpack on a deserted table. "Tell."

"You're too young."

"Seventeen as of yesterday."

"Oh? *Oh.* Um . . . sorry." Eve looked deeply ashamed. "I . . . Happy birthday. Man, I can't believe I forgot that. Well, in my defense, I was kinda pissed at you."

"Yeah, I noticed that. It's okay. But you owe me a cake."

"I do?" Eve flopped into the chair across from her. "Okay. It'll probably suck, though."

Claire found herself smiling. "I hope so. Anyway. What happened with Michael?"

"Oh, you know. The usual." Eve traced a black fingernail in some carving on the tabletop—apparently Martin + Mary = HOT, or at least it had once. "We talked. He played guitar for me. It felt . . . normal for a change."

"And?"

"Like I'm going to tell you."

Claire stared at her.

"Okay, I'll tell you. *God,* don't nag, okay?" Eve scooted her chair closer. "So. We kissed for a while—did I mention what an awesome kisser he is? I did, right?—and . . ."

"And?"

"And I'm not going to end up on Blood Bank Row

because I told you dirty little stories about me and Michael, Miss Barely Seventeen. So just, you know, imagine." Eve winked. "You can be really vivid if you want."

"You suck." Claire sighed.

Eve opened her mouth, then closed it again without saying a single word. Before either of them could think what to say next, a shadow fell across the table.

Claire had never seen him before, but he had the typical cool-boy-on-campus look ... a loose black T-shirt over a nice expanse of shoulders, comfortable jeans, the usual pack full of books. Dark hair, kind of an emo cut, and expressive dark eyes beneath his bangs.

"Hi," he said, and shuffled from one foot to the other. "Umm, do you mind if I ... ?" He pointed to the remaining chair at the table. Claire looked around. All the other tables were full.

"Knock yourself out," Eve said, and pushed his chair out with her foot. "Hope you're not allergic to girl talk."

"Not likely. I have four sisters," he said. "Hey. I'm Dean. Dean Simms." When he extended his hand for Eve to shake, Claire automatically checked his wrist. Not a Morganville native; there was no bracelet, and no sign that there had ever been one. Even those who'd gladly ditched the symbols of Protection still had the tan lines.

"Eve Rosser." From the wattage of Eve's smile, she liked what she saw across the table. "This is Claire Danvers."

"Hey." He gravely shook hands with Claire, too; she thought it was a kind of forced, formal thing for him. He seemed a little nervous. "Sorry to bust in on you. I just need a place to go over my notes before my test." He dug around in his backpack and came up with a battered spiral notebook, which had an elaborate ink-pen drawing of some kind of car doodled all over the front. He saw Claire looking at it, and a faint pink blush worked up over his cheeks. "Core classes. You get bored, right?"

"Right," she said. She'd skipped core classes—tested out of them—but she understood. She'd gotten so bored that she'd read the entire Shakespeare library of plays, and that had been her freshman year in high school. But she'd never been a doodler. "Nice drawing."

"Thanks." He flipped open the notebook, past pages of tight, neat handwriting.

"What class?" Eve asked. "Your test."

"Um, history. World History 101."

Claire had easily bypassed that one. "Seems like you've got all the notes you need."

He smiled. It was awkward and nervous, and he quickly looked down at his pages again. "Yeah, I scribble a lot when I'm in class. It's supposed to help with memory, right?"

"Does it?" Eve asked.

"I'll tell you after the test, I guess." He focused on his notes, looking even more uncomfortable. Claire looked at Eve, who gave a tiny little *whatever* shrug.

"So," she said. "Plans for today?"

"Apart from . . ." Nothing Claire could say in front of an innocent bystander. "Well, not really. Did you know that Richard Morrell's gone missing? Monica asked me to find him."

"Back up. What?"

"Monica asked me to—"

"Yeah, that's what I thought you said. Now you're doing favors for the Morrell family? Girlfriend, there's nice, and then there's utterly dumb. You don't need to do Monica any favors. What has she ever done for you?"

"That's why it's called a favor," Claire pointed out. "Not an evening of the score. It's something you do *before* they owe you one."

"You're just asking for it. Stay out of trouble, okay? Just keep your head down. I *know* that's what Michael told you. If Shane was here, that's what he'd say, too."

Dean was doing a very good imitation of studying, but the tips of his ears had been turning pink, and now, he looked up and stage-whispered, "Yeah, about that. I kind of know Shane."

Which brought the conversation to a quick halt. Dean looked around and lowered his voice even more. "I also know his dad."

"Oh God, please. *Tell* me you're not one of Frank Collins's lame-ass vampire hunters." Eve sighed. "Because if you are, dude, way to go low-profile. Buy some life insurance today, and please, make me the beneficiary."

"Not exactly a vampire hunter, but . . . I do work for Frank Collins, sort of."

Eve looked at Claire. "I think we found a good choice to replace Captain Obvious." Captain Obvious had been part of the secret vampire-hating underground when Claire had first arrived in Morganville; he'd ended up being a little *too* obvious toward the end. Obviously dead.

"Because he'd be dead before he got his first sentence out when he came face-to-face with a vampire?" Claire asked, deadpan.

"I was thinking just put him in a custom T-shirt that says, 'Hello, my name is Dean and I'm here to kill you, evil bloodsucking creatures of the night.' With an arrow pointing at his neck that says, 'Bite here.'"

Dean was flipping his attention back and forth between them in obvious consternation. "Okay, let me start over. I've been trying to find out where Shane and his father are. Do you have any idea?"

"Friend," Eve said, and pointed toward her skull-graphic-covered self. "Girlfriend." The black fingernail turned toward Claire. "Housemates." The finger gestured to include them both. "So yeah, we know. How exactly do *you* know Shane?"

"I . . . I met him when he and his mom and dad were on the run. Did he tell you about that?"

Both girls nodded. Shane's sister had been killed in a house fire; the Collins family had done the forbidden in response—they'd packed up and fled Morganville . . .

with some kind of vampire help, because that was the only way to get past the barriers if you were wearing a Protection mark. Out in the world, though, things hadn't gone well. Shane's parents had each gone crazy in their own special way: his dad had become a cold, hard, vampire-hunting drunk, and his mom had turned into a depressed, possibly suicidal drunk, leaving Shane to make his way as best he could.

"I was there," Dean said. "When Mrs. Collins died. I mean, I was in the motel court. I saw Shane after he found her. Man, he was totally fucked-up."

"You were there?" Claire repeated.

"My brother was running with his dad by then, so yeah. I was around. Me and Shane kind of hit it off, because we were both getting dragged around without any say in what was happening."

"Wait a minute. Shane never said anything about coming back to Morganville with a friend," Eve said.

"Yeah, he wouldn't, because he doesn't know I'm here. Mr. Collins—Shane's dad—sent me after him. I was supposed to stay to keep an eye on Shane, kind of watch his back." Dean shook his head. "Except nothing was the way he said it would be. I didn't know where to hide, so I enrolled at TPU because it gave me an excuse to hang around. Then I kind of lost track of everybody a few weeks ago." He looked at them hopefully. "So? What do I do now?"

Claire and Eve stared at him in silence for a moment, and then Eve said, very seriously, "Look. We know Frank Collins—know, hate, whatever. And you need to give up on that evil old loser. You seem like kind of a sweet kid. Pack it in and go away. Get out while you still can."

"It wasn't supposed to be like this," Dean said. "It was supposed to be easy. I mean, the good guys were supposed to *win,* you know? The vampires were supposed to die."

"And then what, you guys take over and run the town?" Claire sighed. "Not likely. And I've met Mr. Collins. Not a good idea to give him the keys to the city, either."

Dean looked at her like he thought she was crazy, and that it really was a pity. "At least he's not a *vampire*."

"They're not all bad," Claire said.

For a split second, she thought she saw an altogether different Dean watching her—same guy, same emo haircut, but his eyes were weird. Not vampire weird. Odd weird.

Then he blinked, and it was gone, and she thought it was just her imagination. If you couldn't be paranoid in Morganville, though, where could you?

"Well, that's new to me," Dean said. He smiled, and it was a real smile. A warm one, not at all nervous. "I just always thought the whole bloodsucking thing made being bad a lock."

"What you know about vampires could fit into a mosquito's ass," Eve said, irritated. "All you know is what you grew up seeing on TV. You ever actually *meet* one?"

Dean didn't answer that, but the tips of his ears grew red and his smile disappeared as he faced Eve directly. "Yeah, well, I'm not some collaborator who's willing to apologize for what these monsters do. Maybe that's the point. Anyway—it wasn't really my choice. I just came because Frank asked, and I didn't have anyplace else to go. My brother was running with Frank, and he was all I had."

Eve's eyes remained watchful. "So where's Big Scary Bro now?"

"Dead," Dean said softly. "He got killed in the fighting. I'm all alone."

Claire stared down at the table, suddenly not interested at all in her mocha, no matter how delicious. The truth was that some of those guys—the foot soldiers, the ones who'd come along to Morganville with Frank Collins as his shock troops—well, some of those guys hadn't fared well, either in the fight or in jail. She didn't know who they were, not by name. Up until this moment, they'd just been labeled in her head as Frank Collins's minions. But they all had names, friends, lives. They all had families. Claire wouldn't know Dean's brother from any of his fellow muscle-bound biker dudes, but that didn't mean Dean didn't mourn him.

That led Claire to a terrifyingly real waking nightmare— Bishop summoning her, telling her that he'd decided to let Shane go. Shane lying there, not moving . . .

"Hey, Claire?" Eve snapped her fingers under Claire's nose, and Claire jerked so hard she slopped coffee onto the table. "Damn, girl. You space so hard, you ought to look into a career at NASA. So. We agree that Mr. Dean here is a terrible excuse for a vampire hunter, is in a whole lot of trouble if he doesn't keep his head down, and he should head for the hills if he knows what's good for him?"

"Sure," Claire said, but Dean was already looking oddly stubborn.

"I'm not going anywhere," he said. "My brother would have wanted me to finish what I started. I told Frank Collins I'd look out for Shane. I'm staying until I know they're okay."

"That's sweet, but how exactly are you going to look out for him, seeing that he's in jail?" Eve said. "Unless you want to look after his girl instead." She winked at Claire.

The tips of Dean's ears turned even redder. "That's not what I meant."

Except that Claire had the funny feeling that he did.

She avoided Eve's gaze for another few seconds, then pulled out her cell phone and checked the time. She had nowhere to be, but this was turning weirdly uncomfortable all around.

"Gotta go," she said, and grabbed up her backpack. She'd had about all the Dean time she wanted.

Eve blinked. "You barely touched the mocha!"

"Sorry. You have it."

"I *work* in a coffee bar. No. Here, Dean. Knock yourself out."

The last she saw before she ducked off into the crowds, heading for nowhere in particular, was Eve handing Dean her abandoned drink, and chatting like old friends.

Claire really didn't have a lot of ideas about what to do for the rest of the day, but one thing she did *not* intend to do was go against Michael's instructions. No way was she going anywhere near Vampire Central today. Going home didn't have much appeal, either, but it seemed the safest thing to do. As she walked, she dialed Richard Morrell's cell phone number. It went to voice mail. She tried the new chief of police next.

"Hannah Moses, go," said the brisk, calm voice on the other end.

"Hey, Hannah, it's Claire. You know, Claire Danvers?"

Hannah laughed. She was one of the few people Claire had ever met in Morganville who wasn't afraid to really laugh like she meant it. "I know who you are, Claire. How are you?"

"Fine." That was stretching the truth, Claire supposed, but not according to the standards of Morganville, maybe. "How does it feel to be in charge?"

"I'd like to say good, but you know." Claire could almost hear the shrug in the older woman's voice. "Sometimes being a know-nothing spear carrier's comforting. Don't have to know about how the war's going, just the battle in front of you." Hannah was, in real-world terms, a soldier—she'd just come back from Afghanistan a few months ago, and she was as badass a fighter as Claire could even imagine, outside of ninja TV stars. She might not do the fancy high kicks and midair spins, but she could get the job done in a real fight.

Even against vampires.

Hannah finally said, "I'm guessing you didn't call just because you missed me."

"Oh. No . . . I just . . . Did you know Richard Morrell is missing?"

"All over it," Hannah said, without a change at all in her tone. "Nothing to be concerned about. Let me guess, Monica put you onto it. I already told her it's handled."

"I don't think she believes you."

On the other end of the phone, Hannah was probably grinning. "No shit? Well, she's bad; she's not stupid. But her brother's safe enough. Don't worry. Richard can take care of himself, always has."

"Is something going on? Something I should know about?" Hannah said nothing, and Claire felt a hot prickle of shame. "Right. I forgot. I'm wearing the wrong team jersey, right?"

"Not your fault," Hannah said. "You were drafted; you didn't join up. But I can't talk strategy with you, Claire. You know that."

"I know." Claire sighed. "I wish . . . you know."

"I really do. You go home, and stay there. Understand?"

"On my way," Claire promised, and hung up.

On the other side of the street, college-adjacent businesses were starting to close up shop, even though it was still early. Nobody liked to be caught outside as night approached; it was unsafe during the day, but it was a hell of a lot worse at twilight, and after.

Claire slowed as she passed Common Grounds. The security shutters were still down, the door was closed, but there was something . . . something . . .

She crossed the street, not really sure why she did, and stood there for a few seconds, staring like an idiot at the locked door.

Then she heard the distinct, metallic sound of a dead bolt snapping back, and in slow motion, the door sagged open just a bare inch. Nothing showed but darkness.

I am not *going to say, "Hello, is anyone there," like some stupid, too-dumb-to-live chick in a movie*, Claire thought. *Also, I am not going in there.*

I'm really not.

The door opened another inch. More darkness. "You've got to be kidding," Claire said. "How stupid do you really think I am?"

This time, the gap opened to about a foot. Standing well back from any hint of sunlight was someone she knew: Theo Goldman, vampire and doctor.

"I'm sorry," he said. "I couldn't come to you. Will you do me the honor . . . ?"

There were a lot of vampires in Morganville who scared Claire, but Theo wasn't one of them. In fact, she liked him. She didn't blame him for trying to save his family, which included both humans and vampires. He'd done what he had to do, and she knew it hadn't been for any bad motives.

Claire stepped inside. Theo shut the door and locked it securely after her. "This way," he said. "We keep all the lights off in the front, of course. Here, allow me, my dear. I know you won't be able to see your way."

His strong, cool hand closed around her upper arm in a firm, but not harsh grip, and he guided her through blind darkness, zigzagging around (she assumed) tables and chairs. When he let go, she heard a door close behind them, and Theo said, "Shield your eyes. Lights coming on."

She closed her eyes, and a flare of brightness reddened the inside of her lids. When she looked, Theo was stepping away from the light switch and moving toward the group of people sitting at the far end of the room. His dark-haired wife rose from her chair, smiling; except for her generally pale skin, she didn't look much like a vampire, really. Theo's kids and grandkids—some physically older than Claire, some younger—sat in a group playing cards. In the dark, because all the ones playing were vampires. The humans weren't here at all.

"Claire," Patience Goldman said, and extended her hand. "Thank you for coming inside."

"Um . . . no problem," she said. "Is everything okay?"

It hadn't been for a while. Bishop had been thinking of killing all the Goldmans, or making them leave Morganville. Something about their being Jews. Claire didn't really understand all the dynamics of it, but she knew it was an old anger, and a very old feud.

"Yes, we are fine," Theo said. "But I wanted to tell you that we will be leaving Morganville tonight."

"You ... what? I thought Bishop said you could stay—"

"Oh, he did," Theo said, and his kindly face took on a harder look. "Promises were made. None that I believe, of course. It's no sin for a man like him to break a promise to a man like me; after all, I am hardly better than a human to him." His wife made a sound of protest, and Theo blinked. "I did not mean that to slight you, Claire. You understand what I mean."

"Yeah." Bishop had carried over some prejudices from his human days, and a big one had to do with a dislike of Jewish people, so maybe he didn't look at Jewish vampires as being any different—any better—than mere humans, who weren't real to Bishop, anyway. "But ... why tell me? You can't trust me, you know." She rubbed her arm under the long-sleeved T-shirt, feeling ashamed all over again. "I can't help it. If he asks me, I have to tell him about you."

Theo and his wife exchanged a look. "Actually," Patience said, "you don't. I thought you knew."

"Knew what?"

"That the influence of the charm he used on you is fading." Patience stepped forward. "May I?"

Claire had no idea what she was asking for, but since Patience was holding out her cool white hands, Claire hesitantly extended hers. Mrs. Goldman pushed the shirt sleeve up to expose the tattoo, turning it this way and that, studying it.

"Well?" Theo asked. "Can you tell?"

"It's definitely significantly weakened," his wife said. "How much, it's hard to tell, but I don't think he can compel her without a large effort. Not anymore."

That was news to Claire. Good news, actually. "Does he know what I'm thinking?"

"He never did, my dear," Patience said, and patted her hand before releasing it. "Mr. Bishop's skills are hardly all-powerful. He simply uses our fear to make them seem so." She nodded to her husband. "I think I can safely mask her from him, if he should look for her."

"Wait, what?" Claire asked.

Their eldest son, Virgil, threw down a handful of cards in annoyance and crossed his arms. "Oh, just tell her," he said. "They want to take you with us."

"*What?*"

"It's for the best," Theo said quickly. "We can escort you safely out of town. If you stay, he'll kill you, or turn you vampire so he can control you better. You simply have no options here, my dear. We only want to help you, but it has to be now. Tonight. We can't risk waiting any longer."

"That's . . . kind of sweet," Claire said carefully, and measured the distance between where she stood and the door. Not that she could outrun one vampire, much less six. "But I'm okay here. Besides, I really can't leave now. Shane—"

"Ah." Theo snapped his fingers, and his smile took on a wicked sort of tilt around the edges. "Yes, of course. The boy. As it happens, I did not forget young Mr. Collins; Clarence and Minnie have gone to fetch him. Once they arrive here, we will make sure you both are safely away."

Claire's eyes widened, and suddenly she couldn't get a breath. Her heart started to pound, first from anticipation, then from outright fear. "You . . . you decided to break Shane out of jail?"

"Call it our last good act of charity," Theo said. "Or our revenge on Mr. Bishop, if you like. Either way, it's of benefit to you, I think."

"Does Amelie know what you're doing?"

Theo's expression smoothed out into a frighteningly

blank mask. "Amelie finds it better to skulk in the shadows, while people die for her lack of courage. No, she does not know. If she did, she'd no doubt have a dozen reasons why this was a mistake."

It *was* a mistake. Claire couldn't say why, but she knew it, deep down. "She promised me she'd take care of him," Claire said. "She's got a plan, Theo. You shouldn't have interfered."

"Amelie's plans are subject to her own needs, and she never bothered to include me," Theo said. "I am offering you and your boy a way out of Morganville. Now. *Tonight*. And you need never return here again."

It wasn't that simple. "My parents."

"We can take them with us as well."

"But ... Bishop can find us," Claire said. "Vampires found Shane's family when they left town before. They killed his mother."

"Shane and his father blame vampires for what was only a very natural human despair. Shane's mother took her own life. You see that, don't you? Claire?" Theo seemed to want her to agree, and she wasn't sure why. Maybe he doubted it himself. When she didn't, he looked disappointed. "Well, it's too late now, in any case. We can discuss this once we're safely away. We will help you find a place well beyond Bishop's—and Amelie's—reach before we move on ourselves."

One of the grandsons—the middle one, Claire couldn't remember his name—made a rude sound and threw down his cards. "Grandpapa, we don't *want* to leave." The other children tried to shush him, but he stood up. "We don't! None of us do! We have lives here. We stopped running. It was safe for us. Now you want us to go out there again, start over again—"

"Jacob!" Theo's wife seemed shocked. "Don't talk to your grandfather so!"

"You never ask us. You want us all to pretend that we're still children. We're not, Grandmother. I know

you and Grandpapa can't accept that; I know you don't
want to let us go, but we can make our own decisions."

Mrs. Goldman seemed not to know what to say. Theo
looked very thoughtful, and then nodded. "All right. I'm
listening. What decision have you made?"

"To stay here," Jacob said. "We're staying here." He
looked down at his brothers and sisters, who all nodded—
some reluctantly, though. "You can go if you want, but
we're not letting Bishop drive us out. And no matter
what you say, that's what you're doing. You're just saving him the trouble of exiling us."

"If exile was what I was worried about, I would agree
with you. It isn't."

"You think he'll try to kill us?" Jacob shook his head.
"No. It's not the old days, Grandpapa. Nobody's hunting
us here."

"If I have learned anything in my long life, it is that
someone is *always* hunting us," Theo's wife said. "Now
sit down, Jacob. The rest of you, sit down. We'll have no
more of this. You're being rude in front of our friend."

Claire wanted to apologize, somehow; Jacob shot her a
borderline-angry look, but he dropped back in his place on
the floor, shoulders slumped. She'd never thought about
it, but she supposed for a lot of vampires Morganville was
about as good as it could get—no looking over your shoulder, waiting to be discovered. No worrying about putting
down roots, making friends, having some kind of a life.

"Theo," Mrs. Goldman said, and nodded toward the
door where they'd come in. "I hear someone coming."

"She has better ears than I do," Theo confessed to
Claire. "Stay here. I will let them in."

"But—"

"Stay here. There's nothing to fear. You'll be with
your young man soon."

He left, shutting the door behind him. Mrs. Goldman
drifted quietly over to speak to her children and grand-
children in a low, urgent voice—the way moms always
talked to kids who were throwing tantrums in front of

company—and Claire was left not quite knowing what she ought to do. If they *had* managed to bust Shane out of jail, well, that was good, wasn't it? Maybe not according to Amelie's plan, but that didn't make it a bad thing. Not automatically.

Claire took her cell phone out and speed-dialed the Glass House. No answer, at least not on the first three rings.

On the fourth ring, she thought she heard someone pick up, but it was drowned out by a warning cry from Mrs. Goldman from behind her.

The door smashed open, and Theo came flying through, crashing into Claire and sending her to the floor. The phone skittered out of her hands and underneath the shadowy bottom of an old, upholstered chair. She couldn't breathe; Theo's shoulder had hit her in the stomach, and as she struggled to get her muscles working again, she saw black spots swimming at the edge of her vision. Her whole body felt liquid and hot, and she wasn't sure what had just happened, except that it was bad. . . .

Mrs. Goldman vaulted over Claire's body and grabbed Theo, who was feebly trying to right himself. She pulled him back into the corner, with the children, and fearlessly stood in front of all of them, fangs flashing white as she faced their enemies.

"Now, don't be doing that," said a honey-dark voice from the doorway's shadows. "There's no need for violence, is there?" The light caught on the vampire's face, and Claire felt sick. Ysandre, Bishop's icky little pet slut. She was dressed for business just now, in black leather pants and a long-sleeved heavy jacket with a hood. She could have been drawn in black and white, except for the slash of red that was her mouth. "Got something for you, missus."

She reached back, grabbed two people by the hair, and propelled them both inside. It was the Goldmans' other son and daughter, Clarence and Minnie. Vampires didn't often look beaten up, but these two did, and

Claire felt a little sick at the sight of the fear on Mrs. Goldman's face.

"Let them go," she said. "Children! Come here!"

"Not so fast," Ysandre said, and yanked on the hair she was holding. "Let's talk about this first. Mr. Bishop is not too pleased with your family breaking its word to him. He allowed you to stay here, alive and free, and in return you were supposed to stay out of his business. Did you stay out of his business, sugar? Because it really doesn't look like you did, since you sent these two fine children of yours to try to break his enemies out of jail."

Claire stopped moving at all. She was curled on her side, still struggling to breathe, shaking, and now it felt like the whole world was crashing in on her. *Try. Try to break his enemies out jail.*

They hadn't done it. Shane was still a prisoner.

Ysandre hadn't come alone. She shoved the Goldman boy and girl over into the arms of their mother, and behind her a solid army of vampires filled the darkness. "Didn't know about this place," Ysandre remarked. "Didn't know it had a tunnel going right up under it, anyway. That's real convenient. Didn't even have to take a sunburn to get to you." She brushed her shiny hair back, and as she did, her gaze fell on Claire. She gave her a slow, deadly smile. "Why, lookit. It's little Miss Perfect. Oh, I think Mr. Bishop is going to be *very* disappointed in you."

Claire tried to get up and almost fell. She wasn't hurting yet, but she knew she would be. Bruises, mostly, maybe a couple of strained muscles.

Theo Goldman caught her. He'd gotten to his feet when she wasn't looking, and now he helped her stand up. At close range, she saw the misery in his eyes before he put on a fake smile for Ysandre's benefit.

"I suppose we will be going with you," he said. "For another interview with our benevolent master."

"Some of you will," she agreed. "And some of you won't." She snapped her fingers and pointed at Claire.

Two big, muscular vampire guys lunged from behind her and grabbed Claire by the arms to haul her off. When Theo protested, they shoved him back with his family. "I want to introduce you to an old friend of Mr. Bishop's. This is Pennywell. I believe you may already be acquainted, though."

As she was dragged out of the room, into the dark open area of Common Grounds, Claire passed the stranger she'd seen in Bishop's office on her birthday. He—she? it was hard to tell—walked past Claire as if she didn't exist, heading into the room where the Goldmans were being held.

"Wait!" Claire yelled. "What are you going to do?"

Pennywell didn't even pause. Ysandre looked back and winked at her.

"Don't you worry about any of this, now," she cooed with false sympathy. "You've got plenty of your own problems to worry about. Good-bye, Claire."

7

There was a hidden ladder down to a surprisingly large, well-lit tunnel underneath Common Grounds. It had a false brick wall that led into one of the maze of tunnels that was big enough for cars—and there was one waiting, a big idling limousine. One of Claire's vampire captors opened the back and pushed her inside before getting in with her. The other one took the front seat, and before more than a few seconds passed, they were driving on into the hidden world underneath Morganville. "Hey," Claire said. The vampire sitting next to her in the back glanced at her, then away. He was about twice her size, and she had a feeling that he could have broken her in half with a harsh word and his little finger. "What's going to happen to them?"

He shrugged, not like he didn't know—more like he just flat didn't care enough to tell her. The Goldmans didn't mean much to him. Claire meant even less.

"What's your name?" she asked, and surprised herself. But for some reason, she wanted to know. Dean's brother—he hadn't been just some nameless Bad Guy Number Four. This vampire wasn't, either. He had a name, a history, maybe even people who cared what happened to him.

"My name is none of your business," he said, and continued to stare out the window, even though there was nothing but blurry brick out there.

"Can I call you None for short?" It was an Eve joke, but Claire didn't think she delivered it very well, because the vampire didn't even blink. He just shut her out.

She concentrated on not thinking about what might have happened to Shane.

The car burst out of the tunnel at a high rate of speed, rose up a ramp, and exited from what looked like an industrial building—another of Morganville's secret roads. They turned onto a residential street near Claire's parents' house—she recognized two of the burned-out homes and the carefully clipped hedge animals in front of the yellow clapboard house on the corner. She'd always thought the squirrel looked kind of crazy.

They didn't slow down as the limousine sped through the streets. People got out of the way—bikes, cars, even one or two pedestrians hurrying home into the sunset. The vampire driver had a blacked-out windshield, but he was still wearing sunglasses, gloves, and had most of his face covered as well. *Young,* Claire thought. Older vampires wouldn't care about the sun that much. It hurt them, but it wouldn't kill them. So maybe Bishop had recruited some new guys.

Before she could think of anything else to say that wouldn't get her killed, the limousine took a turn down a shaded wide street. At the end of it, Claire saw familiar buildings, and the big green expanse of Founder's Square.

They were taking her to Bishop.

She slid over to the far side, taking her time about it, and as the car slowed for the next turn, she tried to open the door and throw herself out.

Locked. Of course. The vampire in the back didn't even bother to look at her.

Another ramp, this one leading down under the streets, and thirty seconds later they were parked underground. Claire tried to come up with a plan, but honestly, she didn't have much. She'd lost her cell phone when Theo had crashed into her, not that she had even a vague idea of who she could call, anyway. There was a stake hidden at the bottom of her backpack that maybe, *maybe* she could use—but only if it was one-on-one, and the one was a lot less scary than the two currently escorting her around.

"Get out," the vampire in the back said, as the door locks clicked open. "Don't try to run."

She didn't want to. She wanted to save her strength for something more useful.

Whatever that useful thing was, it didn't become clear as they headed for the elevator and crowded inside. Phony not-really-music was piped into the steel-and-carpet box, making it seem that much more like a nightmare.

The elevator doors opened in a big formal room, the round one where she and Myrnin had circulated in their costumes before Mr. Bishop's welcome feast, the one that had been the starting point for everything going so wrong in Morganville. The doors to the banquet hall were closed, and her vampire guards marched her up the hallway to Bishop's office instead.

Michael opened the door. He hesitated, and almost lost his cool, then nodded and stepped aside for the three of them to come inside. There was nobody else in the room.

Not even Mr. Bishop.

"What's going on?" Claire asked. "I thought . . . Where is he?"

"Sit down and shut up," her vampire backseat guardian snarled, and shoved her into a chair. Michael looked like he might have been tempted to come to her defense, but she shook her head. *Not worth it.* Not yet, anyway.

The office door opened, and Mr. Bishop came in, wearing what looked like the same black suit and white shirt he'd been wearing the day before. There was something savage in the look he threw Claire, but he didn't pause; he walked to his desk and sat down.

He never did that. She couldn't imagine it was a good sign.

"Come here," he said. Claire didn't want to, but she felt the power woven into the tattoo on her arm snap to life. It responded to Bishop's voice—only to his—and the harder she tried to resist it, the worse it was going to hurt. But Patience Goldman was right . . . it hurt a lot less than it had before. Maybe it really was fading.

Better not to fight it and tip him off, if that was the case. She took a deep breath and let it pull her closer, right in front of his desk. Bishop leaned forward, staring up at her with cold, empty eyes, elbows braced on the polished wood surface. "Did you know what Goldman was going to do?" he asked. "Did you put him up to it?"

"No," she said. She wasn't sure whether it would help Theo if she took the blame, anyway.

Bishop stared a hole into her, then sat back and let his eyes drift half closed. "It hardly matters," he said. "I knew those people could not be trusted for any length of time. I kept watch on them. And you—I know you can't be trusted, either, little girl. I tethered you, but I didn't tame you. You're harder than you look, like my daughter, Amelie. No wonder she took you under her Protection."

"What are you going to do to the Goldmans?"

Bishop slapped his palm down on the desk, hard enough to leave his imprint half an inch deep in the wood. "I am done with restraint. This town will *learn* I am not to be taunted, not to be toyed with, not to be mocked. *You will learn.*"

Claire wanted to shoot back some smart-ass remark, but she could see the vicious anger in him, and knew it was just waiting to pounce. She stood there, silent, watching him, and then he slowly relaxed. When she started to back away, he said, "Stay there. I have something for you."

He snapped his fingers, and when the door opened, Shane walked in. She hadn't noticed it in the cell, but he was thinner than he'd been a few months ago—and he was also bruised and simmering with fury. When he saw Bishop, he lunged for him.

"No!" Claire yelled. "Shane, stop!"

He didn't, but he also didn't have to. Michael flashed across the room and got in his way, wrapping Shane in a bear hug and bringing him to a sudden halt.

"Let go!" Shane's voice was ragged, splitting and tearing under the strain of his anger. "Screw you, Michael; *let go!*"

He tried to break free. Michael didn't let him. He pushed him back, all the way to the wall, and held him there. Claire couldn't see Michael's face, but she could see part of Shane's, and she saw something change in it. Shane stopped fighting, as if he'd received some message she hadn't seen.

"I am a good master," Bishop said, as if none of that had happened. "You asked me for a birthday favor, Claire. I granted you a visit. Today, I have decided that it was a poor gift. I will give you what you want. Shane will be free to go."

Claire didn't dare to breathe, blink, move. She knew this was a trick, a cruel way to crush her hopes, and Shane's, too. "Why?" she finally said. Her lips felt numb. "Why now?"

"Because I intend to teach you both what it means to defy me, once and for all, and let you carry the tale for me," Bishop said. "Michael. Hold them, but make sure the two of them see everything. I won't have my students failing their lessons."

Bishop's control let go, and Claire stumbled backward into Michael. His arm went around her waist, and she felt the pressure of his lips close to her ear. "Stay still," he whispered. "No matter what happens, just *stay still.* Please. I'll protect you."

On Michael's other side, Shane was very, very quiet.

He wasn't looking at Bishop. He was looking across at Claire, and he was scared—scared that something was going to happen to her, she realized. She tried for a smile, but wasn't sure how it came out.

Shane opened his mouth to say something, but before he could, a vampire guard came in, bringing a thin, scraggly man with a mess of graying, curling hair and a nasty scar down his face.

Shane's dad. He looked older, thinner, and even more vulnerable than he had back in his cell—nothing like the big, scary monster who'd terrified her when she'd first met him.

"Are you watching, Shane?" Bishop asked. "I want you to learn, so that you don't make the same mistakes again."

"Dad," Shane said. "Dad?"

Frank Collins put his hand out to stop Shane from trying to break free. "It's all right. Nothing he can do to me now." He faced Bishop straight on. "Been there, done that, not scared of anything you can bring to this party, bloodsucker. So just kill me and get it over with."

Bishop slowly rose from his chair, staying behind the desk.

"But, Mr. Collins, you mistake me. I'm not going to kill you. I'd never do such a thing. You're far too valuable to me."

His pale hands flashed out, grabbed Shane's dad, and jerked him forward over the desk. Claire shut her eyes as the fangs came out, and Bishop's eyes flashed red. She didn't see the actual biting, but she heard Shane screaming.

It was over in about thirty seconds. Shane never stopped fighting to get free of Michael's hold.

Claire didn't fight at all. She just couldn't.

She heard a thud as Mr. Collins's body hit the floor, and when she opened her eyes she realized that she'd been wrong about everything. Very wrong.

Bishop wasn't finished.

He gnawed at his wrist, pried open Frank Collins's mouth, and poured blood into it as he spread his other hand over the top of the man's head. Claire had seen this before—Amelie had done it to Michael—but Amelie had found it difficult and exhausting to make a new vampire.

For Bishop, it seemed easy.

"No," Shane said. "No, *stop.*"

Right there, right in front of them, Frank Collins coughed, choked, and came back to life. It looked painful, and it seemed to take forever for the thrashing and screaming to stop.

When it did, he wasn't Frank Collins. Not anymore.

He opened his eyes, and they were red.

"You see?" Bishop said, and wiped excess blood from his wrist on his black jacket. "I am not cruel. You'll never lose your father, Shane. Never again."

Claire could hear Shane's breath coming fast and ragged—more sobbing than gasping—but she couldn't look at him. She knew him; she knew he wouldn't want her to see him like this. *That's Shane. Always trying to protect me.*

Michael let Claire go. After a quick glance at her, he turned to Shane. "Don't freak out on me," he said. "Don't. This isn't the time, and it isn't the place."

Shane wasn't even looking at him. He was looking at his dad.

Frank Collins, standing next to Bishop, kept staring back at his son, and Claire didn't think that look was concern.

More like hunger.

"I hope everyone learned something today," Mr. Bishop said. "First, I know everything that goes on in Morganville. Second, I don't tolerate foolish attempts at rebellion. Third ... well. I am so kind and merciful that no one else will die for it today. No, not even the Goldmans, before you bleat the question at me. They have been confined somewhere safe, for now, until I

decide on a fitting punishment." He flicked his fingers
at Michael. "See your friends home, boy. It would be a
dreadful irony if they should be drained along the way
by some passing stranger. Or relative."

Emphasis on the *dreadful*, Claire thought. She grabbed
Shane's cold, shaking hand and forced him to look at
her.

"Let's go," she said. "We have to *go*, Shane. Right
now."

She wasn't really sure he understood her, but Michael
helped nudge him along when he slowed down.

It was a long ten seconds until they were on the other
side of the closed door, being eyed by Bishop's vampire
guards. Claire felt like the last sandwich on the lunch
counter.

Shane broke out of his trance when they got into the
elevator.

Unfortunately.

Michael was pushing the garage button on the elevator panel, and he didn't quite see it coming. Shane got
in a lucky shot to his face, fast and vicious, as Michael
turned. It was hard enough that Michael, even with vampire strength, felt it, and crashed back against the wall,
denting it in an uneven outline of his shoulders.

When Shane tried to follow up with a second punch,
Michael caught his fist in an open palm. "There was
nothing I could do, Shane," he said, but there was something behind the words. Something far kinder. "Let's
wait to do the cage match when Claire isn't trapped in
the middle, all right?"

She wasn't exactly in the middle, but close enough.
No way could she come out of it unbruised if Shane and
Michael decided to really go at it in a small, enclosed
space.

Shane stopped, and, as if he'd forgotten that she was
there at all, he turned to look at her. For a second there
was no expression on his face, and then it all flooded
in—pain, fury, relief.

And then horror.

He lowered his fist, gave Michael a look that pretty clearly said, *Later*, and turned toward Claire. There were two feet of space between them, and about a mile of separation.

"I'm so sorry," she whispered. "God, Shane, I am so *sorry*."

He shuddered and stepped forward to put his arms around her. As hugs went, it was everything wrapped together in a tangled mess—tight, a little desperate, filled with need. He needed her. He really did.

He didn't say anything as the elevator slowly descended. She listened to his breathing, and finally, he made a faint, wordless sound of pain, and pulled away from her. She held on to his hand.

"Come on," she said, and Michael held the door as the two of them stepped out into the darkened garage. Claire knew there were probably threats out there in the dark, but she didn't care. She was tired, and right now, she hated all of them so much for hurting Shane that she would have staked anybody. Amelie. Sam. *Michael*. She couldn't believe he hadn't done anything to stop it from happening. She was just now realizing that he'd stood by and ... watched.

Shane was eerily quiet. Michael moved around them and opened the back door of his Morganville-standard vampmobile; Claire climbed in with Shane, leaving Michael alone in the front seat.

If he had any objections to the seating arrangements, he kept them to himself.

Shane held her hand tightly all the way—through the dark tunnels, then as they traveled the darkened streets. She didn't pay attention to where they were going. Right now, one place was as good as the next, as long as she still had his hand in hers. As long as they stayed together. His misery was a thick black cloud, and it felt like it was smothering them both, but at least they could cling to each other in the middle of it. She couldn't imagine what it would be like all alone.

When Michael braked the car and opened the back door, though, Claire realized that he'd taken Bishop's instructions literally.

He'd brought them home.

The decaying Victorian glory of the Glass House stretched up into the night. Live oaks fluttered their stiff little leaves in the breeze, and in the distance black, shiny grackles set up a loud racket of shrieks and rattles in a neighbor's tree. Grackles loved dusk, Claire remembered. It was their noisiest time of the day. The whole neighborhood sounded like broken glass in a blender.

She got Shane out of the car and opened the front gate. As they moved up the steps, the front door opened, and there stood Eve—not in black tonight, but in purple, with red leggings and clunky black platform shoes. She had a stake in one hand and a silver knife in the other, but as she saw them coming up the steps, she dropped both to the floor and lunged to throw herself on Shane.

He caught her in midair, out of self-defense.

"You're out!" she cried, and gave him an extra-hard squeeze before jumping back to the top of the steps and doing a victory dance that was a cross between something found in an end zone and a chorus line. "I knew you'd beat the rap, Collins! I just knew it! High five . . . "

She held up her hand for him to smack, but he just looked at her. Eve's smile and upraised palm faltered, and she looked quickly at Claire, then Michael.

"Oh God," she said, and lowered her hand. "What is it? What happened?"

"Not out here. Let's get inside," Michael said. "Now."

Shane didn't make it very far. In fact, five steps down the hallway, he gave up and just . . . stopped. He put his back to the wall, slid down to a sitting position, and sat there, staring down at his hands.

Claire didn't know what she ought to do, other than stay with him. Before she could sit down next to him, though, Eve grabbed her by the elbow and shook her hard. "Hey! What *happened*? You called the house but you got cut off. I've been out looking for you ever since, calling everybody I could think of. Hannah's out looking for you, too. What is it?"

"It's Shane's dad," Claire said. Eve let go and covered her mouth with one hand, eyes wide. She already had a sense of what was coming. "Bishop ... he ... he turned him into a vampire. Right in front of us." Claire looked down at Shane. "Right in front of him."

Eve didn't know what to say. She just looked at them, and finally at Michael. "You couldn't do anything about it?"

He kept his head down. "No."

"Nothing? Nothing at all?"

Michael turned and slammed his fist into the wall with so much violence the whole house seemed to shake. Eve yelped and jumped back, and almost tripped over Shane in her stacked heels.

"No," Michael said, with a kind of forced calm that made Claire ache inside. "Nothing at all. If I had, Bishop would have known he didn't have me anymore, and that was what he was waiting for. This wasn't about Shane and Claire, or about Shane's dad. This was more about finding out if I was still his bitch."

Shane slowly raised his head, and the two boys stared at each other for a long, quiet moment.

Michael crouched down. "I'd have killed him if I could have," he said. "I'm not strong enough, and he knows it. That's why he likes to keep me right there, because he knows that deep down I want to rip his head off. It's fun for him."

"So my dad was just your object lesson," Shane said. "Is that it?"

Michael reached out and put his hand on Shane's

knee. He'd split the skin over his knuckles, and there was plaster dust all over his skin.

It wasn't bleeding.

"We're going to get him, Shane. We will."

"Who's we?" Shane asked wearily, and let his head fall back against the wall as he shut his eyes. "Just leave me alone, man. I'm tired. I just can't . . . I'm tired."

Eve put her hand on Michael's shoulder. "Come on," she said. "Leave him alone. He needs time."

Shane laughed dryly. It was a rattle in his throat, like the sound the grackles were making outside. "Yeah. Time. That's what I need." He didn't sound like himself. Not at all.

Michael didn't want to go, but Eve insisted, tugging on his hand until he stood up and followed her out into the living room.

Leaving Shane sitting alone on the floor.

"Hey," Claire said, and sat down beside him, arms wrapped around her knees. "You going to sit here all night?"

"Maybe."

"I just thought—"

"What? I'd snap out of it and go play some video games? Eat a taco? It's not that easy, Claire. He's my—" Shane's voice broke, then got stronger. "He was my *dad*. There was one thing in the world he was afraid of, and I just watched it happen to him. I can't even think about this right now."

"I know," she said, and leaned her head on his shoulder. "I'm so sorry."

They sat there together for a long time. Eve and Michael looked in on them from time to time. After a while, they quit looking, and Claire saw them head upstairs.

The house grew quiet.

"It's cold," Shane finally said. She was getting a little drowsy, despite the discomfort; his voice shocked her back upright again.

"Yeah, kinda. Well, it's the floor." Although it wasn't really the floor's fault, Claire supposed.

He considered that in silence for a few long seconds. "I guess it's pretty stupid to sit here all night."

"Maybe not. If it makes you feel better . . ."

He stretched out his legs with a sudden thump and sighed. "I don't see how getting cold and losing feeling in my body is going to help. Also, I need a bed that isn't a bunk, and hasn't been the previous property of some dude named Bubba with a farting problem."

That was—almost—the old Shane. Claire sat up straight and looked up at him. After a second, he met her eyes. He didn't look happy, but he looked . . . better.

He was trying to be better.

"I forgot to say hello," he said. "Back in Bishop's office, when I saw you."

"Given the circumstances, I think we can let that slide." She swallowed, because he wasn't looking away. "It's been a while. Since . . . you know. Bishop put you behind bars."

"I did notice," he said, deadpan. "Are you asking if I have any wild men-behind-bars stories to tell you?"

"What?" She felt a blush start to burn along her jawline, then spill over her cheeks. "No! Of course not! I just . . . I don't know if—"

"Stop stammering."

"You make me stammer. You always have, when you look at me like that."

"Like what?"

"Like I'm dessert."

He licked her on the nose. She squealed and pulled back, swiping at the moisture, but then he was holding her, and his lips were warm and soft and damp, pressing on hers with genuine urgency. He didn't taste like dessert, not at all; he tasted like she imagined really good wine would taste, dark and strong and going straight to her head. Her muscles warmed and purred where he touched her, and it felt like, just for a moment, there was nothing in the world.

Nothing but this.

He broke off the kiss and pressed his hot cheek against her burning one; she felt his breath fluttering the hair above her ear. She felt him draw in a breath to say something, but she got there first.

"Don't," she whispered. "Don't tell me all the reasons why this isn't a good time, or a good idea. Don't tell me we ought to be thinking about your dad or my parents or what Bishop is doing right now. I want to be here with you. Just . . . here."

Shane said, "Well, I don't want to be here."

The world went out of focus, and her heart shattered. She'd known it was coming; she'd known that he'd changed his mind, that all that time apart had given him time to think about what he wouldn't like about her. . . . Why would somebody like Shane love her, anyway? He'd dated other girls. Better girls. Prettier and smarter and hotter. It had just been a matter of time before he noticed that she was a skinny geek.

But it hurt; oh God, it hurt so badly, like she'd been stabbed with a dagger made of ice.

She couldn't help the tears that flooded her eyes, and she couldn't hold back the sob. Shane went tense, and pushed her back to arm's length. "What?" he asked. "What did I say?"

She wanted to tell him it was all right, but it wasn't, it just *wasn't,* and it never would be. She felt like half of her was dying, and he looked at her in confusion and acted like he didn't understand what he'd done to her.

Claire scrambled away from him and bolted. It was usually Shane who ran away, but this time, she couldn't stay. She couldn't stand to be here, humiliated and stupid and hurting, and try to be nice to him, even though he needed it. Maybe even deserved it.

"Claire!" Shane tried to get up, but his feet wouldn't stay under him. "Dammit, wait—my legs went to sleep; *wait!* Claire—"

She didn't wait, but somehow, he managed to follow

, lunging after her with feet that must have been like running on concrete blocks. He tripped into her and they fell onto the couch. Claire smacked at him and tried to struggle free. "Let go!" she said around her sobs. "Just let go!"

"Not until you tell me what just happened. Claire, look at me. I don't understand why you're upset!"

He really didn't know. He was all but begging her to tell him. All right, then, fine. "Fine," she said aloud, in a voice that trembled more than she wanted. "I get it. You don't want to be with me right now. Maybe not ever. I understand, it's been a long time, and . . . your dad . . . I just . . . I can't . . . Oh, just let me *go*!"

"What in the hell are you talking about?" And then he got it. She saw him run it through his head, and his eyes widened. "Oh my God. Claire, you thought I meant I didn't want— No. God, no. When I said, 'I don't want to be here,' I meant I didn't want to be *there*. You know, sitting on the cold floor with my ass turning into an iceberg. I wanted you. I just wanted you somewhere *else*." He shook his head. "I meant it as a joke. I was going to say, 'I want to be on the *couch*.' Okay, it was stupid, I know. Sorry. I never meant you to think— Wait. Why would you think I'm not into you, anyway?"

Because I'm a girl, Claire thought. She was barely able to contain the relief welling up inside her. *Because we're all stupid and insecure and think that we're never, ever good enough.* She didn't say that, though. Some things it was better for boys not to know. "I just . . . It's been a tough day." She was still crying, and she couldn't seem to stop. "I'm sorry, Shane. I'm sorry your dad—"

"Hey." He touched her cheek. "It's bad, but I can deal. I'm more worried about you."

He always was. "Why?"

He wiped away the tears that trickled down her cheeks. "Because I'm not the one doing the crying, for one thing."

She nodded, shuddered, and started to gulp back

the sobs. He waited, holding her, until she was finally quiet—relaxed in a way she hadn't been before.

Weirdly happy just to be here, with him, no matter what had happened or would happen. *This moment*, she thought. *This moment is perfect.*

"Shane?" she asked. She felt drowsy now, lazy in the warmth of his body.

"Yes?"

"*Do* you have any wild men-behind-bars stories?"

"Not really. Sorry to tease you," he said, and traced his finger down her cheek and over her lips. Slowly. "You know I spent a lot of time thinking about you, don't you? About how you look, how you smell, how you taste . . ."

"Creepy stalker boy."

He kissed her. There was something new in it, something fierce and hot and wild, and she felt needs explode inside her she didn't even recognize. Her whole body lifted, like she'd become metal to his magnet. Shane groaned and rolled her over on her back, his weight on top of her, and kept on kissing her like it was the most important thing in his world.

His lips left hers gasping for air, and traveled down her neck, around the collar of her T-shirt, and his hand dragged the fabric down to expose more skin to his kisses.

Off, Claire thought incoherently, and tried to pull the hem of her shirt up.

Shane's hand stopped hers. She looked up at him.

"Not here," he said. She waited. He looked wary. "What?"

"I was just waiting for you to say, 'Not now,' too. You know, like always."

He smiled, and it was pure Shane—full of edges and yet oddly sweet. "Claire, I just got out of *jail.* Do you honestly think I'm bucking for sainthood or something?"

Her whole body burned with a sudden burst of furious energy. *He just said yes. Oh my God.* All she could think of to say was, "Tell me how much you missed me."

"Not everything needs a speech." He was right about that. She could feel the wild energy in him, trembling right under his skin—a match for hers. "But I have to know, do you want to do this? Really?"

She'd been trying not to think about the scary mechanics of the moment. She'd asked Eve once, in that conspiracy-whisper voice girls used when they were embarrassed not to already know, whether or not the first time really hurt. Eve had said, very matter-of-factly, yes, and gone on to tell her all about her horrible first-time guy. So part of Claire's body was dreading the unknown, and part of it was screaming to jump in, no matter what happened.

"Yes," she said, and her whole body went quiet, stunned into silence. "Yes, Shane. I want to do this. I want to do it with you."

He let out his breath in a shaky laugh. "Nobody else? Not even the hot nude guy from that movie? No? Okay. No pressure." He gave her another kiss, this one fast and warm. "Upstairs?"

They slid off the couch together, hand in hand, and he led her up the stairs, looking back at her in warm glances, stopping every few steps to kiss her. By the time they made it to the top, she was tingling and shaking all over.

Shane pointed questioningly at his own door, but she shook her head. Her room was bigger, and it was at the end of the hall. More private.

He pulled in a quick, shaking breath. "Five minutes," he said. "I need a shower."

She nodded, although somehow being parted from him made it feel risky. They could change their minds at any second.

She opened her bedroom door as Shane went into the bathroom.

It hadn't occurred to Claire, but she supposed that Eve could have turned her former bedroom into anything—a Goth wardrobe warehouse, for instance, filled with skull-themed outfits. Or storage for her growing collection of vampire-slaying implements. Instead, the room was just the way Claire had left it—neat, kind of sterile, no trace of her own stuff left behind. There was a layer of dust on the sparse furniture, and the air felt cold for a few seconds, then began to warm up, as if the house sensed her presence and was eager to make her welcome again.

The big, soft bed still had sheets and layers of blankets and comforters.

She closed and sat down on the bed. Her hands were cold and shaking, and now that Shane wasn't here, she felt sense trying to knock itself back into her head.

No, she thought stubbornly. *No, not this time.*

It was less than five minutes before he came in, hair damp around his face, beads of water on his skin and dampening his shirt.

He leaned against the door after closing it, watching her.

"So," he said. "Maybe I should just—"

"Shut up, Shane," she said, and went to kiss him for a long, warm, lingering moment.

Then she reached behind him and locked the door. Just her and Shane, no friends banging on the door, no family ready to drag them apart. Not even a single vampire hiding in the shadows to spoil things.

For once, nothing to make either of them change their minds.

"Don't you dare ask me again if I'm sure," Claire said, and raised the hem of her T-shirt and pulled it off. The cold air glided over her flushed skin and made her shiver. She knew she was blushing, and she couldn't stop trembling, but that was all right, somehow. As she dropped the shirt to the floor, she thought, *He's seen me like this before. It's okay.*

Shane sat down on the edge of the bed, watching her with absolute concentration. She toed off her shoes, stripped away her socks, unbuttoned her jeans and unzipped them, and kicked them off into the same pile.

He's seen me like this before, too.

She reached behind her for the clasp of her bra. *But not like this.*

"Wait," he said, and pulled his own shirt off. Beneath it, his skin was paler than she remembered, his muscles more defined underneath. "I just want to keep it even."

She swallowed a nervous laugh. "Then you have to get rid of the pants."

Shane grinned at her and leaned back to work the button and zipper. "Don't blame me for the underwear," he said. "It's prison-issue."

"I am so glad you didn't say that before. Oh, and don't say that to my parents, ever."

Shane's pants hit the floor, along with his shoes and socks. Claire's gaze skimmed over him, and she felt dizzy at the sight of so much exposed skin.

"Come over here," he said. "It's cold."

He folded back the covers and slid in. She followed, feeling awkward and made of angles that didn't quite seem to know how to fit together.

Lying beside him felt strange and, at the same time, completely right. They lay inches apart, turned toward each other on their sides. Yearning, and not touching.

Shane lost his smile for a second. "You can tell me to stop anytime. Always."

"I *know.*"

"I won't be angry about that."

"Shane—"

"Anyway, I just wanted to tell you something."

"What?"

He reached out and touched the back of his hand to her face. "I love you."

Somehow, she managed not to cry, although she knew he'd see the glitter of tears in her eyes. "You said it first this time."

He looked relieved. "Yeah. Finally, huh?"

"Finally," she whispered. "I love you, too."

His arms pulled her against him, and she felt small

and breathless and utterly secure. It was just a hug, a hug like all the other hugs ... but it was different, too.

"God, you're beautiful," he said, and she felt his fingers press on her back. Oh—he was working the hooks on her bra. He'd had practice, some part of her noticed; the rest was too busy screaming in utter joy.

Then she wasn't able to think about much at all.

It wasn't like in the movies. In the movies, it was all graceful, pretty people and hot camera angles; in real life, it was a weird mix of tremendously exciting and totally awkward. Shane still had condoms in the wallet that he retrieved from his jeans. That was something they never showed in the movies (at least the ones Claire watched). He was kind of embarrassed about it, too. It made it feel real to her—a lot more real than all her old fantasies.

Shane asked a lot of questions, which felt odd at first, but then she realized that he was nervous, just as nervous as she was, and that was all right. He wanted to make her happy.

He *did* make her happy.

Despite what Eve had told her, the pain still came as a shock, leaping in an electric current through her entire body. If Shane hadn't held her and helped her through it, Claire didn't know how she would have felt about it later ... but he did, and it got better.

And then it was all right.

And then it was *amazing*. She cried a little, and she didn't even know why, except that the emotions were just too big for her. Too overwhelming.

"It's different," Claire whispered to him in the dark, as they lay there wrapped up together, warm and content. "It's different from what I thought."

"Different how?" He sounded suddenly worried. Claire kissed him.

"Good different. Different like it means something. Like right now—it doesn't feel like we're naked at all, does it?" She didn't know why she said that, but it was true; she didn't feel exposed with him. Just ... accepted. "I'm not afraid with you. You know what I mean?"

He made a lazy *uh-huh* sound that meant he might possibly not be listening. "So it was okay."

"Okay?" She rose up on one elbow to look down on him. "Is this you fishing for compliments on your hotness?"

"Why? Did I catch one?"

"Idiot." She flopped back down and cuddled up against him. His hand caressed the small of her back in tiny circles. "I won't lie to you: that was intense. And it hurt. But ... yeah. It was ... amazing."

"I hate that it hurt," he said. "Next time—"

"I know. It wasn't so bad, though. Don't worry." The warm cushion of his arm under her head felt like the best pillow in the world. "I feel different. Do I look different?"

Shane brushed hair back from her face. "It's pretty dark in here, but yeah, I can see it."

She felt her eyes widen. "You can?"

"Sure." He traced a finger over her forehead. "Claire is not a virgin. Says so right there."

She felt her cheeks and forehead heat up, and smacked his arm. "You are *awful.*"

"Ah, the truth comes out."

"Seriously. I just feel ... I do feel different. I feel like I'm someone else than I was before. You know?"

"Yeah," he said somberly. "I know. But I feel like that every day I wake up in Morganville."

She kissed him, and tasted the sadness in him. His sigh seemed to come all the way from his toes. "God, I needed you," he murmured. "I can't even tell you how many times I thought about this. The funny thing is, I don't need you any less now. I think I need you *more.*"

That, Claire thought, was a pretty good definition of love: needing someone even after you got what you thought you wanted.

After a long moment, he said, "Your dad is going to kill me. And he's probably got a right to."

She hadn't thought about her parents, but now it flooded in with a vengeance. This was going to get messy. And complicated. "It'll be okay," she whispered, and spread her hand out over his chest. He put his own hand over hers. "We'll be okay."

They fell asleep in each other's arms, and woke up late in the morning to the sound of birds.

Not grackles.

Songbirds.

8

"You are so busted," Eve said, as Claire, fresh from a shower, ran down the steps shouldering her book bag.

Eve was sitting at the dining table, sipping a Coke and reading a *Cosmo* article with great concentration. She was wearing pink today—or, as Eve liked to call it, Ironic Pink. Pink shirt with poison skull and bones logo. Matching pink pedal-pushers with skulls embossed at the hems. Little pink skull hair ties on her pigtails, which stood out from her head aggressively, daring someone to mock them.

"Excuse me?" Claire kept moving. Eve barely glanced up from the article.

"Don't even try," she said. "I know that look."

"What look?" Claire shoved open the kitchen door.

"The now-I-am-a-woman look. Oh God, don't tell me, please, because then I have to feel guilty that you're seventeen and I should have been more of a den mom, right?" Claire couldn't think of anything to say. Eve sighed. "He'd better have been a good, sweet boy to you, or I swear, I'll kick his ass from here to— Hey, is that Shane's shirt?"

It was. "No." Claire hurried into the kitchen.

Michael was standing at the coffeepot, pushing buttons. He looked over at her and raised his eyebrows, but he didn't say anything.

"What?" she demanded, and dumped her book bag

on the table as she poured herself a glass of orange juice. "Do I owe back rent?"

"We've got some things to talk about other than the rent."

"Like what?" She kept her stare focused on her OJ. "Like how far you're going to take this whole undercover-cop thing with Bishop, and whether or not you're going to get yourself killed? Because I'm wondering, Michael."

He took in a deep breath and ran his hands through his curly golden hair as if he wanted to rip a handful out in frustration. The cut on his hand, Claire noticed, was neatly healed without any trace of a scar. "I can't tell you anything else. I already took a huge risk telling you what I did, understand?"

"And did I rat you out? No. Because according to Patience Goldman, this"—she yanked back her sleeve and showed him the tattoo, which was barely a shadow now under her skin, and hardly moving at all—"this thing is running out of juice. I don't think he's noticed yet, but he probably will soon."

"That's why I told you to stay away from him."

"Not like I came on my own! Theo ... " It struck her hard that she hadn't even asked, and she felt all of her good vibes of the morning flee in horror. "Oh God. Theo and his family—"

"They're okay," Michael said. "They were taken to a holding cell. I checked on them, and I told Sam. He'll get word to Amelie."

"That'll do a lot of good."

Michael glanced up at her as he poured his coffee. "You seem different today."

She was struck speechless, and she felt a blush burn its crimson onto her face. Michael's eyebrows rose, slowly, but he didn't say anything.

"Okay, that's ... not what I meant. And don't ever play poker." He gave her a half smile to show her he wasn't going to harass her about it. Yet. "You moving back in?"

"I don't know." She swallowed and tried to get her racing heartbeat under control. "I need to talk to my parents. They're really . . . I'm just scared for them, that's all. I thought that maybe if I stayed with them, it would make things better, but I think it's made it worse. I wish I could just get them out of Morganville. Somehow."

"You can," said a voice from the kitchen doorway. It was—of all people!—Hannah Moses, looking tall, lean, and extremely dangerous in her Morganville police uniform, loaded down with a gun, riot baton, pepper spray, handcuffs, and who knew what else. Hannah was one of those women who would command attention no matter what she was wearing, but when she put on the full display, it was no contest at all. "Mind if I come in?"

"I think you're already in," Michael said, and gestured to the kitchen table. "Want some coffee to go with that breaking and entering?"

"It's not breaking and entering with a badge, especially if someone lets you in."

"And that would be . . . ?"

"Eve. Actually, I'll have some orange juice, if you've got more," Hannah said. "All coffeed out. I've been patrolling all night." She did look tired, as she settled in a chair and stretched her legs out, although tired for Hannah just looked slightly less focused. She was wearing her cornrowed hair back in a complicated knot at the nape of her neck; having it away from her face emphasized the scar she'd gotten in Afghanistan, a seam that ran from her left temple over to her nose. On some women it might have been disfiguring. On Hannah, it was kind of a terrifying beauty mark. "It's getting nasty out there."

For Hannah to say that, it had to be worse than nasty. Claire poured some orange juice into a Scooby-Doo cup and handed it over before sitting down herself.

Michael said, "You're talking about getting Claire's parents out of town? How is that possible, without tipping off Bishop?"

"Oh, there's no doubt he'll know," Myrnin said, from right behind Claire—close enough that his cool breath touched the back of her neck, and she squealed and spilled her drink all over the table. "What he knows no longer matters. We *want* him to know."

"How did you get in here?" Michael asked, and from the shock on his face, he clearly hadn't seen Myrnin make his appearance, either. Myrnin, when Claire turned to look at him, was smirking. He'd had a bath; his hair, face, and hands were clean, although his clothes still held on to their well-lived-in filth.

"You'd hardly understand it if I told you. But to answer your question, Chief Moses has complete cooperation from me in bypassing the safeguards around the town. We need to get specific groups of people out of Morganville, and among those people are your parents, Claire."

She wet her lips. "Any special reason we're moving so fast now?"

"Yes," he said, and Hannah sent him a sharp look that would have stopped anybody sane. Didn't work on him, of course. "We are ready. Once Bishop starts killing, he will start with the ones we love first. That includes your parents, Claire, who will have no way to defend themselves."

He knew something. She could see it, and it scared her to death. "When?"

He spread his hands. "Unknown. But I can tell you that it's coming. Michael knows this as well."

Michael didn't say anything, but he studied the table very hard. Claire resisted an urge to fling some orange juice his way. "When can we get them out of town?"

"I'll handle getting them packed and ready to go," Hannah said. "I'm filling two buses with the most likely targets, and those are getting a mandatory evac out of Morganville in the next two hours." Claire saw a movement at the door, and noticed that Eve had slipped inside the kitchen, but was standing silently against the wall. As she watched, Shane came in, too, fresh from a shower, hair sparkling with drops. His gaze locked with hers, but he didn't come to her; he took up wall space next to Eve.

Hannah noticed them, too. "You two," she said. "You're on the bus today. Grab a bag. Pack for a couple of days. If you need more, we'll get it for you."

Eve and Shane both talked at once, an out-of-tune duet of angry denials. Eve slapped Shane on the shoulder and shut him up so she could go first. "No way. I'm not going anywhere, Hannah. End of story."

Shane added, "I'm not going anywhere if Claire stays here."

"Then she goes, too," Hannah said. "I was going to do that anyway."

But both Michael and Myrnin were shaking their heads. "She can't," Michael said. "Faded or not, that tattoo links her directly to Bishop. He'd still be able to track her down—and all the others who went with her."

"Not necessarily," Myrnin said. "There are vampires who could block his perception of her, if they traveled with her. But they are not available at present."

"Patience Goldman," Claire said. "Right?"

"If Theo had only waited one more day, this could have been avoided. I had planned to use her for that very purpose. But I suppose the fault is ours; if we'd kept him closer in our plans, he would not have acted so stupidly." Myrnin shrugged.

"I still wouldn't have gone," Claire said. "I'm not leaving Michael all by himself, pretending to be Bishop's best friend."

"Oh, thanks for that. Glad I inspire such confidence."

"Well, you don't. You're not a spy, Michael. You're a *musician*."

"The two," Myrnin said dryly, "are not mutually exclusive. But Michael is right. Our little Claire cannot leave the boundaries of Morganville, as matters stand just now. Besides, I need her at my side."

"Well, if she's not going," Shane said, "count me out of the running away party."

"Ditto," from Eve.

Hannah gave them both looks that should have made suitcases magically appear in their hands, but then she gave up and shook her head. "I can't promise you I'll be able to keep you safe. Understand?"

Eve rolled her eyes. "Have we ever *asked* for that? Like, *ever*? You know us, Hannah. We all went to the same high school—well, except for Claire. We Morganville kids have dodged vamps our whole lives. Not like it's new territory."

"Not true," Myrnin said, very soberly. "You might have played games with Morganville's tamed vampires, restrained by rules and laws. You've never really faced someone like Bishop, who has no conscience and no restraint."

"Don't care," Eve shot back. "That just means it's more important that we all stick together."

"Always some crazy fool who stays with a hurricane coming. Can't save everybody." Hannah drained her orange juice down to a pale froth on the bottom of the glass. "All right. I'm moving on. We're pulling people from the Founder Houses first, then anybody who has ties to Amelie, then people who were in the old Morrell administration. And yeah, the Morrells, too."

"Isn't Richard missing?"

"No," Hannah said. "Richard's just been working with us to get people lined up for evacuation. I told his damn sister to cool it, but she's still ringing every alarm bell she can find. Wish I could find a special bus just for her. A stinky, slow one. Preferably with a backed-up toilet."

Claire smiled at that, then remembered someone else. "The Goldmans," she said. "They need help, too. Can you get them?"

"No idea where they are," Hannah said.

"I know." Myrnin looked thoughtful. "I'm not sure, but I can try," he said. "They have no blood ties to Amelie or to Bishop, so they would be safe enough if we could get them on their way. But it's a risk including vampires in your evacuation."

"Then again, it means that we have some vampires fighting on our side if things go wrong outside of town," Hannah pointed out. "Not a bad thing."

"Provided the Goldmans will alight." He seemed about to say something else, but then he shook his head and made his hands into fists. "No, that isn't what I meant. Will *fight*. No. Provided that . . . provided . . . "

He was losing it. Claire got up and opened her backpack. She took out a small box of red crystals and handed it over; for most vampires, it would have been a massive dose. For a human, it was certain, gruesome death.

For Myrnin, it was like taking a handful of candy. He choked, swallowed, and nodded as he tossed the empty box back to her. Then he turned away, face to the corner, and braced himself with outspread arms, head down. His whole body shook.

That's not supposed to happen.

Then he spasmed so badly she thought he was going to fall. "Myrnin!" Claire touched his shoulder; she'd never seen this happen before—not this bad, anyway. "What's wrong?"

He whispered, "Get away. Get them all away from me, now."

"But—"

"Everything smells like blood. *Get them away.*"

Claire let go and backed up, gesturing for Hannah and even Michael to follow. Nobody said a word. Shane held open the kitchen door, and they all left.

All except Claire, who stayed at the exit, watching Myrnin fight for his life and sanity, one slow second at a time.

She saw his shoulders relax, and felt her tide of worry begin to recede—until he turned toward her.

His eyes weren't red. They were *white*. Just . . . white,

with the faint shadow of an iris and pupil showing through. The eyes of a corpse.

"Claire," he said, and took a step toward her.

Then he fell, hit the ground, and went completely limp.

"We could take him to the hospital," Hannah said, but not as if she thought it was a good idea. Claire was kneeling next to Myrnin, with Michael hovering near her, ready to yank her out of the way if Myrnin should suddenly surge back to bloodsucking life.

He was quiet. He looked *dead.*

"I think this is a little beyond the hospital," Claire said. "It's part of the disease. It's in his notes—he charted the progress; sometimes this happens. They just . . . collapse. They revive, but usually when they do, they're not—" Her voice failed her, and she had to clear her throat. "Not the same." Myrnin's notes, what she could remember of them, seemed to indicate that when—or if—the vampire recovered from the coma, he didn't have much left of his original personality.

Myrnin had been sick a long time. He'd lost the ability to create other vampires more than a hundred years ago; he'd begun behaving weirdly about another fifty years after, and from there it had progressed rapidly. Amelie, by contrast, was just now getting to the early physical symptoms—the occasional loss of emotional control, and the shakes. Oliver . . . well. Who knew if Oliver's problem was the disease or just a bad attitude?

The fact that Myrnin had held out longer than at least thirty other vampires confined underground in cells was either proof that the disease didn't work the same way in everyone, or that Myrnin was incredibly determined. He hadn't wanted to take the cure . . . but there wasn't a choice now. He *had* to take it.

And she had to get him to Dr. Mills.

*   *   *

They carried him through the portal—well, Michael and Hannah carried him; Claire concentrated on getting them to their target location, the basement of Morganville High. "Stay here," Claire said. "I'm going to get the doctor."

"We can carry him up," Michael said. He was being charitable; he could have done it on his own, no problem, but he was letting Hannah take half the weight.

"I know," Claire said. "I just don't want to lead a really obvious parade to a secret hideout."

She didn't wait for an answer, just dashed up the steps, through the broken-locked door, and out into the hallways, dodging around oblivious teens her own age who were hustling to and from class. It was early morning, but Morganville High was in full session, and Claire had to shove her way through the crowd with a little more force than usual.

Somebody grabbed her by the back of her shirt and hauled her to a sudden stop. She flailed for escape, but it was just like always—she was too small, and he was *way* too big.

Her captor was wearing a shirt and tie, and had the drill sergeant hairstyle of school officials everywhere. He glared at her as if she was some bug he'd caught scurrying across his dinner table. "What do you think you're doing?" he demanded. "No shoving in the halls!"

"I'm not a student!" she yelled. "Let go of me!"

He got a glance at the gold bracelet on her wrist, and his eyes went wide; he quickly focused back on her face. "You're that girl—Claire. Claire Danvers. The Founder's—Sorry." He let her go so suddenly she almost toppled over. "My apologies, miss. I thought you were just another of these rude punk kids."

There were a few moments in her new, weird life when it was all worth it—worth being the freak of nature with all the baggage that had been loaded on her in Morganville.

This was one of them. She braced herself, put her

hands on her hips, and glared at him with the kind of icy calm that she imagined Amelie would have brought down like a guillotine blade. "I *am* a rude punk kid," she said. "But I'm a rude punk kid you don't get to order around. Now, I'd like you to leave me alone and go to your office. And shut the door. Now."

He looked at her as if he couldn't quite believe his ears. "Excuse me?"

"You heard me. I don't need you out here causing trouble right now. *Go!*"

He looked confused, but he nodded reluctantly and headed for a door marked ADMINISTRATION farther down the hall.

"Eat your heart out, Monica," Claire murmured. "Thanks for the bitch lessons." She broke into a full run, leaving him and his petty kingdom behind.

Myrnin had taken her through darkened corridors, but she remembered the turns; she also remembered a little too late that the way was dark, and wished she'd thought to grab a flashlight somewhere along the way. There was little light coming into the hall during the last leg, and desks and chairs stacked randomly in her path; she had to slow down or end up taking an epic spill.

Finally, she saw the locked doors at the end of the hallway, and lunged around a dusty teacher's desk to batter at the heavy wood panel.

"Hey!" No answer. She knocked again. "Dr. Mills! Dr. Mills, open up; it's Claire! I need your help!"

There was no answer. She tried the door handle.

"Dr. Mills?"

The door opened without the slightest resistance.

The room was empty. No sign of a struggle—no sign of anything, actually. It looked like nobody had ever been here. All of the equipment was back on the shelves, sparkling and clean; there was no sign of the production of serum and crystals that had been going on here. The only thing that gave it away was the lack of a coating of dust.

Claire dashed for the room behind—the teacher's office and locked storage, where the Mills family had been living.

Same story. Nothing there to show they'd ever been here, not so much as a scrap of paper or a lost toy. "Oh God, they were *moved*," Claire whispered, and turned to run back to where she'd left her friends. She hoped the Mills family had been moved, at least. The alternative was much, much worse, but she couldn't see Bishop—or his henchmen—taking the time and energy to clean up after themselves. They certainly hadn't in Myrnin's lab.

Claire let out an involuntary yell because a ghostly woman—black and white, shades of gray, no color to her at all—blocked the way out.

She looked like she'd stepped right out of a photograph from the Victorian ages. Big full skirts, hair done up in a bun, body slender and graceful. She stared straight at Claire, hands clasped in front of her. There was something so creepy and *aware* about her that Claire skidded to a sudden halt, not sure what she should do, but absolutely sure she didn't want to go anywhere near that image.

Claire could see the room behind right through her body. As she watched, the ghost broke up into a mist of static, then re-formed. She put a finger to her lips, gestured to Claire, and glided away.

"Ghosts," Claire said. "Great. I'm going crazy. That's all there is to it."

Only, when she checked the other room, the ghost was still there, hovering a couple of inches above the floor. So at least she was consistently crazy.

The phantom beckoned for Claire to follow, and turned—getting thinner and thinner, disappearing, then widening again to show a back view. Not at all like a real person, more like a flat cardboard cutout making a one-eighty. It was startling and eerie, and Claire thought, *I'm not hallucinating this, because I'd never imagine that on my own.*

She followed the ghost back out into the science lab, then out into the hallway. Then into another classroom, this one empty except for desks and chalkboards. The same dusty sense of disuse lay over everything. It didn't feel like anyone had been here in years.

The ghost turned to the chalkboard, and letters formed in thin white strokes.

AMELIE HAS WHAT YOU NEED, it wrote. FIND AMELIE. SAVE MYRNIN.

"Who are you?" Claire asked. The ghost gave her a very tiny smile. It seemed annoyed, and more than a little superior.

Three letters appeared on the chalkboard. ADA.

"You're the *computer*?" Claire couldn't help it; she laughed. Not only was she talking to a blood-drinking computer, but it liked to think of itself as some gothic-novel heroine. Plucky Miss Plum the governess. "How do you— Oh, never mind, I know it's not the time. How can I find Amelie?"

USE BRACELET. Ada's black-and-white image flickered again, like a signal getting too much interference. When she re-formed, she looked strained and unhappy. HURRY. NO TIME.

"I don't know how!"

Ada looked even more annoyed, and wrote something on the board—but it was faint, and faded almost before Claire could read it. B-L-O . . . "Blood?" Claire asked. Ada herself was fading, but Claire saw her mouth the word *yes*. "Of course. What else? Why can't any of you guys ever come up with something that uses *chocolate*?"

No answer from the computer/spirit world; Ada disappeared in a puff of white mist and was gone. Claire looked around and found a thumbtack pressed into the surface of a bulletin board. She hesitated, positioned the thumbtack over her finger, and muttered, "If I get tetanus, I'm blaming you, Myrnin."

Then she stabbed the sharp point in, and came up with

a few fat drops of red that she dripped onto the surface of the symbol on Amelie's bracelet.

It glowed white in the dim light. The blood disappeared into the grooves, and the whole bracelet turned warm, then uncomfortably hot against her skin. Claire gritted her teeth until she felt a scream coming on, and finally, the burning sensation faded, leaving the metal oddly cold.

And that was it. Amelie didn't magically appear. Claire wasn't sure what she'd expected, but this seemed really anticlimactic.

She stuck the thumbtack back on the board and went back to tell Hannah and Michael that she'd completely failed.

Dejected, she headed back to the basement. The hallways were deserted now, since classes were back in session. As she passed the administration office door, it opened, and the man she'd sent to his room like a little kid looked out. "Miss Danvers?" he asked. "Is there something I can do for you?"

This was every high school kid's fantasy, Claire thought, and she was tempted to tell him to do something crazy, like strip naked and run around the auditorium. But instead she just shook her head and kept on walking.

He came out of the door and got in her way.

"Could you put in a good word for me?" he asked, and when she tried to go around him, he grabbed her by the arm. He lowered his voice to a fast, harsh whisper. "Tell Mr. Bishop I can help him. I can be of use. Just tell him that!"

The big double doors leading out into the sunlight at the end of the hall crashed open, and a whole troop of people came flooding in. They all wore long, dark hooded coats, and they moved fast, with a purpose.

Faster than humans.

The two in the lead threw back their hoods, and Claire was relieved to see that one of them was Amelie, perfectly composed and looking as in charge as ever, even if she wasn't queen of Morganville anymore.

The other leader of the pack was Oliver, of course. Not so comforting.

"Milton Dyer," Amelie said. "Please take your hand off of my friend Claire. *Now.*"

The man went about as pale as his white shirt, and looked down at Claire, and his hand wrapped around her arm. He let go as if she'd suddenly become electrified.

"Now go away," Amelie said to him in that same calm, emotionless voice. "I don't wish to see you again."

"I . . . " He wet his lips. "I'm still loyal to my Protector. . . ."

"Your Protector was Charles," Amelie said. "Charles is dead. Oliver, do you have any interest in picking up Mr. Dyer's contract?"

"I really don't," Oliver said. He sounded bored.

"Then that settles things. Leave my sight, Mr. Dyer. The next time you cross my path, I'll finish you." She said it without any particular sense of menace, but Claire didn't doubt for an instant that she meant it. Neither did Mr. Dyer, who quickly retreated to his office. He didn't even dare to slam the door. It closed with a soft, careful click.

Leaving Claire in the hallway with a bunch of vampires. Old ones, she thought—Amelie and Oliver were obviously old, but the others seemed to have come through their sunlight stroll without a mark, too. Ten of them in total. Most of them didn't bother to put their hoods back and reveal their faces.

"You used the bracelet in a way that I did not teach you," Amelie said. "Who showed you how to use it to summon me?"

"Why?"

"Don't play games with me, Claire. Was it Myrnin?"

"No. It was Ada."

Amelie's gray eyes flickered, just a little, but it was enough to tell Claire that she had knowledge that Amelie wished she didn't. "I see. We'll talk of that later," she said. "Why did you use the blood call? It's intended to alert me only if you are seriously injured."

"Well, someone is. Myrnin's very sick. He's downstairs. I need to get him some help. I came to find Dr. Mills, but—"

"Dr. Mills has been relocated," Amelie said. "I thought it best, after Myrnin's ill-advised visit here. I can't tell you where he is. You understand why."

Claire knew. And she felt sick and a little angry, too. "You think I might give him away. To Bishop. Well, I wouldn't. Myrnin knew that."

"Whatever Myrnin believes, I can't take the risk. We are close to the endgame, Claire. I risk only what I must."

"You're not happy that Myrnin introduced me to Ada, are you?" Claire asked.

"Myrnin's judgment has been . . . questionable of late. As you say, he is ill. Where can we find him?"

"Downstairs, by the portal," Claire said. Amelie nodded a brisk dismissal and turned to go, along with all of her followers. "Wait! What do you want me to do?"

Amelie said nothing. Oliver, lingering behind for just a moment, said, "Stay out of our way. If you value your friends, keep them out of our way, too."

Then they were gone, moving fast and silently through the basement doorway.

Claire stood in the empty hallway for a few deep breaths, hearing the sounds of lectures continuing on inside of classrooms, student voices raised in questions or answers.

Life went on.

So weird.

She started to go down to the basement, but a vampire she didn't know blocked the entrance. "No," he said flatly. "You don't go with us."

"But—"

"No."

"Hannah and Michael—"

"They will be taken care of. Leave."

There wasn't any room for negotiation. Claire finally got the hint, and turned away to walk out of the high school the old-fashioned way ... into the sunlight, the way Amelie and her gang had come. She had no idea where they'd come from, or where they were going.

Amelie wanted it that way.

Claire sat down on the steps of the high school for a few long minutes, shivering in the cold wind, not much warmed by the bright sun in a cloudless sky. The street outside the school looked empty—a few cars making their way around Morganville, but not much else going on.

She heard the door behind her open, and Hannah Moses clumped down in her heavy boots and offered Claire a big, elegant hand. Claire took it and stood. "Amelie's taking care of him?" she asked. Hannah nodded. "Michael went with?"

"He'll see you later," Hannah said. "Important thing is to get you out of here. I need you to help me get your parents on that bus."

"Bishop's going to find out," she said. "You know that, right? He's going to find out what you're doing."

Hannah nodded. "That's why we're doing it fast, girl-friend. So let's move."

Mom and Dad were having an argument; Claire could hear it from where she and Hannah stood on the front porch of their house, ringing the doorbell. Claire felt a sinking sensation in the pit of her stomach. Her parents didn't fight very often, but when they did, it was usually over something important.

The shouty blur of voices broke off, and about ten seconds later, the door whipped open. Claire's mom stood there, color burning high in her cheeks. She looked stricken when she caught sight of Claire, very obviously a guilty-looking earwitness to the fighting, but she rallied and gave a bright smile and gestured them both inside.

"Sheriff Hannah Moses, ma'am," Hannah said without waiting for introductions. "I don't think we've met in person before. I've known your daughter for a while now. She's good people."

She offered her hand, and Claire's mother took it for a quick shake as her eyes darted anxiously from Claire to Hannah, then back. "Is there some kind of problem, Sheriff Moses?"

"Hannah, please." Hannah really was turning on the charm, and she had an awful lot of it. "May I talk with you and your husband at the same time? This concerns both of you."

With only a single, worried look over her shoulder, her mother led the way down the long hallway and into the living room area. Same floor plan as the Glass House, but so wrenchingly different, especially now. Claire got mental whiplash from expecting to see the familiar battered couch and Michael's guitar and the cheerful stacks of books against the wall; instead, her mother's ruthlessly efficient housekeeping had made this room magazine-feature-ready, everything carefully aligned and straightened.

The only thing that wasn't ready for the photo shoot was Claire's father, who sat in one of the leather armchairs, face flushed. He had a stubborn set to his jaw, and an angry fire in his eyes that Claire hadn't seen in, well, forever. Still, he got to his feet and shook hands with Hannah, politely gesturing her to the couch while Claire's mom sank down on the other end, with Claire left to take the middle seat. Normally, her mom would have been fluttering around offering coffee and cookies and sandwiches, but not this time. She just took the other armchair and looked worried.

Hannah said, "Let's put all our cards on the table.

There's a town emergency. Mr. and Mrs. Danvers, you are going to need to come with us. Pack a bag for a few nights, take whatever you need that you can't live without. I can give you about fifteen minutes."

That was ... blunt. Claire blinked. She expected a flood of questions from her parents, but she was surprised by the silence.

Claire's parents looked at each other, and then her father nodded. "Good," he said. "I've wanted to do this for a while. Claire, go with your mother and pack. I'll be up in a second."

"Um ..." Claire cleared her throat and tried not to look as awkward as she felt. "I'm not going, Dad."

They both looked at her as if she'd spoken in Chinese. "Of course you are," her mom said. "You're not staying here alone. Not with what we know about how dangerous it is."

"I'm sorry, but you know just enough about Morganville to get yourselves in trouble," Hannah said. "This really isn't up for discussion. You have to pack, and you have to go. And Claire can't come with you, at least not yet."

One thing about Hannah: when she said something like that, she clearly meant it. In the silence that fell, Claire felt the weight of both her parents' stares directly on her, so she looked down at her clasped hands instead. "I can't," she said. "It's complicated."

"No, it's not," her dad said, with a steely undertone in his voice she couldn't remember hearing before. "It's absolutely simple. I'm your father, you're under eighteen, and you're coming with us. I'm sorry, Chief Moses, but she's too young to be here on her own."

"Dad, you *sent* me here on my own!" Claire said.

"Why do you think we were fighting, Claire?" her mom replied. "Your father was just reminding me that I was the one who thought sending you to a school close by, just to get some experience with it, would be a good idea. *He* wanted you to go straight to MIT, although how we were going to pay for that, I really don't have any—"

Dad interrupted her. "We're not going to start this up again. Claire, we were wrong to let you go off on your own here in the first place, no matter how safe we thought it would be. And we're fixing that now. You're coming with us, and things will be better once we're out of this town."

Claire's hands formed into fists as frustration boiled up inside her. "Are you *listening* to me? It's too late for all that stuff! I can't go with you!"

She should have guessed that they'd make the wrong assumptions . . . and, in a way, the right one. "It's the boy, isn't it?" Claire's mother said. "Shane?"

"What? No!" Claire blurted out a denial that, even to her own ears, sounded lame and guilty. "No, not really. It's something else. Like I said, it's complicated."

"Oh my God . . . Claire, are you *pregnant?*"

"*Mom!*" She knew she looked as mortified as she felt, especially with Hannah looking on.

"Honey, has that boy taken advantage of you?" Her father was charging full speed down the wrong path; he even stood up to make it more dramatic. "Well?"

Claire stared at him, openmouthed, unable to even try to speak. She knew she should lie, but she just couldn't find the words.

In the ringing silence, her father said, "I want him arrested."

Hannah asked, "On what charge, sir?"

"Are you kidding? He had sex with my underage daughter!" He gave Claire a look that was partly angry, partly wounded, and all over dangerous. "Go ahead, tell me I'm wrong, Claire."

"It . . . wasn't like that!"

Her dad transferred his glare over to Hannah. "You see? I'll swear out a complaint if I need to."

Hannah looked perfectly comfortable. "Sir, there's no

complaint to be sworn out here. Fact is, Claire is seventeen years old, which by Texas law makes her able to give consent on her own. Shane's only a year older than she is. There's no laws being broken here, beyond maybe the law of good sense, which I think you'll admit is often a casualty of our teen years. This is a family matter, not a matter for the police."

Her father looked shocked, then even angrier. "That's insane! It has to be illegal!"

"Well, it's not, sir, and it has nothing to do with why I'm telling you Claire needs to stay in Morganville. That has to do with the vampires." Hannah had deftly moved the whole thing off the subject of Shane and sex, for which Claire was spine-meltingly grateful. "I'm telling you this for your own good, and for Claire's own good: she stays here. She won't be unprotected; I promise you that. We're committed to keeping her safe."

"Who's *we*?" Claire's dad wasn't giving up without a fight.

"Everybody who counts," Hannah said, and raised her eyebrows. "Time's a-wastin', Mr. Danvers. We really can't debate this. You need to go right now. Please go pack."

In the end, they did. Claire went to help her mother, reluctantly; she didn't want the subject to come back to her and Shane, but it did as soon as the door was closed. At least her father wasn't in the room. God, that had been awkward.

"Honey." Claire paused in the act of dragging a suitcase out from under her parents' bed, took one look at the serious expression on her mother's face, and kept on with what she was doing. "Honey, I really don't like your getting involved with that boy—that man. And it's not appropriate for you to be living in that house with him. I just can't allow that."

"Mom, could we *please* focus on not getting killed today? I promise, you can give me the I'm-so-disappointed-in-you speech tomorrow, and every day after, if you will just pack!"

Her mother opened a drawer of the dresser by the window, grabbed a few handfuls of things at random, and threw them into the open suitcase. *Not* normal. Mom made those people who worked retail clothing stores look sloppy about how they folded things. She moved on to the next drawer, then the next. Claire struggled to neaten up the mess.

"Just tell me this," her mother said as she dumped an armload of clothes from the closet onto the bed. "Are you being safe?"

Oh *lord,* Claire did not want to have the birds-and-bees part two conversation with her mother. Not now. Not ever, to be honest; they'd suffered through it once, awkwardly, and once was enough. "Yes," she said, with as calm and decisive a tone as she could manage. "He insisted." She meant that to reflect well on Shane. Of course, Mom took it the wrong way.

"You mean you *didn't*? Oh, Claire. It's your body!"

"Mom, of course I—" Claire took a deep breath. "Can we just pack? Please?"

She winced as a rain of shoes descended on the bed.

Hannah was waiting when she finally dragged the suitcase downstairs. Claire's father had come in for a few minutes, just long enough to add his few things to the pile, and then he'd tried to tote the bag himself, but Claire had insisted on doing it. The thing was fifty pounds, at least.

Hannah raised her eyebrows at Claire. *What happened?*

Claire rolled her eyes. *Don't ask.*

It was a cold, silent ride to the bus.

Richard Morrell had commandeered two genuine Greyhound buses, with plush seats and tinted windows. According to the hand-lettered sign in the front window, it was a charter heading to Midland/Odessa, but Claire suspected they'd go somewhere else as a destination.

The first bus was already being loaded by the time

Claire arrived with her parents; in line to board were most of the town officials and Founder House residents, including the Morrells. Eve was there, too, holding a clipboard and checking people in at a folding table.

"Oh, look, there's your friend," Claire's mom said, and pointed. "She doesn't look very happy."

She wasn't pointing at Eve, but at Monica. Monica definitely wasn't happy. She had to be forced onto the bus, arguing the entire time with her brother, who looked harassed and angry. She'd somehow managed to shoehorn her two friends into the evacuation along with her, although Gina and Jennifer looked a lot more relieved at being given a chance to leave town. Monica was probably thinking that she stood a better chance of social queen bee-ness with Bishop than if Amelie was in charge, but she was thinking short-term; if what Myrnin said was right, and Claire had no reason to think it wasn't, then the entire social order of Morganville was about to get shattered, and being the most popular wouldn't get you anything but more face time with the firing squad.

The argument with Monica came from the fact that Richard Morrell refused to get on the bus. Well, Claire had seen that coming. He wasn't the type to run. "There's a whole town here that can't get out," he snapped at his sister, who was stubbornly resisting getting pushed toward the idling bus. "People who need looking after. I'm the mayor. I have to stay. Besides, since Dad's gone, I'm on the town council. I can't just go."

"You have got such an ego, Richard! Nobody's counting on you. Most of the stupid people in this town would claw one another apart to get out, if they thought they could."

"That's why I'm staying," he said. "Because those people need order. But I need for you to go, Monica. Please. You need to look after our mom."

Monica wavered. Claire, looking up, could see Mrs. Morrell sitting on the bus, looking out the window with a distant, remote expression. Monica had said her mother wasn't dealing very well, and she did look thin and frail and not entirely in this world.

"That is such emotional blackmail!" Monica spat. Behind her, Gina and Jennifer looked at each other, took a few quiet steps back, and mounted the stairs to board the bus, leaving Monica on her own. "Seriously, Richard. I can't believe you're sending me away like this!"

"Believe it. You're getting on, and getting out of here. Now. I need you to be safe." He hugged her, but she stiff-armed him with an angry glare, and turned and boarded without another word. She slumped into the seat behind Jennifer and Gina, next to her mother, and folded her arms in silent protest.

Richard breathed a sigh of relief, then turned to Claire's parents. "Please," he said. "We need to get these buses moving."

Claire's father shook his head.

"Dad," Claire said, and tugged on his arm. "Dad, come on."

He still hesitated, staring at Hannah, then Richard, then Claire. Still shaking his head in mute refusal.

"Dad, you have to go! Now!" Claire practically shouted. She felt sick inside, worried for them and relieved to think they'd be safe, finally, somewhere outside of Morganville. Somewhere none of this could touch them. "Mom, please. Just make him go! I don't want you here; you're just in the way!"

She said it in desperation, and she saw it hurt her parents a little. She'd said worse to them over the years; she'd had her share of *I hate you* and *I wish you were dead*, but that had been when she was just a kid and thought she knew everything.

Now, she knew she didn't, but in this case, she knew more than they did.

Frustrating, because they'd never see it that way.

"Don't you talk to us like that, Claire!" her mother snapped. Her dad put a hand on her shoulder and patted, and she took a deep breath.

"All right," Dad said, "I can see you're not going to come without a fight, and I can see your friends here aren't going to help us." He paused, and Claire swallowed hard at the look in his eyes as he locked stares with Hannah, then Richard. "If anything happens to our daughter—"

"Sir," Richard said. "If you don't get on the bus, something is going to happen to all of us, and it's going to be very, very bad. Please. Just go."

"You need to do it for your daughter," Hannah added. "I think you both know that, deep down. So you let me worry about taking care of Claire. You two get on the bus. I promise you, this will be over soon."

It was a sad sort of farewell, full of tears (from Mom and Claire) and the kind of too-strong hug that meant Claire's father felt just as choked up, but wasn't willing to show it. Her mother smoothed her hair, just like she'd done since Claire was a little girl, and kissed her gently on the cheek.

"You be good," she said, and looked deep into Claire's eyes. "We're going to talk about things later."

She meant about Shane, of course. Claire sighed and nodded, and hugged her one last time. She watched them walk up the stairs and onto the bus.

Her parents took a seat near the front, with her mom next to the window. Claire gave a sad little wave, and her mom waved back. Mom was still crying. Dad looked off into the distance, jaw set tight, and didn't wave back.

The bus closed its doors with a final hiss and pulled away from the deserted warehouse that served as a dropoff point for the departures. Three police cars fell in behind it, driven by people Hannah had handpicked.

Claire shivered, even though she was standing in the sun. *They're leaving. They're really leaving.* She felt very alone.

The bus looked so vulnerable.

"Cold?" A jacket settled around her shoulders. It smelled like Shane. "What did I miss?"

She turned, and there he was, wearing an old gray T-shirt and jeans. His leather jacket felt like a hug around her body, but it wasn't enough; she dived into the warmth of his arms, and they clung together for a moment. He kissed the top of her head. "It's okay," he said. "They'll be okay."

"No, it's not okay," she said, muffled against his chest. "It's just not."

He didn't argue. After a moment, she turned her head, and together they watched the caravan stream away toward the Morganville city limits.

"Why is it," she asked in a plaintive little voice, "that I can fight vampires and risk death and they can accept that, but they can't accept that I'm a woman, with my own life?"

Shane thought about that for a second; she could see him trying to work it out through the framework of his own admittedly weird childhood. "Must be a girl thing?"

"Yeah, must be."

"So I'm guessing you told them."

"Um ... not on purpose. I didn't expect them to be so ... angry about it."

"You're their little girl," Shane said. "You know, when I think about it, I'd feel the same way about my own daughter."

"You would?" There was something deliciously warm about the fact that he wasn't afraid to say that to her. "So," she said, with an effort at being casual that was probably all too obvious. "You want to have a daughter, then?"

He kissed the top of her head. "Hit the brakes, girl."

But he didn't sound angry about it, or nervous. Just—as was usual with Shane—focused on what was in front of them right now. A sense of calm was slowly spreading through her, sinking deeper with every breath. It felt better when she was with him. Everything felt better.

Shane asked, "What about the Goldmans? Were they on the bus, too?"

"I didn't see the Goldmans," Claire said. "Hannah?"

Hannah Moses was still standing nearby, signing papers on a clipboard that another uniformed Morganville cop had handed her. She glanced toward the two of them. "Couldn't get to them," she said. "Myrnin was going to arrange that, but we've got no way to get them out of Bishop's control right now. The clock's running, and it's only a matter of minutes before Bishop finds out what we just did, if he hasn't already."

Richard Morrell's phone rang. He unclipped it from his belt and checked the number, then flipped it open and walked away to talk for a moment. Claire watched him pace, shoulders hunched, as he had his conversation. When he folded up the phone and came back, his face was tense. "He knows," he said. "Bishop's calling a town hall meeting for tonight at Founder's Square. Everybody must attend. Nobody stays home."

"Oh, come on. You can't get everybody in town to a meeting. What if they don't get the message? What if they just don't want to do it?" Claire asked. Even in Morganville, making people stick to rules—whatever the rules were—was like herding cats.

Richard and Hannah exchanged a look. "Bishop's not one for taking excuses," she said. "If he says everybody has to be at the meeting, he'll make it open season on anybody who isn't there. That's his style."

Richard was already nodding his agreement. "We need to get word out. Knock on every door, every business. Lock off the campus and keep the students out of this. We've got six hours before sundown. Let's not waste one minute."

Shane was drafted into helping a whole crowd of people load supplies into the warehouse—food, water, clothing, radios, survival-type stuff. Claire wasn't sure why, and she didn't think she really wanted to know; the atmosphere was quiet, purposeful, but tense. Nobody asked questions. Not now.

The first of Bishop's vampires showed up about two hours later, driving slowly past the perimeter in one of the city-issued cars with tinted windows. Hannah's strike team stopped the car, and Claire was surprised to see them fling a blanket over the vampire as he was dragged out of the shelter into the sun, and hauled off to be confined under cover.

"Most of Bishop's people are really Amelie's," Hannah explained. "Amelie would like us to keep them alive, if we can. She can turn them back, once Bishop's gone. Call it temporary insanity—not a killing kind of offense, even for vampires. We just need to keep them out of commission, that's all."

Well, that sounded deceptively easy to Claire's ears; she didn't think Bishop's converts—even the unwilling ones—would be all that eager to be put on the bench. Still, Hannah seemed to know what she was doing. Hopefully. "So that's the plan: we just grab every vamp who comes looking?"

"Not quite." Hannah gave her a slight smile. "You do know I'm not telling you the plan, right?"

Right, Claire was still on the wrong side. She glared down at her much-faded tattoo, which was still moving under her skin, but weakly, like the last flutters of a failing butterfly. It itched. "I wish this thing would just *die* already."

"Has Bishop tried to reach you through it?"

"Not recently. Or if he has, I can't feel it anymore." That would be excellent, if it really was a bad connection. Maybe she was in a no-magic-signal dead zone. "So what can I do?"

"Go knock on doors," Hannah said. "We've got a list of names that we're still looking for, for the second bus. You can go with Joe Hess."

Claire's eyes widened. "He's okay?" Because she had

an instant sense memory of the feeling of that death warrant in her hands, the one she'd given to him.

"Sure," Hannah said. "Why wouldn't he be?"

Claire had no idea what had happened, but she liked Detective Hess, and at least riding around with him would give her a feeling of forward motion, of doing something useful. Everyone else seemed to have a purpose. All she could think about was that her parents were on a bus heading out of town, and she didn't know what was going to happen to them. Or *could* happen to them.

She wished she'd said a better good-bye. She wished they hadn't been so upset with her about Shane. *Well, they're going to have to get used to it*, she thought defiantly, but even to herself, it felt weak and a little selfish.

But being with Shane wasn't a mistake. She knew it wasn't.

Joe Hess was driving his own car, but it had all the cool cop stuff inside—a radio, one of those magnetic flashing lights to go on the roof, and a shotgun that was locked into a rack in the back. He was a tall, quiet man who just had a way about him that put her at ease. For one thing, he never looked at her like some annoying kid; he just looked at her as a person. A young person, true, but someone to take seriously. She wasn't quite sure how she'd earned that from him, considering the death warrant delivery.

"I'm locking the doors," he told her as she climbed into the passenger seat, half a second before the *click-thump* sound echoed through the car. "Nice to see you, Claire."

"Thanks. It's good to see you, too. What about the buses?" she said. "Are they out of town yet?"

"Amelie herself escorted them through the barrier a few minutes ago," he said. "There was a little bit of trouble at the border, nothing we couldn't handle. They're on their way. Nobody was hurt."

That eased a tight knot in her chest that she hadn't

even known was there. "Where are they going— No, don't tell me. I probably don't need to know, right?"

"Probably not," he agreed, and gave her a sidelong look. "You okay?"

She looked out the car window and shrugged. "My parents are on one of those buses, that's all. I'm just worried."

He kept sending her looks as he drove, and there was a frown on his face. "And tired," he said. "When you left me, did you go back to Bishop? Did he hurt you?"

There really wasn't an easy answer to that. "He didn't hurt me," she finally said. "Not . . . personally."

"I guess that's part of what I was asking," he said. "But that doesn't answer my question, really."

"You mean, am I in need of serious therapy because of all this?" Another shrug seemed kind of appropriate. "Yeah, probably. But this is Morganville. That's not exactly the worst thing that could happen." She turned her head and looked directly at him. "What was on the scroll I gave you?"

He was quiet for so long she thought he was blowing off the question, but then he said, "It was a death warrant."

She already knew that. "Not yours, though."

"No," he said. "Someone else's."

"Whose?"

"Claire—"

"It doesn't matter. We got it reversed. It's not an issue anymore."

"I delivered it. I have a right to know."

For answer, Joe dug into the pocket of his sports jacket and pulled out a folded piece of paper, still curling at the edges, with fragments of wax clinging to the outside. He held it out to her.

Claire unfolded it. The paper was stiff and crackly, old paper, with a faintly moldy smell to it. The handwriting—Bishop's—was spiky and hard to read, but the name was done larger and underlined.

Eve Rosser.

"That's not happening," Joe said. "I just wanted you to know that. If he tells you about it, I wanted you to understand that Eve is perfectly safe, all right? Nothing will happen to her. Claire, do you understand me?"

She'd carried an order to him to kill her best friend.

Claire couldn't think. Couldn't feel anything except a vast, echoing sense of shock. She tried to read the rest of the paper, but her eyes kept moving back to Eve's name, going over and over it.

She folded up the paper and held it clutched tightly in one hand. *Breathe.* She felt light-headed and a little sick.

"Why you?" she asked faintly. "Why give it to you?"

"That's Bishop's style. He picks out people least likely to do what he wants, so he can punish them when they refuse to carry out the order. Object lessons for the rest of Morganville. He knew I wouldn't kill Eve. Not a chance. This was less about his wanting to get rid of Eve than to get rid of me."

She still felt cold. Sure, Detective Hess wouldn't have done it, but what if she'd been told to take it to someone else? Monica, maybe?

Eve might be dead right now, and it would have been all her fault.

She felt the death warrant being tugged out of her fingers. When she opened her eyes, fighting back tears, Detective Hess was slipping it back into his pocket. "I just wanted you to understand what we're up against," he said. "And to understand that no matter what happens, some of us will never do what he wants."

Claire realized that she couldn't count herself in that club. She'd already done what Bishop wanted.

More than once.

God, she *really* didn't want to think about how far she'd wandered into that swamp, but she was definitely up to her butt in alligators.

"All right, back to business." Hess handed her a piece of paper. "These are the people we still need to find," he said. "I heard about what happened with Frank Collins. You and Shane were there?"

She really wasn't up to talking about that. "Dr. Mills is with Amelie," she said. "You can cross him off this list. She isn't going to send him out of town."

All around Morganville, as they drove, there were signs things were happening—people gathering in groups, whispering at fences, and pausing to stare hard at the passing car. No vampires in sight, but then Claire wouldn't expect there to be so close to noon. "What is this?" she asked. Hess shook his head.

"There's still a pretty strong antivampire movement in town," he said. "It got stronger these last few months. I've been trying to keep them calmed down, because if they start this now, they'll just get themselves killed. And most of them aren't looking at Amelie's side as anything but another target. We can't afford that until Bishop's gone."

"So what do we do about it?"

"Nothing. Nothing we can do right now. Bishop's the one pushing the agenda, not us. If he wants a fight tonight, he's going to get one. Maybe bigger than he wants."

The fourth address on the list was an apartment—there weren't many apartment buildings in Morganville, since most people lived in single-family houses, but there were a few. Like in any small town, the complexes varied from crappy to less crappy; there was no such thing as luxury multifamily housing.

The apartment complex they stopped at was on the crappy end of the short spectrum. It was stucco over brick, painted a sun-faded pink, with two stories of apartments built into an open square on a central . . . well, Claire guessed you could call it a courtyard, if you liked a view that included a dry swimming pool with dark scum at one end, some spiky, untrimmed bushes, and an overflowing trash can.

Joe Hess checked apartment numbers. If the run-down appearance of the place bothered him, he didn't show it. When they reached number twenty-two, he banged loudly on the door. "Police, open up!" he yelled, and pushed Claire out of the way when she tried to stand next to him. He gave her a silent *stay there* gesture, and listened. She couldn't hear a thing from inside.

Neither could he, apparently. He shook his head, but as they turned to go, Claire clearly heard someone inside the apartment say, "Help."

She froze, staring at Detective Hess. He'd heard it, too, and he gestured her even farther back as he pulled his gun from the holster under his jacket. "Willie Combs? You okay in there? It's Joe Hess. Answer me, Willie!"

"Help," the voice came again, weaker this time.

Hess tried the door, but it was locked. He took in a deep breath. "Claire, you stay right there. *Do not come in.* Hear me?"

She nodded. He whirled and kicked into the door, and the cheap hollow wood splintered and flew open on the second try, sending wood and metal flying.

Detective Hess disappeared inside. Claire saw curtains fluttering and blinds tenting as people looked out to see what was going on, but nobody came outside.

Not even in the middle of the day.

It seemed like a very long time until Detective Hess came out with someone held in his arms. It was a girl about Claire's age, pretty, dressed in a Morganville High T-shirt and sweatpants, like she'd just dropped in from gym class.

She wasn't moving, and he was holding a towel on her neck.

"Call an ambulance," he ordered Claire. "Tell them it's a rush, and bring the bite kit."

"Is she—"

"She's alive," he said, and stretched her out on the concrete, still holding the towel in place. Hess looked up at her with fury shining in his eyes. "Her name is Theresa. Theresa Combs. She's the oldest of the three kids."

Claire went cold, and looked at the doorway of the apartment. "They're not—"

"Let's focus on the living," he said. "Hold this on her throat, just like this." She knelt beside him and pressed her small fingers where his larger ones were. It felt like she was pressing too hard, but he nodded. "Good. Keep doing that. I'm going to make one more sweep inside, just to be sure."

As he stepped over the girl and back into the apartment, Theresa's eyes fluttered, and she looked at Claire. Big, dark eyes. Desperate. "Help," she whispered. "Help Jimmy. He's only twelve."

Claire took her hand. "Shhhh. Just rest."

Theresa's eyes filled up with tears. "I tried," she said. "I really tried. Why is this happening to us? We didn't do anything wrong. We followed all the rules."

Claire couldn't do anything to help her, except hold her hand and keep the towel over her throat, just like Detective Hess said. When he came back to the doorway, drawn by the distant howl of an approaching siren, she looked up at him in miserable hope.

He shook his head.

They didn't speak at all until the paramedics took Theresa away. Claire stayed where she was, on her knees, staring at the blood speckling her trembling fingers. Detective Hess crouched down and handed her a moist wipe, with the attitude of somebody who'd done that sort of thing a lot. He patted her gently on the shoulder. "Deep breaths," he said. "I'm sorry you had to see that. Good job taking care of Theresa. You probably saved her life."

"Who did that to them?" Once she started wiping her hands, she really couldn't stop. "Why?"

"It's been happening all over town," Hess said. "People whose Protectors went over to Bishop. People who lost their Protectors in the fight. People whose Protectors never cared enough in the first place. Half of this town is nothing but a mobile blood supply right now." The look on his face, when she glanced up, was enough to make her shiver. "Maybe the crazies are right. Maybe we should kill all the vampires."

"Yeah," Claire said, very softly. "Because people never kill people, right?"

He had Eve's death warrant in his pocket.

He didn't argue about it.

They found another five people on Hannah's list, all safe and alive—well, one of them was drunk off his butt at the Barfly, one of the scarier local watering holes, but he was still breathing and unfanged. One by one, they were put on the bus.

By four p.m., the last bus was motoring out of Morganville, heading for parts unknown (to Claire, at least), and she was left standing with those who were left. Richard Morrell. Hannah Moses. Shane and Eve, standing there together, whispering. Joe Hess, talking on the police car radio. There were other people around, but they stayed in the shadows, and Claire had the strong suspicion that they were vampires. Amelie's vampires, getting organized for something big.

Without warning, Claire felt a burning sensation on her arm.

When she pulled back her sleeve, she saw the tattoo was swirling, like a pot of stirred ink under her skin. Bishop was trying to pull her in. She could feel the impulse to walk out of the warehouse and head for Founder's Square, but she resisted.

When she was afraid she couldn't hold back anymore, she told Shane. He put his arms around her. "I'm not letting you go anywhere," he promised. "Not without me."

The impulse felt like a string tied around her guts, pulling relentlessly. It was annoying at first. Then it hurt. Finally, she pulled free of Shane's embrace and walked in circles around the open space of the warehouse they'd used for the bus staging area, making wider and wider arcs. He intercepted her when she came close to the door, and she looked at him in silent misery. "I hate this!" she blurted. "I want this thing *out*!" And she burst into tears, because it felt overwhelming to her, this feeling of despair and anguish, of not being where she was supposed to be. This time, even Shane's presence couldn't help. The misery just came in waves, crushing her underneath. She heard Shane yelling at Richard Morrell, and then Hannah was there, saying something about helping.

Claire felt a hot sting in her arm, and then calm spread like ice through her veins. It was a relief, but it didn't touch the burning on her arm, or the anxiety boiling in her stomach. Her body still wasn't her own.

"She'll sleep for a while," Hannah said, from a long way off. "Shane, I need you."

Claire couldn't open her eyes, or tell them that she wasn't really asleep at all. She seemed to be—she got that—but she was desperately awake underneath. Painfully awake.

Shane kissed her, warm and gentle, and she felt his hand smooth her hair and trace down her cheek. *Don't leave me,* she wanted to tell him, but she couldn't make herself move or speak.

Her heartbeat thudded, slow and calm, even though she felt the panic building inside her.

She felt herself carried somewhere, tucked into a warm bed and piled with blankets.

Then silence.

Her eyes opened, as if someone else was controlling them, and as she sat up, she saw someone standing in the corner of the darkened room where they'd left her.

Ada.

The ghost put a pale, flickering finger to her lips and motioned for Claire to sit up. She did, although she had no idea why.

Ada drifted closer. Once again, she wasn't three-dimensional at all, just a flat projection on the air, like a TV character without the screen. She didn't really look human; in fact, she looked more like a game character, all smoothness and manufactured detail.

Somewhere in the dark, a cell phone rang. Claire walked over to a pile of boxes labeled EMERGENCY COM-MUNICATION EQUIPMENT and ripped away tape to retrieve a cell phone. Fully charged, from the battery icon on the display. She lifted it to her ear.

"Bishop is trying to pull you to him," Ada's tinny, artificial voice said. "But I need you elsewhere."

"*You* need me."

"Of course. With Myrnin deactivated, I require someone to assist me. Take the portal to reach me."

"There's a portal?" Claire felt slow and stupid, and she didn't think it was the drugs that Hannah had given her. Ada's ghostly representation gave her a scorching look of contempt.

"I have *made* a portal," she said. "That's what I do, you silly fool. Take it, now. Six steps forward, four to your right. Go!"

The connection died on Claire's borrowed phone with a lost-signal beep. She folded the clamshell and slid it back in her pocket, and realized that someone—Shane, she guessed—had taken her shoes off for her. She put them on and walked six paces forward into the dark, then four steps to the right.

Her fourth step sent her falling through freezing-cold blackness, and then her foot touched ground, and she was someplace she recognized.

She came out in the cells where Myrnin and Amelie had confined the vampires who had become too sick to function on their own. It was an old prison, dark and damp, built out of solid stone and steel. The tornado that had raged through Morganville a few months back had damaged part of the building; Claire hadn't been involved in tracking down the escaped patients, but she knew it had been done, and the place repaired. Not that Bishop had cared, of course. Amelie had done that.

But all the cells were empty now.

Claire stumbled to a halt and wrapped her arms around her stomach, where the tug from Bishop's will felt like a white-hot wire being pulled through her skin. She braced herself against the wall, breathing hard. "I'm here," she said to the empty air. "What do you want me to do, Ada?"

Ada's ghost glided down the corridor ahead of her— still two-dimensional, but this time the view was from the back. Her stiff belled skirts drifted inches above the stone floor, and she looked back over her shoulder toward Claire in unmistakable command. *Great,* Claire thought. *It's not bad enough that Bishop has his hooks in me; now it's Myrnin's nutty computer, too. I have way too many bosses.*

Eve would have told her she needed a better job, which would include sewage treatment.

"Where are we going?" she asked Ada, not that she expected an answer. She wasn't disappointed. The prison was laid out in long hallways, and the last time Claire had been here, most of the cells had been filled with plague victims. She'd delivered their food—well, blood—to them to make sure they hadn't starved. Some had been violent; most had just been lying very still, unable to do much at all.

Where were they now?

At the end of the line was the cell where Myrnin had spent his days, off and on, when he was too dangerous to be in the lab or around anybody—even other vampires. It had been furnished with his home comforts, like a thick Turkish rug and a soft pile of blankets and pillows, his ragged armchair, and stacks of books.

No sign of Myrnin, either.

Ada glided to the end of the hall, then turned to face

Claire, flickering from a back view to a front view like a jump cut in a movie.

"That's really creepy," Claire said. "You know that, right?"

Her phone rang. She opened the clamshell. "You were seeking Dr. Mills," Ada said. "He is here."

"Where?"

"Follow. He requires assistance."

Claire kept the phone to her ear as Ada turned around again and misted right through the stone wall. Claire stopped, her nose two inches away from the surface of the barrier. She slowly reached out, and although the stone looked utterly real—it even smelled real, like dust and mold—there was nothing under her hand but air. Still, her brain stubbornly told her not to take another step, or she'd end up with a bruised face at the very least. In fact, her whole body resisted the order to walk on.

Claire forced her foot to rise, inch forward, and step *into* the stone. Then the other foot, shuffling forward to match it. It didn't get any easier, not for five or six torturous inches, and then suddenly the pressure was gone, and she stepped through into a large, well-lit room.

A room full of vampires.

Claire froze as dozens of pallid faces turned toward her. She'd never gotten to know the inmates—they'd mostly been anonymous in the shadows—but she recognized a few of them. What were they doing out of their cages?

The voice on the phone at her ear snapped, impatiently, "Would you *come,* then?"

Claire blinked and saw that Ada was drifting in the middle of the room, staring at her in naked fury. "They're not going to—"

"They will not hurt you," Ada said. "Don't be absurd."

It really wasn't all that absurd. Claire had seen some of these same vampires clawing gouges in stone with their fingernails, and gnawing on their own fingers. She was like a doggie treat in a room full of rabid rottweilers.

None of them lunged at her. They stared at her as if she was a curiosity, but they didn't seem especially, well, hungry.

She followed Ada's image across the room to a small stone alcove, where she saw Dr. Mills lying very still on a cot.

"Oh no," Claire whispered, and hurried over to him. "Dr. Mills?"

He groaned and opened reddened eyes, blinking to focus on her face. "Claire," he croaked, and coughed. "Damn. What time is it?"

"Uh—almost five, I think. Why?"

"I just went to sleep at four," he said, and flopped back to full length on his cot. "God. Sorry, I'm exhausted. Forty-eight hours without more than a couple of hours down. I'm not a med student anymore."

She felt a wave of utter relief. "They didn't, you know—"

"Kill me? Other than by working me half to death?" Dr. Mills groaned and sat up, rubbing his head as if he was trying to shove his brains back inside. "Amelie wanted to use the serum to treat the worst cases first. I got everyone housed here, except for Myrnin. I have two doses left. There won't be any more if we don't get blood from Bishop to culture."

She'd almost forgotten about that. "Have you seen Myrnin?"

"Not since Amelie brought me here," Dr. Mills said. "Why?"

"He's sick," Claire said. "Very sick. I was looking for you to try to help him, but I don't know where he is now. Amelie took him, too."

He was already shaking his head. "She didn't bring him here. I haven't seen them."

Claire sensed a shadow behind her and, turning, came face-to-face with a vampire. A smallish one, just a little taller than her own modest height. It was a girl barely out of her teens, with waist-length blond hair and lovely dark eyes, who smiled at the two of them with an unsettlingly knowing expression.

"I am Naomi," she said. "This is my sister Violet." Just behind her was a slightly older girl, same dark eyes, only a little stronger in the chin, and with midnight-black hair. "We wish to thank you, Doctor, for your gift. We have not felt so well in many years."

"You're welcome," Dr. Mills said. He sounded tense, and Claire could understand why; the vamps were all on their best behavior, but that could change, and she saw a shadow of it in Naomi. "I'm sure Amelie will be along to get you soon."

The two vamps nodded, bobbed an old-fashioned curtsy, and withdrew back into the main room. There was a soft buzz of conversation building out there, a kind of whisper that sounded like a calm sea on the shore. Vampires didn't have to speak loudly to be heard, at least by one another.

"*Is* Amelie coming?" Dr. Mills asked. "Because I'm starting to feel like the special of the day around here."

Oh. He thought Claire was the scout riding ahead of the vampire cavalry. She looked around for Ada, but she didn't see any sign of her now. She'd just faded out. Claire folded up the phone and put it back in her pocket, feeling a little stupid. "I don't know," she said. "I was told you needed help."

He gave a jaw-cracking yawn, murmured an apology, and nodded. "I've got sacks of crystals, and some of the liquid. We need to distribute it all over town, make sure everybody who needs it gets medicated. It won't last for long, and it isn't the cure, but until I can get Bishop's blood, it'll have to do. Can you help me measure it into individual doses?"

Claire realized, as she was scooping measuring spoons of red crystals and putting them in bottles, that the burning urgency in her guts had finally, slowly faded away.

She pulled up her sleeve.

The tattoo was barely a shadow under her skin.

As she stared at the place where it had been, Naomi the vampire leaned over her shoulder and studied it with her. Claire flinched, which was probably what the vamp had intended, and Naomi chuckled. "I see Bishop marked you," she said. "Don't fear, child. It's almost gone now. He marked my sister once." The smile left her face, and it set in hard, cold lines. "Then he marked us both forever. Sister Amelie told us he was dead, long ago, but he isn't, is he?"

Claire shook her head, unable to say anything with fangs so close to her neck. Naomi didn't seem to be threatening, but she didn't seem to be *comforting,* either.

"Then it's come to it," Naomi said. "It's time for us to fight him. Good. For my sister's sake, I'll be happy to face him again." Naomi's cool hand stroked Claire's cheek. "Pretty child. You smell warm."

Claire shuddered. "Yeah, well, I, uh, am. I guess."

"Warm as sunlight. So was I, once." Naomi's sigh brushed Claire's skin, and then the vampire was gone, moving in a blur. The vampires were all moving faster now—recovering, Claire guessed. Growing stronger.

Dr. Mills was looking at them in satisfaction, but Claire couldn't quite get there from here. Great, they were feeling better; she could get behind that.

But now they were *healthy* vampires. Which meant they could make more vampires, and that changed everything. It changed the entire dynamic of Morganville.

Didn't it?

Her phone rang. No number displayed on the caller ID. Claire flipped it open and said, "What, Ada?"

"You must take Dr. Mills and leave," Ada said. "I will dial the portal for you. Go now."

"Would you mind telling me what—"

"Do as I say or I will leave you both alone in a room full of vampires who may crave an instant hot meal."

Myrnin's computer was such a *bitch*.

Claire snapped the phone shut. "Grab what you need," she said. "It's time to go."

Dr. Mills nodded. He'd loaded the individual doses into a couple of duffel bags, and he handed one to her as he hefted the other. He opened up a padded silver box and checked the contents.

Two syringes.

"Those are the last two doses of the serum, right?" Claire asked. "Maybe I'd better . . . ?"

He handed them over. "Make sure Myrnin gets one, and Amelie gets the other," he said. "Oliver will try to hijack one for himself. Don't let him."

Like she stood a chance of saying no to Oliver on her own, but she nodded anyway. Dr. Mills seemed relieved to have the stuff out of his hands. He looked around at the vampires, who were all turning toward them. "Maybe we should be going," he said. "I'm sure they're all grateful, but—"

"Yeah," Claire said. "Let's."

Walking through the crowd was like walking through a giant pride of lions. They might be calmly observing, but there was no mistaking the predatory gleam in their eyes as they did it. Claire caught the glitter of fangs in one or two mouths, and made sure not to make eye contact.

Naomi stepped into her path. The young vampire— well, young-*looking*—blocked the way out. "May I beg a favor?" she asked. "A small one, I assure you."

Claire licked her lips. "Sure."

"Give this to my sister Amelie," she said, and lifted a silver necklace off of her alabaster neck. It was a beautiful little thing, thin as a whisper, and it had a white cameo dangling from it. "Tell her that we are with her if she requires it."

Claire put the necklace in her pocket, and nodded. "I'll tell her." Naomi didn't move. "Did you want something else?"

"Oh, yes," Naomi said faintly. "Very badly. But you see, I know my sister. I know she would not forgive me if I did anything untoward. So you and your kind doctor must go, before we forget our promises."

Still, she didn't move.

Claire went around her. Naomi turned to watch her.

Stepping through the stone illusion seemed a whole lot easier this time, maybe because she knew staying was definitely not a good idea at all.

Ada's ghost stood in the hallway, looking furiously out of sorts with the delay. She turned and glided away at top speed. Claire broke into a run to keep up, and Dr. Mills kept pace. Ada suddenly stopped and spun her image to face them like a flat cardboard cutout, and the speaker on Claire's phone shrieked with static.

Dr. Mills went down.

"Run!" Ada screamed through the speakerphone, but Claire couldn't. She couldn't leave him behind.

Claire stopped to reach down to help him up, but he wasn't moving. There was a cut on his head, and although he was breathing, he was completely unconscious.

The cut was on the *back* of his head. He hadn't fallen that way.

Someone had hit him.

Ada tried to tell her to run away, but she stayed where she was. Ada's ghostly image screamed silently in frustration and burst into a storm of misty static.

Gone.

In the darkness, Claire felt fingers brush her hair.

"Naomi?" she asked in a faint whisper.

A dry chuckle sounded next to her ear, shockingly close. "Never met the lady. You know who I am," a male voice said. "Don't you, Claire?"

She closed her eyes.

"Hello," she said, "Mr. Collins."

9

Shane's dad turned on an electric light overhead, and the sudden glare made Claire wince and blink. She looked down quickly at Dr. Mills to confirm that he was still breathing, and not moving. Good. She needed all her concentration right now.

Frank Collins looked the same as he had the last time she'd seen him alive, there in Bishop's office—thin, lean, with his long graying hair down around his face, only now he was paler. He looked like a man who'd lived hard and died the same way—and there was definitely a shadow in him that hadn't been there before. A crazy, scary shine in his eyes, like a silver film. He had a few things in common with Oliver, but where Oliver came across as tough, frightening, and ultimately rational, Collins missed that last one entirely.

He was *way* too close. Claire stayed very still, trying not to let her pulse pound too hard.

"I see what my son likes about you," Frank Collins said. "You're tougher than you look."

"Thanks," she said. "Now back off."

He laughed again. It echoed off of the stone, as if he'd brought three or four copies of himself to enjoy the show. "No," he said. "I don't think so. Never done it before. Never will." He paused "I'd like to talk to my son."

"Never going to happen," Claire said. "He doesn't want to talk to you."

Mr. Collins's smile showed more than teeth. His fangs slowly unfolded, and the edges caught the dim light. "You think he'd want you sucking plasma, too, sweetheart? It would kill him if something like that happened. So you might try to be a little more polite."

She wanted to vomit at the thought of Frank Collins biting her. "He'll kill *you*," she said. "You know he would."

"Maybe he'd try." Frank shrugged. "He wouldn't hurt you, though. I know my boy well enough to know how head over heels he is for you. He'd never touch a hair on your pretty little head. You're his weakness, Claire."

That was sickeningly true. Shane would do anything to save Claire. He'd even let his father turn him into a vampire—which might be what Freaky Frank was thinking about.

She couldn't let that happen. No way.

Claire slowly let the duffel bag she was holding thump down to the floor, and took stock of what she had to work with. Not much. Frank Collins had been turned by Bishop; he wasn't sick. She had no hope of curing him, or even treating him. This was his *natural* state of crazy.

Her backpack.

Claire let it slide down her arm, hoping that he'd think she was getting ready to make a run for it. It'd be useless to do that; she'd never make it.

Plus, he'd enjoy the chase.

As her backpack caught in the crook of her elbow, she grabbed the front zipper. Gravity helped her pull it down as the weight sagged forward.

Oh, crap.

The stakes weren't in the front pocket. She'd put them in the bigger interior, with her books. There was nothing in the front pocket but some paper clips, a highlighter, and half a candy bar. She didn't think bribing him with chocolate would get it done.

"Relax," Shane's dad said. "I'll let you go."

That seemed . . . too good to be true, but Claire was

willing to take it and run. "Thanks," she said, and bent to grab Dr. Mills to pull him toward the portal.

"I didn't say *he* could go," Frank said, his smile full-tilt crazy. "I deserve a little bonus for being so accommodating."

Claire could feel her heart pounding now, even through the layers of calming drugs that Hannah had dosed her with before. Everything seemed to slow down. She didn't pause to think. She threw all her strength into grabbing the pack in both hands, twirling in place like a shot-putter, and slamming the pack into Frank Collins's back.

There were a lot of books in there, and physics was something not even vampires could ignore, especially when it hit them full force. Frank went sprawling. Claire grabbed Dr. Mills by one arm and dragged him toward the spot where Ada had been standing.

Ada flickered back into existence as she approached. The speaker in Claire's phone activated and Ada shouted, "Leave the man; get the bags!"

"Bite me," Claire snapped. She heaved, got Dr. Mills up to a sitting position, and rolled him through the portal.

Then she dashed back for the duffel bags.

Frank Collins's pale hand grabbed her wrist. She looked up, right into his scarred face and silvery eyes, and screamed. There was no way she could break free, not without leaving her hand behind. He was just that strong.

Shane's dad yanked her down to her knees on the floor. He pulled the strap of her backpack off her shoulder and ripped the tough fabric open, spilling the contents all over the floor. *Advanced Particle Physics* slipped off into the dark, along with *Fundamentals of Matrix Computations*. Out spilled two sharp-pointed wooden stakes. Out of sheer desperation, she made a grab for them, but his foot came crashing down to pin them to the floor before she could get there.

He stood there, staring at the stakes, and she saw something move over his face, like a ripple of real human pain. "Christ," he murmured. "I used to carry some just like that when I was starting out hunting them. What the hell am I doing?"

She knew what that pain was, and all of a sudden she knew how to hurt him. "You're hunting," Claire said. Her heart was beating so hard, it felt as if it would break her ribs. "That's what vamps do. Hunt people."

He shook his head silently, then looked up at her. He almost looked sane again, or as sane as Shane's father ever got. "I've been fighting vampires a long time," he said. "Killed a couple; did you know that?"

She knew. He and Shane had almost been executed for killing Brandon, even though Shane hadn't had anything to do with it. He stared down again at the hand-carved stakes sticking out from under his big, scuffed boot.

"Never ended up using stakes all that much," he said, and looked her right in the eyes. "You know why?"

She was afraid to ask.

"Because if you don't kill a vampire, it just makes them angrier," he said. "You think you can kill me with something like this?"

She swallowed hard. "Sure. Not that you're going to let me try."

"Truth is, the worst thing I ever feared was this. Being this. Shane tell you that?" She slowly nodded. "I'm sorry he had to see what happened to me. I'm sorry for all the things I did to make his life hell over the years. You understand?"

She shook her head, because she really didn't.

"You tell Shane I love him," Frank said. "I always did. Didn't show it right, I know that, but that was never his fault. I'm glad he found you. He deserves something good in his life."

And then he lifted up his boot and picked up the

stakes. Claire opened her mouth, but her voice caught in her throat.

He didn't hurt her.

"You go home," he said. "You tell my son his father says good-bye. Wish I'd gotten to see him one more time, but you're right. It's probably not a good idea."

He turned away toward the darkness, with the stakes in his hand.

"I guess you should know that he loves you, too. He can't help it." Her voice echoed from the stone. She didn't know why she said it, except that she knew, with sad certainty, that she wouldn't see him again.

She thought Shane's dad hesitated, but then he shuffled on, until he was out of sight.

The instant he was gone, Claire grabbed the duffel bags, and lunged to her feet, heading for the open portal.

She stumbled out on the other side, tripped over Dr. Mills's motionless body, and fell into Oliver's arms.

He looked at her with an absolutely disgusted expression, and dropped her on her butt on the plushly carpeted floor of Amelie's study.

"It's gone," Claire said for the four hundredth time, as Oliver turned her arm this way and that, holding it under a light so bright it felt like a laser cutting into her skin. "Hey! I said it's *gone*!"

Oliver held her in place with a grip so hard she knew it would leave its own kind of tattooing. In blue, purple, and black. "And I said that Bishop would very much like us to think that it's gone," he snapped. "You were told to stay where you were. As usual, you ignored that instruction, and now you've placed us all at extreme risk of—"

"Let her go, Oliver," Amelie said from the other side of the vast, polished desk. She drummed her perfect fingernails on the surface, making a light, dry tapping sound like bones dropped on marble. "The girl could

have betrayed us a dozen times or more by now. She
hasn't. I believe we can give her the benefit of the doubt,
for now."

He let Claire go and stalked away, arms folded. This,
Claire thought, was Amelie's war council—Sam Glass
sat next to her in a side chair, looking more like Michael
all the time as his red hair grew out into a mess of waves
and curls. Oliver paced. Richard Morrell stood nearby,
looking as if he *wanted* to pace, but was too tired to
make the attempt.

Michael moved up next to Claire, put his hand on her
shoulder, and led her off to the side, near where Hannah
Moses leaned against the wall, looking fascinated and
worried. Claire knew just how she felt. Being plunged
into the deep end—and this was it—meant swimming
for your life, with sharks. Even the supposedly friendly
ones could turn and take your leg off when they felt
like it.

"Where's Myrnin?" Claire whispered. Michael shook
his head. "Isn't he here? Somewhere?"

"No idea," Michael whispered back. "Amelie stashed
him someplace; I just don't know where. He's not—"

"Michael," Amelie said, "I said I would give her the
benefit of the doubt, not the full story. Please be quiet."
She stood up, and Claire saw that she'd changed clothes
again, this time to a flawless pale pink suit, something
that looked like it belonged on a runway in Paris. Not
what Claire would have thought you'd wear to a show-
down. "Claire. Thank you for bringing the supplies that
I requested from Dr. Mills. Thank you also for retriev-
ing the good doctor. I am told that he will recover from
his wound." Her light-colored, cool eyes focused on
Claire, and shot right through her. "May I also see your
arm?"

Always polite. That was when Amelie was the most
dangerous, Claire knew. She slowly extended her arm,
still holding Michael's hand on the other side for comfort. Amelie's touch was cold and light. She didn't study

the skin, like Oliver had; she ran her fingertips over the surface, and then lowered Claire's arm back to her side.

"Michael," she said, "please take Claire to your friends. I am sure you would both prefer to be with them now."

"But . . ." Claire licked her lips. "Don't you want me here? To help?"

"You'll help when it's needed," Amelie said. "For now, you should be elsewhere. We will be bringing in some of my people to remove them from Bishop's influence. The process can be somewhat unsettling to witness."

Oliver made a rude noise as he continued his relentless pacing. "It's far worse when it fails," he said. "I hope you're not fond of this carpet."

Amelie ignored that. "Myrnin and Dr. Mills had told me that the work could not continue on the serum without more of Bishop's blood. Is that correct?" Claire nodded. "Difficult to achieve, I'm afraid, but I will include that in our calculations."

"We talked about drugging him."

"So Myrnin said." Amelie wasn't going to tell her anything. "It's no longer your concern. I will rely on you and your friends to be in attendance this evening. You should come prepared."

"Prepared for what?" Claire asked.

Amelie's eyebrows rose. "Anything. We are no longer following a plan. We are facing the final moves on the chessboard, and who wins will very much depend on nerve, skill, and the ability to do the unexpected. You may count on my father being ready to do his worst. We must be just as ruthless."

Claire thought about that moment in the tunnels, with Frank Collins. She hadn't felt ruthless at the end. She'd felt sad.

She didn't suppose Amelie, Oliver, or any of the rest of them would have hesitated for a second. Frank Collins was a bad guy. He'd been a bad guy as a human, right? But still . . . there was just that one moment when she'd seen him as a man who loved his son.

Maybe everybody had those moments. Even the worst people.

Maybe it didn't matter, except to her.

The door opened at the far end of the room, and two of Amelie's favorite vamp bodyguards came in, dragging a beat-up human. At least, Claire thought he was human; it was hard to tell, under all the dirt and bruises.

Oh. She knew him. It was Jason Rosser, Eve's crazy-ass brother. He looked like he'd been living in a garbage dump for months—for all Claire knew, he had been. Eve had said he'd been coming by the house, maybe even acting less insane, but right now, Claire couldn't see it. He looked like a rabid sewer rat, and as he scanned the room, he was all gleaming, crazy eyes and bared teeth.

When the guards let him go, at a nod from Amelie, Jason lunged for the Founder of Morganville. She didn't raise a hand to defend herself. She didn't have to.

Oliver met him halfway, grabbed Jason by the throat, and slammed him down onto the carpet flat on his back.

"You see?" Oliver said, and gave Amelie a freakishly calm smile. "You really should have thought about the carpet; you'll never get the smell of him out of it. Really, Amelie, you do insist on bringing home strays."

"I also put them down when necessary," she said. "This one happens to be yours, Oliver, yes? So I leave him to you for proper judgment."

Nobody said a word in protest to that. Not even Claire. Jason was nobody's friend; Claire would never, ever forget the night he'd almost killed Shane, for *nothing.* She wasn't about to speak up on his behalf.

Oliver stared deep into Jason's eyes and said, "You deserve to die, you know. Not only for the fact that you reek of guilt; I'm partial to a bit of mayhem now and then. No, you deserve to die because you broke the laws of Morganville *without my permission.*" Oliver's smile widened into something out of a bad-clown nightmare. "So what then am I to do with you? You broke your word to Brandon. You broke your word to me. You had the bad taste to betray Amelie, in full public view. You took the side of that ancient reptile Bishop."

Jason *laughed.* It sounded like breaking ice. "Yeah, I did," he said. "Vamps are getting a break for doing the same thing. I get to die. Perfect. Nothing ever changes around here, does it? If a vampire does it, they can't help it. If a human does it, they're lunch meat."

Amelie said, "Is there anyone who will speak for him?" Claire knew it was a pro forma kind of question, like, *Speak now or forever hold your peace,* but she was thinking about Eve. About how she was ever going to tell her that she'd watched her brother die, and hadn't said a word . . .

But as it happened, she didn't have to.

"I will," Michael said.

There was a collective intake of breath. Nobody—Claire included—could quite believe he'd spoken up. It even made Oliver turn and lose his bitch face.

"Don't do me no favors, Glass Ass," Jason snapped.

"I'm not." Michael turned to Amelie. "He's a pathetic little worm, but he's just a criminal. He deserves to be punished. Not killed like some rabid dog."

"He's a killer," she said.

"Well, if he is, he's not the only one in this room, is he?"

Amelie showed her teeth briefly in a smile. "Will you take his parole, Michael? Will you put him into your own household and shelter him with those you love?"

Michael didn't answer. He wanted to—Claire could see it—but he just . . . couldn't.

Finally, he shook his head.

"If you won't trust him with those you love, how can I trust him with anyone else's family?" Amelie said, and nodded to Oliver.

Claire blurted, "Wait!"

"May we *please* have done with interruptions from the children's section?" Oliver said.

"Why is he here?" Claire asked, talking so fast that she stumbled over the words. "Why is he *here*? Who brought him *here*?"

"Who cares?"

Amelie held up a warning hand. "It's a reasonable question. Who brought him to us?"

"Nobody," one of the guards said from the door. "He came through the portal."

"*What?*" Amelie crossed to Jason in a flash, knocked Oliver out of the way, and slammed the boy back against the closest wall. "Tell me how you came to work the portals."

"Somebody showed me," Jason said. "He showed me a lot of things. He showed me how to kill. How to hide. How to get around town without anybody knowing."

"*Who?*"

Jason laughed. "No way, lady. I'm not telling. That's all I've got left to bargain with, right?"

Amelie's face twisted with anger, and she was about two seconds from snapping some bones for him. "Then you have nothing, because I will have it out of you one way or another."

Sam Glass, who hadn't said a thing, slowly rose to his feet. "Amelie. Amelie, stop."

"Not until this worm tells me who showed him the portals!"

"Then I'll tell you," Sam said. "I showed him. I showed him everything you showed me."

Silence. Even Oliver looked as if he didn't quite understand what he'd just heard. Amelie stood there like an ivory statue, holding Jason in place with one flattened hand on his chest.

"Why?" she whispered. "Sam, why would you do such a thing?"

It felt, to Claire, like suddenly the room was empty and they'd all turned to ghosts, except for Amelie and Sam. There was something so powerful in the stare between them that it just vaporized the rest of the world. "I did the

best I could," he said softly. "You left me no choice. You
wouldn't see me. You wouldn't speak to me, all those years.
I was alone, and I—I wanted to do something good." He
took in a deep breath and walked toward her, coming close
enough to touch, although he didn't reach out. "Jason was
a victim. Brandon brutalized him, and no one did anything
to stop it. So yes, I taught the boy to fight, to defend himself
from Brandon. I taught him to use the portals to help him
escape when he needed to get away. I couldn't stop Brandon, not without you, but I could try to save his victims. I
thought I was helping."

"Don't worry, man; I wasn't going to throw you under
the bus." Jason laughed. "Fuck it, you were the only one
who was ever good to me. Why should I?"

"The boy rewarded you by showing my father everything you taught him," Amelie said softly. She broke
the stare with Sam and looked at Jason's face. "Didn't
you?"

"It was what I had to trade. You set up the rules, lady.
I just followed them."

Amelie grabbed Jason by the hair and shoved him
at Sam, who caught him in surprise, and then held
him when Jason tried to break free. "He's yours," she
snapped at Sam. "You created this. Deal with it." She
spun to Oliver. "You were right. Bishop does know how
to use the network."

"Then we can take advantage of that," Oliver said.
"Since he assumes we do *not* know that he does."

They'd effectively dismissed Sam and Jason. Sam
stared at Amelie with so much pain in his face that it
made Claire hurt to look at it, then shook his head.
"Let's go," he said, and nodded to Michael and Claire.
"All of us. Now."

No one tried to stop them. When Jason tried to make
one last clever little comment, Sam slapped a hand over
his mouth and dragged him out. "Shut up," he said.
"You're still alive. That's a better outcome than you deserve."

*   *   *

Claire portaled them directly into the Glass House. She breathed an involuntary sigh of relief at finding Shane sitting on the couch, staring at a flickering TV screen like it held the secrets of the universe, and Eve pacing the hallway in her clumpy boots.

Eve spotted them first, screamed, and threw herself on Claire like a warm Goth blanket. "Oh *God*, everybody thought you were dead! Or, you know, Bishoped, which would have been worse, right? What happened? Where did you go?"

Over Eve's shoulder, Claire saw that Shane had gotten to his feet. "You all right?" he asked. She nodded, and he closed his eyes in sudden relief. Claire patted Eve's back, in thanks, love, and a little bit of get-the-hell-off-me. Eve got the message. She backed up, sniffling a little, and couldn't keep a smile from ruining her sad-clown makeup.

"Sorry about that," Claire said. "I ... well. It wasn't exactly my idea, and I can't really explain...."

"But you're okay. No fang marks or ... " Eve's gaze darted past Claire, and she stopped talking. Stopped moving, too.

Shane, on the other hand, moved fast, putting himself between Claire and Jason. "What the hell is he doing here?"

"Fuck you too, Collins."

"Shut up," Sam said, and gave Jason a warning shake that must have rattled his bones. "He's here because I didn't want to kill him. Any other questions?"

Eve still wasn't saying anything. Claire couldn't blame her; she had the same kind of conflicted emotions passing over her face that Shane had when he thought about his dad. Love/hate/loss. That sucked, when Jason was standing right there. She hadn't really lost him. Not yet.

Michael went to her, the same way Shane had gone to Claire—to get between her and her brother. "He's not welcome here," Michael said, and that put the force of the Founder House behind it. Claire felt a pressure building, getting ready to evict Jason and—presumably—Sam, if Sam didn't let go of him.

"Wait," Sam said. "You send him out there, he's dead from all sides, and you know it. Bishop has no use for him, hasn't since Jason's assassination attempt failed. Amelie would kill him without blinking. You really want to do that to your girlfriend's brother?"

"Michael, don't," Eve said. "He won't hurt us." And *everyone* rolled their eyes at that. Even Jason, which was borderline hilarious.

"Look," Jason said, "all I want is a way out of this stupid town. You arrange that, and I'll never show my face around here again. You can keep your stupid hero lifestyle. I just want out."

"Too late," Shane said. "Last bus already left, man. And we're thirty minutes away from Bishop's big town hall meeting. You can run, but you can't hide. Anybody who isn't there is dead. He's going to send out hunters. It'll be open season."

"I could stay here," Jason said quickly. "Upstairs. In the secret room, right?"

They all looked at one another.

"Oh, come *on*, it's not like I'm going to run up your phone bill and watch pay-per-view. Besides, if I was going to kill you in your sleep, I would have already done it." He made a kissy-face at Shane. "Even you, asswipe."

"Jesus, Jason." Eve sighed. "Do you *want* to end up in the landfill, or what?" She touched Michael on the arm, and he glanced back at her and took her hand. "Can you tell if he lies to us?"

"Uh, no. Drinking blood doesn't make me a lie detector."

Sam spoke up somberly. "I can." He shrugged when Michael gave him an odd look. "It's just a skill. You pick it up, over time. People can't control their bodies the way vampires can. I can usually tell when they're lying."

"No offense, but you've been wrong plenty of times,

Sam. Like, deciding that you could trust this little weasel as far as you can throw him," Michael said, then caught a devastating pleading look from Eve. "All right. Go ahead. Ask him whatever you want."

Eve took in a deep breath, looked her brother in the eyes, and said, "Please tell me the truth. Did you kill those girls?"

Because that had been Jason's rep. Murdered girls, dumped all over town, a string of killings that had begun right after Jason had gotten out of jail, just about the time Claire had moved to Morganville. One body had been put here in their own house, in an attempt to implicate Shane and Michael.

Jason blinked, as if he somehow hadn't really expected her to ask. "The truth?"

"Of course, the truth, idiot."

"I've done bad things," he said. "I've hurt people. I need help."

Eve's face fell. "You really did do it."

"It wasn't my fault, Eve."

"Never is, is it? I really thought—"

"He's lying," Michael said. He sounded as surprised as Claire felt. "Right, Sam?" Sam nodded. "My God. You really didn't do it, did you?"

Jason looked away from them. "Might as well have."

"What the hell does *that* mean?" Eve snapped. "Either you did, or you didn't!"

"No," her brother said. "Either I did, I didn't, or I was there when it happened and didn't stop it. Figure it out."

"Then who—"

"I'm not saying. People think I'm a killer; they leave me the fuck alone. They think I'm just some sad-ass ride-along clown. They'll kill me quick." Jason looked up now, right at Eve, and for the first time, Claire thought he looked sincere. "I never killed anybody. Not on my own, anyway. Well, I came close with you, Collins."

"But you won't tell us who did kill them?"

He shook his head.

"Are you afraid?" Eve asked, very gently.

Silence.

"You know what?" Shane said. "Don't care. Street him before we wake up with our throats cut by him *or* his imaginary playmate."

And they might have, except that the doorbell rang. Michael flashed to the window and looked out. "Crap. Our ride's here. We don't have time for this."

"Michael," Eve said. "Please. Let him stay, at least for now. *Please.*"

"All right. Get him upstairs and lock him in. Sam, can you stay with him?

"No," Sam said. "I have to go back to Amelie."

"We have to leave. Claire, can you shut down the portal that leads here?"

"I can try, sure."

As Sam hustled Jason up the stairs to the second floor, Claire touched the bare wall at the back of the living room, and felt the slightly pliable surface of the portal lying on top of it. It was invisible, but definitely active.

"Ada," she whispered, and felt the surface ripple.

Her phone rang. Claire answered it. No incoming caller ID had appeared on the display, just random numbers and letters. She answered.

"What?" the computer snapped. "I'm busy, you know. I can't just be at your constant beck and call."

"Shut down the portal to the Glass House."

"Oh, bother. Do it yourself."

"I don't know how!"

"I hardly have time to school you," Ada said primly. God, she reminded Claire of Myrnin—not in a good way. "Very well. I shall do it for you this one time. But you'll have to turn it on again yourself. And stop calling me!"

The phone clicked off, and under Claire's fingers, the surface turned cold and still, like glass.

Blocked. *Quantum stasis*, she thought, fascinated, and wondered how that worked, for about the millionth time.

She wanted to take Ada apart and figure it out. *Yeah, if you live long enough.* It had taken Myrnin three hundred years to put Ada together; it might take her that long just to figure out the basic principles he'd used.

Michael came back into the living room, leading two other vampires—Ysandre, that smug little witch, and her occasional partner François, an equally nasty reject from some Eurotrash vampire melodrama.

They were walking clichés, but they were also deadly. Claire couldn't even look at François without remembering how he'd ripped the cross off of her neck and bitten her. She still had the scars—faint, but they'd always be there. And she couldn't forget how that had felt, either.

A hot flood of emotion came over her when she saw him smirking at her—hate, fear, loathing, and fury. She knew he could feel it coming off of her in sick waves.

She also knew he enjoyed it.

François gave her an elaborate bow and blew her a kiss. "*Chérie*," he said. "The exquisite taste of you still lingers in my mouth."

Shane's hands closed into fists. François saw that, too. Claire touched Shane's arm; his muscles were tensed and hard. "Don't let him bait you," she whispered. "I was a snack. Not a date."

François closed his eyes and made a point of sniffing the air. "Ah, but you smell so different now," he said, with elaborate disappointment. "Rich and complex, not simple and pure anymore. Still, I was the first to taste your blood, wasn't I, little Claire? And you never forget your first."

"*Don't!*" she hissed to Shane, and dug her fingernails in as deep as she could. It was all she could do. If Shane decided to go for him, she knew how it would end.

Luckily, so did Shane. He slowly relaxed, and Claire saw Michael's tension ease as well. "We talking, or are we walking?" Shane asked. "I thought we had someplace to be."

Claire felt a sunburst of pride in him, and a longing that came with it—she wanted all of this to just *stop*; she wanted to go back to the night, the silence, the touch of his skin and the sound of his whispers. That was real. That was important.

It was a reason to live through all this.

She took Shane's hand and squeezed it. He sent her a look. "What?"

She whispered, "You're just full of awesome; did you know that?"

François made a face. "Full of something. In the car, fools."

Founder's Square at twilight was full of people—rock-concert full. Claire didn't even know this many people lived in Morganville. "Did they grab the students, too?" she asked Michael.

"Bishop's not quite that stupid. It's residents only. University gates were closed. The place is under lock-down."

"What, again? Even the stoners are going to figure out something's going on." Claire certainly would have, and she knew most of the students weren't that gullible. Then again, knowing and wanting to push the status quo were two very different things. "You think they'll stay on campus?"

"I think if they don't, the problem's going to solve it-self," Michael said somberly. "Amelie will try to protect them, but we've got a much bigger issue tonight."

Technically, that challenge was saving Morganville, and everybody in it.

There were no chairs down on the grassy area, but Bishop's vampires were out and about, and they were separating people at the entrances to the park and send-ing them to special holding areas. Or, Claire, thought, *pens*. Like sorting cattle. "What are they doing?"

"Dividing people according to their Protectors," Fran-çois said. "What else?"

Bishop had kept the Protection system, then—or at least, he hadn't bothered to really dismantle it. People were being questioned at the gate. If they didn't name a Protector, they got slapped with a big yellow sticker and herded into a big open area in the middle. "What if their Protector is one of Amelie's rebels?" She knew the answer to that one. "Then they're no longer Protected. They go in the middle, too?"

Michael looked pallid—not just vampire-pale, really stressed and upset, as if he knew what was coming before she did. Claire didn't get it until François said, "Just like your friends," and he grabbed Shane. Ysandre took hold of Eve. They both fought and cursed and tried to get free, but it was no use—they were shoved apart from Michael and Claire.

They were both dragged away to the big cordoned-off area in the center of the square. Claire tried to follow them, but Michael held her back. "Don't," he said. "Bishop may not know you're out of his control yet. Tell him you were drugged by Hannah to keep you out of the way. It's the truth; he'll probably sense that."

"What about Shane? Eve? God, how can you just *stand there?*"

"I don't know," he admitted. "But I know I have to. Claire, don't screw this up. You won't help them, and you'll only get yourself killed." He gave her a grim smile. "And me, because I'd have to get in the middle."

Claire stopped fighting him, but she still couldn't accept it. She saw why Richard had wanted people out of town who were at the highest risk; Bishop intended this to be a public spectacle.

His final act to make himself the undisputed ruler of Morganville. In the bad old days, that meant executing lots of people.

François took Claire's arm and marched her up to the front, past angry, scared men and women she knew by sight, and some she'd never seen before. That section had a symbol taped to the barrier that surrounded it—

she vaguely recognized it as the symbol for a vampire named Valerie, who'd joined Bishop in the first round of fighting. And yes, there was Valerie, standing inside the barricade with her humans, but looking very much as if she wished she was somewhere else. Anywhere else.

Past Valerie's barricades was a big raised stage, at least twenty feet off the ground, with steps leading up to it. There were plush chairs, and carpet, and a red velvet backdrop behind it. Spotlights turned the sunset pale in contrast. The stage was empty, but there was a knot of people standing at the foot of the steps.

Richard Morrell was there, dressed in a spotless dark blue suit, with a sky blue tie. He looked like he was running for office, not about to fight for his life; apparently, he and Amelie had the same philosophy on looking good for the Apocalypse. Next to him, Hannah still wore her police uniform, but no belt—and no gun, handcuffs, baton, stakes, or pepper spray. They'd taken away the human cops' weapons. There were other people, too—mostly vampires, but Claire recognized Dean Wallace, the head of TPU, and a few of the other prominent humans in town, including Mr. Janes, who was the CEO of the biggest bank in town. Mr. Janes had decided to stay. She'd seen his name on Richard's evac list, and she'd seen him driving away from the warehouse instead of getting on the bus.

She wondered how Mr. Janes was feeling about that decision right now. Not too good, she was guessing. He kept looking out at the crowd, probably trying to find friends and family.

She knew how he felt.

Richard Morrell nodded to her. "You okay?"

Why did everybody always ask that? "Sure," she lied. "What's going to happen?"

"Wish I knew," Richard said. "Stay close to Michael, whatever happens."

She was going to do that regardless, but she appreciated that he cared. He patted her on the back, and under cover of shaking her hand, he pressed something into her hand.

It was a silver knife, no bigger than her finger. Razor-sharp, too. She tried not to cut herself—the last thing she wanted was for the vamps around her to smell blood—and managed to get it in the pocket of her hoodie without stabbing herself. From Richard's warning look, she got that it was a weapon of last resort.

She nodded to let him know she understood.

A cordon of vampires closed in around them, including the tall, thin, sexless dude whom she'd last seen with the Goldmans. What was his name? Pennywell. Ugh. He had a thin smile, like he knew what was going to happen, and it wasn't going to be pretty.

"Up," he said, and jerked his chin to indicate that they were supposed to climb the steps. Richard went first—trying to set a good example, Claire supposed—and she followed, along with Hannah and Michael. It seemed like a long climb, and it reminded her of nothing else than those old stories about people getting hanged, or walking the last mile to the electric chair.

Up on the stage, it was a whole lot worse. There were hisses and boos from the crowd, quickly hushed, and Claire was blinded by the white spotlights, but she could feel thousands of people staring at her. *I'm nobody,* she wanted to shout. *I don't want to be up here!*

They wouldn't care about her motives, or her choices, or anything else. She was working for Bishop. That made her the enemy.

Richard took one of the chairs, and Dean Wallace sat next to him. Hannah stayed standing next to Richard's chair, arms folded. Claire didn't quite know what to do, so she stuck close to Michael as Mr. Janes claimed the last plush chair.

Two vampires came up the steps carrying Bishop's massive carved throne, which they set right in the exact center of the carpeted stage.

Mr. Pennywell—if he was a he; Claire still couldn't

really tell—stood next to the throne, along with Ysandre and François. The old friends, Claire thought. The clique.

Bishop came through the curtains at the back of the stage. He was wearing a black suit, white shirt, black tie, and a colorful red pocket square. In fact, he was dressed better than Mr. Janes. No ornate medieval robes, which was kind of what Claire had expected. He didn't even have a crown.

But he had a throne, and he settled into it. His three favorite henchpersons knelt in front of him, and he gave them a lazy blessing.

Then he said, "I will speak with the town's mayor."

Claire didn't know how it was possible, but Bishop's voice echoed from every corner of the square—a pocket microphone, she guessed, broadcasting to amplified speakers hidden in the trees. It was eerie, though. She squinted. Out behind the lights, she saw that Shane and Eve had squeezed their way through the crowd and were standing at the front of the group in the center of the square. Shane had his arm around Eve, but not in a boyfriend way—just for comfort.

The way Michael had his arm around Claire.

Richard Morrell got up and walked over to stand in front of Bishop.

"I demanded loyalty," Bishop said. "I received defiance. Not just from my daughter and her misguided followers, but from *humans*. Humans under your control, Mayor Morrell. This is not acceptable. It cannot continue, this blatant defiance of my rule."

Richard didn't say anything, but then, Claire had no idea what he really *could* say. Bishop was just stating the obvious.

And it was just a warm-up to what was coming.

"Today, I learned that you personally authorized the removal from our town of several of our most valued citizens," Bishop said. "Many members of your own town council, for instance. Leaders of industry. People of social standing. Tell me, Mayor Morrell, why did you spirit these people away, and leave so many of your common citizens here to bear the punishment? Were you thinking only of the rich and powerful?"

Clever. He was trying to make the town think that Richard was like his dad—corrupt, in it for his own sake.

It would probably work, too. People liked to believe that sort of thing.

Richard said, "I don't know what you're talking about. If anyone left town, I'm sure they must have had your permission, sir. How could they have left if you didn't authorize it?"

Which was a direct slap in the face for Bishop on the subject of his authority. And his power.

Bishop stood up.

"I will find out the secrets of this town if I have to rip them bloody from every one of you," he said, "and when I do have my answers, you will pay a price, Richard. But to ensure that we have a loyal and stable government, I must ask you to appoint a new town council now. Since you so carelessly allowed the last one to slip away."

"Let me guess. All vampires," Richard said.

Bishop smiled. "No, of course not. But if they are not vampires, I will, of course, *make* them vampires . . . simply to ensure fairness. . . ."

His voice trailed off, because someone was coming up the steps. Someone Bishop hadn't summoned.

Myrnin.

He looked half-dead, worse than Claire had ever seen him; his eyes were milky white, and he felt blindly for each slow step as he climbed. He looked thinner, too. Frail.

She felt sick when she saw the manic smile on his face, so out of touch with the exhaustion of his body.

"So sorry, my lord," he said, and tried to make one of his usual elaborate bows. He staggered, off balance, and settled for a vague wave. "I was detained. I would never miss a good party. Is there catering? Or are we dining buffet?"

Bishop didn't look at him with any favor. "You might have dressed for the occasion," he said. "You're filthy."

"I dress as nature wills me. Oh, Claire, good. So glad to see you, my dear." Myrnin grabbed Claire and dragged her away from Michael, wrapped her in a tight embrace, and waltzed her in an unsteady circle around the stage while she struggled.

There was nothing vague about his voice when he whispered, "*Do nothing. Something is about to happen. Keep your wits, girl.*"

She nodded. He kissed her playfully on the throat— not quite as innocently as she would have liked—and reeled away to lean on the back of Bishop's chair. "Beg pardon," he said. "Dizzy."

"You're drunk," Bishop said.

"That's what happens when you are what you eat," Myrnin agreed. "I stopped off for a bite. Unfortunately, all that was left in town were pathetic alcoholics, and criminals too fast for me to catch."

Bishop ignored him. He turned his attention back to Richard. "Will you name your town council, Mayor? Or must I name them for you?"

"You'll do what you want." Richard shrugged. "I'm not going to enable you."

"Then I'll have to remove those of your appointees who remain." Bishop snapped his fingers, and Ysandre and François moved to grab Mr. Janes and Dean Wallace. When Hannah Moses tried to interfere, she ended up facedown on the carpet, held there by Pennywell. "And I'll allow my hunters to relieve us of any of your citizens who remain unclaimed, or are loyal to my enemy. There. That should clear the air a great deal."

The screaming started down in the crowd as the people in the center of the square realized they'd been put there to die.

Shane and Eve . . .

Claire grabbed the silver knife in her pocket and tried to get to Bishop. Michael tackled her, probably for her own good.

Myrnin lunged for Bishop. Bishop caught him easily, laughing at Myrnin's flailing attempts to fight, and snapped his fingers at Ysandre. She reached in her pocket and took something out that Claire recognized.

A syringe. From the color of the liquid, it was Dr. Mills's cure.

Bishop plunged the needle into Myrnin's heart and emptied the contents, then dropped Myrnin to lie on the carpet, writhing, as the cure raced through his body.

When he opened his eyes, the white film was gone from them.

He was healing.

But he was also in horrible pain.

"I know your plans," Bishop said, and smiled down at him. "I know you filled yourself with poison before coming here. I know you planned to have me drain you and cripple myself so your mistress could finish me off. Unfortunately, it's wasted effort, my dear old friend."

He gestured, and the curtain at the back opened.

Amelie was dragged out, bound in silver chains. She was still wearing her perfect pink suit, but it wasn't so perfect now—filthy, ripped, bloody. Her pale crown of hair had come down in straggles all around her face.

She had a silver leash around her neck, and Oliver was holding it.

Oliver.

Claire felt hot, then cold, then very still inside. She'd come to believe he wasn't as bad as she'd thought; she'd actually started to think he really was almost . . . trustworthy.

Obviously, Amelie had thought so, too. And Michael, because he went for Oliver in a big way, and was brought down by Pennywell and two others.

Worse, though, was the next prisoner, also wrapped in silver chains, and suffering a lot worse than Amelie from the touch of the poisonous metal. His skin smoked and blackened where it touched him, because he was younger and more fragile than she was.

Sam Glass.

Amelie cried out when she saw him, and closed her eyes. She'd lost her careful detachment, and now Claire could see in her how much she cared. How much she wanted Sam.

How much she loved him.

Bishop smiled, and in that smile, Claire saw everything. He didn't want to just destroy Morganville; he wanted to destroy life, and hope, and reasons for living at all. He could win only if he was the last vampire standing, no matter how many people that meant he had to kill along the way.

"You couldn't have won, Amelie," he said, and the tattoo on Claire's arm flared back into view, weaving its way up from a single spot of indigo on her wrist until it covered her arm. Then her chest. She felt it spreading like poison through her whole body, burning, and then it flared out like a brush fire. Gone for real, this time. "There, you can have your little pet back now. I no longer have need for her. She helped me learn everything I needed to know."

"I doubt that," Amelie said. Her voice was ragged with emotion, but she held her father's stare. "I was careful to keep things from her."

"Not so careful to keep them from Oliver, though. And that was a mistake." He tipped her chin up to meet her eyes. "Morganville is mine. You are mine. Again."

"Then take what's yours," Amelie said. She seemed weak now. Defeated. "Kill, if you wish. Burn. Destroy. When it's over, what do you have, Father? Nothing. Exactly what you've always had. We came here to build. To *live*. It's not something you would ever understand."

"Oh, I do understand. I just despise it. And here," Bishop said, "is where you die."

He yanked Amelie's head to the side, and for a horrible second Claire thought she was going to see him kill her, right there, but then he laughed and kissed her on the throat.

"Though, of course, not at my hands," he said. "It wouldn't be moral, after all. We must set a good example, or so you like to tell me, child. I'll let your humans kill you, eventually. Once you've begged for the privilege."

He shoved Amelie aside, into Pennywell's hands, and instead, he grabbed Sam Glass.

"No!" Michael shouted, and leaped to his feet to stop it.

He couldn't. Claire caught sight of Sam's pale, set face, of a determination she couldn't understand, and of Michael being brought down ten feet away, as Bishop exposed Sam's throat and bit him.

Amelie's scream tore through the air. Myrnin—still shaking and weak—crawled toward her. Ysandre kicked him aside, laughing.

Oliver just *stood there*, like an ice sculpture. Only his eyes were alive, and even they didn't show Claire anything she understood.

Michael wasn't there to hold Claire down anymore. She scrambled to her feet, clutched the silver knife, and plunged it into Ysandre's back as deeply as she could. It dug into bone.

"Oh," Ysandre said, annoyed. She tried to get at the knife, but it was out of her reach. She turned on Claire with a snarl, then staggered. Shock blanked her pretty face, and then worry.

Then fear, as the burning started.

She fell, screaming for help. Claire vaulted over her to kneel next to Myrnin. He was fighting his way back through the pain, panting, and his eyes were bright crimson from the stress, and probably hunger.

He wasn't out of control, though. Not anymore. "Get me up," he demanded. "*Do it now!*"

She offered him a hand, and he used it to haul himself to his feet—unsteady, but stronger than she'd ever seen him. This was a different Myrnin . . . sleek, glossy, dark, and dangerous, with his glowing, angry eyes fixed on Bishop.

"Stop him!" Claire yelled at Myrnin, as he just *stood* there. Sam was dying. Myrnin was letting it happen. "It's Sam! You have to stop him!"

Instead, Myrnin turned and attacked Pennywell.

"No! Myrnin, no! *Sam!*"

Oliver still wasn't moving. He was staring at Bishop. Waiting.

They were all waiting.

Down in the crowd, screaming had started, and as Claire looked out she saw that people were trying to run. There were vampires moving through the crowd—hunters, taking victims. The Morganville humans were fighting for their lives. A lot of people had shown up armed to their own funerals, including Shane and Eve; Claire caught glimpses of them down there, and all she could do was pray they'd be okay. They had each other for protection, at least.

She had to help Michael. Claire didn't dare grab the knife from Ysandre's back—it was the only thing keeping her out of the fight—but she couldn't just stand there, either.

Luckily, she didn't have to. Hannah Moses shouted her name, and as Claire turned, she saw Hannah throwing something at her. She instinctively reached up to catch it.

It was a sharp wooden stake. Hannah didn't wait to see what she was going to do with it; she was already heading for François, who was trying to get hold of Richard Morrell. Hannah leaped on the nasty little vampire, pinned him with an expert shift of her weight, and plunged her own wooden stake through his heart. It wouldn't kill him, probably, but he was out of the struggle until somebody removed it.

Michael had already won his fight by the time Claire got there; he was bloodied and a little unsteady, but he grabbed her arm and yelled, "Get out of here!"

"We have to save Sam!" she protested.

But it was too late for that.

Bishop dropped Sam limply to the carpeted floor, and Claire could see that if Sam was still alive, he wouldn't be for long. The holes in his throat were barely leaking at all, and he wasn't moving.

Fury whited out her good sense.

Claire ran at Bishop as he turned, and rammed the stake at his chest, right on target for where his heart would be, if he had one at all.

He caught her wrist.

"No," he said gently, like someone with a pet who'd piddled on the good furniture. "I'll not be taken by the likes of you, little girl."

She tried to get away, but she knew it was over; there was just no way she was getting out of this. Michael had gotten into a fight along the way to reach Sam. Amelie was down on her knees, still bound by all the silver chains. Hannah and Richard were back-to-back, defending themselves against three vampire guards.

Myrnin was fighting Pennywell, and destroying half the stage along the way. There was some old hate there. History.

Oliver had drifted closer to Amelie, although Claire couldn't see any change in him at all. He still wasn't fighting, for or against, and he certainly wasn't making any heroic effort to save *her*.

"Claire!"

Shane. She heard him scream her name, but he was too far away—twenty feet down, at the foot of the stage, looking up.

He had a knife in his hand. As she looked down to meet his eyes, he flipped it, grabbed it by the blade, and threw it.

The knife grazed her cheek, but it hit Mr. Bishop right in the center of his chest.

He laughed. "Your young man has quite the throwing arm," he said, and pulled the knife out as casually as a

CARPE CORPUS
195

splinter. Not silver. It wouldn't do a thing to him. "Your friends like to think they still have a chance, but they don't. There's no ... "

Then the oddest thing happened.... Bishop seemed to hesitate. His eyes went blank and distant, and for a second Claire thought he was just savoring his victory.

"There's no chance," he started again, and then stopped. Then he took an unsteady step to the side, like he'd lost his balance.

Then he let her go altogether, to brace himself on the arm of his throne. Bishop looked down at the knife in his hand—Shane's knife—in disbelief. He couldn't hold on to it. It slipped out of his fist, hit the seat of the chair, and bounced off to the floor.

Bishop staggered backward. As he did, his coat flapped open, and Claire saw that the wound was bleeding.

Bleeding a *lot*.

"Get the book!" Amelie suddenly screamed, and Claire saw it, tucked in the breast pocket of Bishop's jacket. Amelie's book, Myrnin's book. The book of Morganville, with all the secrets and power.

Seemed only right that it ought to be the thing he lost tonight, even if he won everything else.

Claire darted in, grabbed the book, and somehow ducked his clutching hands.

Bishop lunged after her as she danced backward, but he seemed confused now. Slower.

Sicker?

As if sensing some signal, Oliver finally moved. He took a pair of leather gloves from his pocket, calmly put them on, and snapped the silver chains holding Amelie prisoner. He picked up the end of the silver leash and held it for a second, looking into her eyes.

He smiled.

Then he took that off her neck and dropped it to the floor.

Amelie surged to her feet—wounded, bloodied, messy, and angrier than Claire had ever seen her. She hissed at

Oliver, fangs out, and then darted around him to kneel next to Sam.

His eyes opened and fixed on her face. Neither of them spoke.

She took his hand in hers for a moment, then lifted it to touch the back of it to her face.

"You were right," she said. "You were always right, about everything. And I will always love you, Sam. Forever."

He smiled, and then he closed his eyes ...

... and he was gone. Claire could see his life—or whatever it was that animated a vampire—slip away.

Her eyes blurred with hot tears. *No. Oh, Sam ...*

Amelie put his hand gently back on his chest, touched her lips to his forehead, and stood up. Oliver helped her, with one hand under her arm—that was the only way Claire could tell that Amelie wasn't herself, because she seemed to be more alive than ever.

More motivated, anyway.

Bishop was seriously hurt, although Claire couldn't figure out how; Shane's knife couldn't have really injured him. The old man was barely staying on his feet now, as he backed away from Amelie and Oliver.

That put him to moving toward Myrnin, who picked up Pennywell and threw him like a rag doll way out into the distance—all the way to the spotlight, where Pennywell slammed into the glass and smashed the machine into wreckage.

Then Myrnin turned toward Bishop, blocking him from that side.

The three vampires fighting Hannah and Richard suddenly realized that the tide was turning against them, and moved away. As a parting shot, though, one of them yanked the stake out of François's chest, and the vampire yelled and rolled around for a second, then jumped to his feet, snarling.

Oliver, annoyed, reached down and picked up the silver leash he'd removed from Amelie's neck. In a single, smooth motion, he wrapped it around François's throat and tied him to the arm of Bishop's heavy throne. "Stay," he snapped, and, just to be sure, wrapped another length of heavy silver chain around his ankle. François howled in pain.

Oliver plucked the wooden stake out of Claire's hand, removed the silver knife from Ysandre's back, and drove the stake all the way through her to nail her to the stage. It went through her heart. She shuddered and stopped moving, frozen in place.

"There, that should keep them for a while," Oliver said. "Claire. Take this." He tossed the knife to her, and she caught it, still numb and not entirely understanding what had just happened.

"You're . . . you're not—"

"On Bishop's side?" He smiled thinly. "He certainly has thought so, since I sold myself to him the night he came to Morganville. But no. I am not his beast. I've always been my own."

Amelie took a step toward her father. "It's over," she said. "You've done your worst. You'll do no more."

He looked desperate, confused, and—for the first time—really afraid. "How? How did you do this?"

"The key was not in guessing whom you would choose to kill," she said, and her voice was light and calm and ice cold. "You taught me endgames, my father. The key to winning is that no matter what move your opponent makes, it will be the wrong one. I knew you'd kill at least one of us personally; you enjoy it far too much. You couldn't resist."

Like Bishop, she lost her balance. Oliver caught her and held her upright.

Bishop's face went blank. "You . . . you poisoned me. Through Myrnin. But I didn't drink."

"I poisoned Myrnin," she said. "And myself. And Sam. The only one who didn't take poison was Oliver, because I needed him in reserve. You see, we knew about Claire after all. We counted on your knowing where we would be, and what we'd planned, at least insofar as she witnessed it." A pawn. Claire had always been a pawn.

And Sam—Sam had been a *sacrifice*.

Amelie looked unsteady now, and Oliver put an arm around her shoulders. It looked like comfort, but it wasn't; he took a syringe from his pocket, uncapped it with a flick of his thumb, and drove it into the side of Amelie's neck. He emptied the contents in, and she shuddered and sagged against him for just a moment, then drew in a deep breath and straightened.

She nodded to Oliver, who took out another syringe, which he pitched to Claire. "Give it to him."

For a second she thought he meant to Bishop, but then she realized, as Myrnin's strength failed and he went to his knees, who it was really meant to help. She swallowed hard, looking at Myrnin uncertainly, and he moved his hair aside to bare the side of his pale neck. "Hurry," he said. "Not much time."

She did it, somehow, and helped him back to his feet.

When he looked up, she could see that he was better. *Much* better.

Amelie said, "In case you have any doubt, Father, that was an antidote to the poison that is taking hold inside you. Without the antidote, the poison won't kill you, but it will disable you. You can't win against us. Not now."

Down among the crowds, the fights were dying down. There were casualties, but many of them were Bishop's people; the humans of Morganville weren't quite as easy to lead to slaughter as he'd expected. All their anger and vampire-slaying attitude had helped, after all.

And now, pounding up the steps on the side of the stage, came Shane and Eve, backed by a party of grim-looking humans, including Detective Hess and several other cops. All held weapons. Eve had a crossbow that she aimed at Bishop's chest.

Michael took an extra stake from Hannah.

All of Morganville on one side, and Bishop alone on the other.

He backed up, toward the back of the stage.

Behind him, the curtain took on a silvery shimmer.

"Portal!" Claire yelled, but it was too late; Bishop had activated an escape hatch, and in the next second he stumbled through it and was gone. Amelie was too far away, and too weak to go after him anyway.

Claire didn't think; she just jumped forward, put her hand on the portal's surface, and yelled Ada's name.

"What?" the computer asked. The sound this time boomed out of the portal.

"I need to track Bishop!" Claire said.

"I don't work for you anymore, human," Ada said, and shut down the portal with a snap. Claire turned to look at Myrnin, who was watching a few feet away, eyes fading back to his normal black. He walked toward her, bare feet gliding over the carpet, and studied the empty space where the portal had been.

Then he reached out and drew a wide circle with a sweep of his arm, and the silver shimmer flickered back into view.

"Don't be rude, Ada," he said. "Now, I know you can hear me. Where did our dear Mr. Bishop take himself off to?"

"I can't tell you," Ada said primly. "I don't work for you, either."

Myrnin placed his palm flat on the surface of the shimmer and looked at Claire. "He's reprogrammed her," he said. "He must have gone to her and given her his blood while we were making our own plans. I didn't expect him to move so quickly. I wasn't thinking as clearly as I should have been." He removed his palm, and Claire realized he'd done it as a kind of mute button, so Ada wouldn't hear what they had to say. "Ada, my darling, I put you together from scraps and my own blood. Are you really going to say you don't love me anymore?" Claire had never heard him sound that way before—so in control of himself, so assured and darkly clever. It made her shiver somewhere deep inside. "Let me come to you. I really want to see you, my love."

Ada was silent for a moment, and then her ghostly image appeared on the surface of the portal—a Victorian woman, dressed in the big skirts and high collar of the times. She smoothed her pale hands over the fabric of her dress. "Very well," she said. "You may call on me, Myrnin."

"Excellent." He grabbed Claire by the hand and stepped through the portal.

Her foot came down on something soft that ran off with a shrill squeak, and she jumped and gave out a squeal of her own. *Rats.* She hated rats. It was too dark to see, but in the next second the lights flickered on around the cavern, and there was the monster tangle of pipes and elaborate bracing that was Ada.

Her ghost stood in front of the clumsy giant type-writer-style keyboard, smiling at Myrnin like a lovesick girl, but the smile faltered when she saw Claire. "Oh," she said, through the tinny speakers of the computer. "You brought *her.*"

"Don't be jealous, love. You're the only girl for me." Myrnin strode up to the keyboard, *through* Ada's two-dimensional form, and Claire saw Ada make a startled face and turn toward him.

"What are you doing?" she demanded. "Myrnin!"

"Fixing you, hopefully," he said. "Claire."

She headed for his side, but Ada turned on her, and the prim Victorian image turned into . . . something else. Something dark and corrupt and horrible, snarling at her.

She flinched and veered off, but Myrnin's hand reached out and grabbed her to drag her in, past Ada. "Ignore her," he said. "She's in a mood." Myrnin tapped symbols, then uncovered the sharp needle on the control panel, and slammed his hand down on the point. "Ada. You will no longer accept commands from Mr. Bishop; do you understand me?"

"He was nicer to me," Ada said sulkily. "He gave me better blood."

"Better than mine? I believe I'm offended."

Ada's giggle sounded like a rattle of finfoil. "Well, you haven't been yourself, you know. But you taste *much* better now, Myrnin. Almost like your old self."

"Imagine that. Well, then, I promise that you'll get all the lovely sweet blood you'd like from me, if you will block Bishop from access, my sweet."

Ada made a long, drawn-out humming sound, as if she was thinking, and then she finally said, "Well . . . all right. But you have to give me a full pint."

"I haven't moved my hand at all, my dear. Drink away." He let almost a minute go by, then gestured to Claire to come closer. "Nearly done, Ada?"

"Mmmmmm." Ada sighed. "Yes. Delicious. I feel ever so much— What are you doing?"

He yanked his hand off the panel, grabbed Claire's, and slammed it down on the needle. She knew better than to try to fight him this time, just winced and bit her lip and tried not to wonder if, say, having Myrnin's blood infecting hers would have any nasty side effects, like a sudden craving for blood and an allergy to the sun.

"Sorry," he said, not as if he was, and altered his voice again to that velvety, dark, seductive tone. "Ada, my love?"

No answer.

"Ada, Claire is my very good friend, and I really must insist that she have the same access I do."

Ada made a retching sound.

"Ada."

"No."

He sighed. "List for me who has access to the system, please."

Ada said, "There are currently six individuals with full access to the portals, not including you. I have removed Mr. Bishop, because you asked so very nicely. That leaves Amelie, Oliver, Michael, *Claire*, Jason, and

Dean. Although Claire is no good for you, Myrnin. You should eat her immediately."

"Thank you, I shall think that over." He frowned down at the console. "Jason. Jason Rosser? Why did I not know this? And who is *Dean*?"

"That's for me to know and you to find out," Ada said, and laughed. Myrnin blinked.

"She's not supposed to do that, right?" Claire asked.

"Right. Oh dear. I think that my blood might have carried an infection deep into her systems. This may be a very bad thing."

"Can't you give her the cure?"

"It's not quite that simple," Myrnin said, and shifted his focus again. "Ada, my love? Can you tell me how Jason and Dean have access to the system?"

"Sam Glass gave it to Jason," she said. "But not full access, of course. Just to use open portals. Dean is Jason's friend. I revoked Sam's access, obviously. Because he's no longer functional."

Claire fidgeted uncomfortably. The white-hot pain in her hand was starting to eat away at her calm. "Um— Myrnin, can I please stop now?" She figured that Ada must have drained at least a pint by now.

"Please," Ada said. "I don't like your blood anyway." She made a computerized spitting sound. Claire yanked her hand away in relief and cradled it against her chest, squeezing her fist tight to stop the bleeding. "Disgusting. Too sweet."

Claire stuck her tongue out at the computer.

"I saw that."

"Good," she snapped. "Where did Bishop go?"

"Why should I—"

"Ada!" Myrnin's voice cracked across the computer's sulky response, and she went quiet. "I want you to block access to the portals for anyone except me, Amelie, Oliver, Michael, and Claire. Do you understand?"

"I'm not your slave." Ada's image flickered, then went out completely.

"I'm sorry," Myrnin said, and put his hands on the machine, almost like a caress. "My dear, I will come back and talk to you soon, and we'll work all this out. But you must promise me this. It's important."

Ada's sigh echoed through the speakers. "I can never say no to you," she said. "All right. I've locked out Dean and Jason, too."

"I guess that's it," Claire said, and felt a little bubble of relief that quickly popped when Myrnin shook his head.

"One more thing. I need to know where Bishop went when he traveled the last portal. Ada, love, can you do that for me?"

Behind them, Claire felt the subtle warping of a portal forming. She and Myrnin both turned to look. Ada's ghost reappeared, and then drifted off to the side, hands clasped behind her back. Definitely sulking.

Michael stepped through, holding Eve's hand. Behind him came Shane.

"Really." Ada sighed. "There's just no getting rid of *any* of you, is there?"

"Ada! Tell me where Bishop is!" Myrnin was out of patience, and she must have heard it in his voice. She shrugged.

"The university," she said. "I expect he can hide there for some time without detection. Plenty of snacks, after all."

If by *snacks* she meant *students*, then Claire supposed she was right. And the university was full of cavernous buildings, many of which were deserted at night. She was right. It was the perfect hiding place for Bishop, if he wanted to regain his strength and regroup.

They had to get him before that happened.

Myrnin was already on it. He stepped up to the portal Michael and the others had come through, tapped the surface, and listened. Claire heard it, too, faintly—a kind of ringing sound. A frequency. *Of course.* The portal worked on frequencies, like a radio—tune in to the right one, and you arrived at the correct destination. She'd been doing it without understanding consciously how, but now that she focused, she could hear the tone clearly.

"Here," Myrnin said, and stepped through. Claire reached back for Shane's hand, and walked into the unknown with him.

10

They came out in the Administration Building, in a deserted room that Claire remembered. Myrnin was already gone, but the door was still swinging on its hinges from where he'd headed through it. Claire made sure everybody was through, then took a second to look at the other three.

"You guys sure you want to do this?" she asked them. Michael looked more adult than she'd ever seen him—and more like Sam. He'd lost his grandfather, she realized—someone who wasn't supposed to be lost, ever. And that had fired up something in him that made him different.

More like Sam than ever.

Eve was still unmistakably Eve. She twirled the stake in her fingers, lifted the crossbow in her right hand. "How often do I get to go vamp stalking?" she asked, and smiled. "Let's do it."

"Shane?"

He'd been uncharacteristically quiet. Now, he just nodded. "Watch yourself," he said, and brushed the back of his hand gently across her cheek. "You scare me."

She burst out laughing, shakily. "You're insane."

There was a short hallway outside of the room, deserted and dark; at the end of the hallway was a fire door, and one of the doors was still open a little. Myrnin had gone that way, Claire figured.

She set out after him.

As she stepped outside into the cool evening air, something grabbed her. Not Myrnin.

Bishop.

He looked bad—unsteady, but still stronger than a mere human. He fumbled at her clothes; for a second she thought, *Oh my God, he's going to rape me,* and then his flailing hand brushed the book she'd shoved into her pocket. She'd forgotten about it.

Now, as he tried to pull it away from her, she fought back. Hard. Bishop was weaker than he'd ever been, and she was panicked. Bishop heard Shane calling her name, and pulled her farther into the darkness—then he headed for a nearby building, and dragged her *up* as he climbed. They ended up on the flat roof of the maintenance shed.

"Over there!" she heard Michael shout, and then he was heading toward them in a blur, with Shane and Eve in hot pursuit.

Bishop had his fingers on the book. *No!* She couldn't let it happen. Claire didn't fully understand what was in those pages, but she'd seen how he could use it. She felt it, in that tattoo.

She wasn't going to take the chance there was more he could do with it.

Bishop screamed something at her, and his fangs came down. Claire planted both feet in his chest and heaved with all her strength.

Bishop tumbled away from her, skidding on the loose roof gravel. Claire flipped over and scrambled to her feet, running for the edge. She had no idea what she'd do when she got there. Fly, maybe. Or take the fall, no matter how hard it was.

She didn't have to. Michael swooped in, grabbed her by the waist, and jumped with her. He landed lightly on the ground, let her slide down him, and looked up.

Bishop was leaning over, breathing hard. His fangs and crazy eyes caught the moonlight.

"Oh, crap," Eve said. "He's still not exactly Mr. Fluffy."

Shane summed it up. "Run!"

They did. Shane took Claire's hand; she had the shortest legs, but the most motivation, and she kept up with them as they raced out into the open green soccer field in front of the Admin Building.

Bishop landed on the grass behind them and began to chase them.

"He's going to catch us!" Eve yelled. "Head for the library!"

The TPU library was a big, columned building catty-corner to the Administration Building. It had its lights on, and there were still students coming and going up the steps, oblivious to what was coming their way. "Get out of here!" Claire shouted, and ran full speed to the top of the stairs. Shane was just ahead of her, Eve somewhere behind.

Michael had stopped at the foot of the steps, and was turning to face Bishop. When Claire hesitated, Eve grabbed her by the collar of her T-shirt and yanked her forward. "Don't stop!" she said, panting. "Damn, I need more exercise. Head into the stacks. Don't stop for anything, Claire!"

As they blew through the metal detectors, sirens went off. Students popped out of study carrels and up from tables like prairie dogs, then yelped and scattered as they realized something bad was heading their way, leaving a trail of notebooks and open computers. As they flashed past rows of library books, Shane skidded to a halt, grabbed two volumes with black covers, and tossed one to Eve. She nodded and shoved it in the waistband of her pants.

There was a crash somewhere behind them, and the glass doors blew into a million jagged pieces that flew across the marble floor. Students scrambled for cover. Somebody yelled to call the campus cops; somebody smarter yelled to shut up and hide.

Michael hit the marble floor and rolled, leaving trails of blood. He landed on his hands and knees, facing Claire, Shane, and Eve, who'd paused halfway down the stacks. "Go!" he told them, and got to his feet as Bishop stepped inside. He didn't seem as unsteady now.

The poison was wearing off, way too fast.

Shane pushed Claire into a run. Eve stumbled after them, looking over her shoulder to see if Michael was going to follow.

He didn't.

The aisle ended in a brick wall, with windows way up high, but there was an exit sign pointing to the left. The three of them turned the corner and headed for it, dodging past students wearing headphones, oblivious to the trouble in the stacks.

Shane hit the fire door first, setting off another alarm, and they raced down another flight of concrete steps.

This side of the library faced the big fountain—only the fountain was gone, and had been for a couple of months. What was in its place, at the center of six converging sidewalks, was the big concrete rim of what had been the pool, and in the center, a bronze statue of Mr. Bishop, holding a book in his hand.

There was one of those eternal flames burning in front of his statue—the light of knowledge, or something stupid like that. Claire had been revolted by the statue when it went up.

Now, she had an idea.

"Split up!" she yelled. "Make sure he sees that you have the books!"

Shane and Eve peeled off, heading right and left.

Claire went straight for the statue.

When Bishop emerged from the library, there was no sign of Michael. He paused on the steps, and he must have realized that two of the three of them were obvious decoys—but which two? Claire was betting that he'd assume she'd switched books with Shane.

She guessed right. Bishop jumped off of the stairs to the grass, and headed at a run after Shane. That gave Claire precious time to reach the stone rim of the fountain, climb over, and get to the eternal flame of knowledge—which was just a gas jet, really.

That was all she needed.

Claire pulled the book from her pocket and held it over the flame. *Yes. Finally.*

"Hey!" she distantly heard Eve shouting. "Hey, Bishop! Tag!" When she looked up, Eve was jumping up and down, waving her leather-bound book like a demented Goth cheerleader.

Bishop ignored her.

Shane zigzagged, doing the best broken field running Claire had seen outside of a football field, but Bishop was faster and more agile, and he cut him off and bowled Shane over.

Claire looked at the book in her hand.

It wasn't burning. She frantically turned it, trying the side with the gilded pages. "You've *got* to be kidding me!" she yelped, and kept trying.

It wouldn't even scorch.

Bishop took the book from Shane, examined it, and flung it away in disgust. He headed straight for Claire. Eve saw him coming, and got to Claire first, leaping over the rim of the fountain and skidding to a halt. "What are you waiting for?" she asked, panting. "Burn the damn thing already!"

"Trying!" Claire gritted out, and out of desperation, grabbed a handful of paper in the middle of the book and twisted.

The pages ripped out. When she held them out over the flames, they immediately caught like flash paper.

"Yes!" Eve cheered and jumped up and down, pumping her fists. "Go!"

Claire tore loose more pages and flung them into the fire.

Bishop landed flat-footed in front of her, red-eyed and growling, and backhanded Eve as she tried to get between him and Claire.

Claire ripped more pages and burned them. She'd done about half the book.

"You evil little beast," Bishop said, and held out his hand. "Give it to me."

She ripped pages and backed away, dodging around the other side of the brazier. Most of the paper made it to the fire. What didn't drifted lazily around her feet in the breeze. Sparks drifted on the wind and landed on her clothes.

Bishop lunged for her as she tore more pages free. She thrust the handful into the fire a second before he hit her, driving her back against his bronze statue. She landed hard enough to make the metal ring, not to mention her ears.

Bishop reached out to take the ragged remains of his book.

A shadow flashed by them, barely visible in the moonlight, and then Claire felt the statue shake as something leaped on top.

Myrnin, sitting on the shoulders of Bishop's statue, reached down and plucked the book from Claire's hand an instant before Bishop grabbed it. "Ah, ah, ah," he said. "Don't be rude, old man. This was never yours in the first place." He ripped loose a page, balled it up, and pitched it neatly into the brazier, where it burst into flame and was consumed. "Leave the girl alone. You're finished now."

Bishop grabbed Claire and pulled her against his chest, claws out and at her throat. "Give me the book or I kill her!"

"Oh, go ahead, then," Myrnin said, and ripped loose the last handful of pages. He studied the writing on them and smiled. "I remember this. Good times. Ah, well." He flung them toward the fire. Bishop desperately grabbed at one of the fluttering leaves and managed to pluck it out of the air before it caught fire. "Oh, dear. Now you have a memoir of my secret relationship with Queen Elizabeth. The first one. I hope it does you a lot of good, Bishop. If you're seeking spells and magic, you won't find it on that page. Now, *this one* . . ." Myrnin produced, by sleight of hand, another sheet, neatly folded. "This one could easily give you rule of Morganville. Maybe even the entire human world. I promised Amelie I would never let it fall into evil hands, but then again, it's in mine already, isn't it? So that might already be a moot point." He lost his smile. "Let the girl go, and you shall have it."

"Myrnin, don't," she whispered.

"I'm not doing it for you," he said. He quickly folded the paper into a toy airplane and sailed it toward Bishop, who snatched it out of the air with a greedy cry.

Myrnin's eyes flickered bright red. "Oh dear," he said. "I might have given you the wrong page. *Ardentia verba!*"

The page burst into purple fire, and it traveled from the page through Bishop's skin, over his hand, onto his clothes. The paper was ash in seconds. Bishop staggered back, engulfed in fire.

Myrnin reached down and grabbed Claire. He pulled her up and settled her safely on the metal arm of Bishop's statue—the one holding the open book.

"The goal of the wise," Myrnin said softly, "is good works. Here endeth your lesson, old man."

Claire swallowed. She couldn't stand to watch him burn, and shut her eyes. "I thought . . . I thought we needed his blood for the cure," she said. She didn't want to save him. She just hated to see anyone suffer.

"Why, you're right—we do." Myrnin snapped his fingers, and the purple fire went out. Bishop toppled to the stone floor of the empty fountain, too weak to escape.

Myrnin jumped down from the statue, pinned Bishop to the ground, and bit him. He didn't drain him—not quite—and rose, wiping blood from his lips. "I've got all his blood I need," he said. "Now I have something for you, Bishop. Don't worry—I won't kill you. I won't even allow you to die." He reached into his pocket and pulled out another syringe, this one filled with blood. He injected Bishop with it, straight into the heart. "My blood," Myrnin said. "Before you cured me. Now I hope you can enjoy a long, slow decline into madness, just like mine. I wish you the joy of it."

Bishop didn't move. He blinked up at the moon, the cold stars, and finally closed his eyes.

Not dead, though.

Claire wasn't sure _that_ was a great idea.

"Hey," Eve said, and sat up, holding her head. "Ow. What is that smell— Oh. Is he—"

"No," Michael said, and stepped over the rim to help Eve to her feet. "He's alive." He looked up at Claire and smiled, and it was a full-on Michael Glass special smile, one that turned on the sun and made the stars dance. "We're all alive."

"Relatively speaking," Myrnin said. "Ah. Your white knight has arrived. A bit dinged, but intact."

Shane. He was more than a little dinged, but Claire knew he'd be okay with that. They'd all given up hope of coming out of this alive, at some point; she could see in his smile, like Michael's, the joy of being wrong.

"Wish I had a camera," Shane said, staring up at her. "Is this some kind of college thing? Like flagpole sitting or something?"

"Shut up," she said, and jumped.

He caught her.

The kiss was worth the fall.

Two days passed in a blur. Claire spent most of it sleeping; she'd never felt so exhausted, or so glad to simply be alive.

On the third day, when she came down for dinner, she found the others sharing a massive platter of chili dogs and looking somber. Shane stood up when he saw her, which made her heart turn cartwheels, and he pulled out her chair. Eve and Michael shared an amused look.

"So cute," Eve said. When Shane glared, she smiled. "No, really. It is. Dude, chill."

There was something forced about it, and Claire didn't know why; she didn't get the sense that she'd walked in on an argument or anything like that. "What's going on?" she asked as she loaded her plate with a couple of hot dogs. She wasn't sure she really wanted to know. She'd just gotten used to the idea of not being marked for death. *Please don't let it be about Bishop escaping, or something horrible like that . . .*

It wasn't. Michael took a shallow sip of whatever was in his coffee mug and said, "Sam's funeral is tonight."

Oh *God.* Somehow, she hadn't expected that, and she really didn't even know why. The chili dog lost its taste, and she had to work to swallow it.

"They haven't had one before," Eve put in. "A funeral, I mean. For a vampire. At least, not one that's been open to the public. But this one was posted in the newspaper, and they ran it on the nightly news, too. Everybody's invited."

Most people would come out of curiosity, but for the four of them, it would be real loss. Under the table, Claire saw that Eve was holding Michael's hand. He was taking care not to look at any of them.

"It's in a couple of hours," Eve continued. "The three of us were going to go . . ."

"Sure," Claire said. "I want to go." She didn't, because it already hurt to think about it, but she thought they ought to be there for Michael. "I should find something to wear."

"You should finish your dinner first," Eve said. "One bite does not equal a balanced meal."

"Neither does a whole chili dog," Claire said.

"Do not diss the dog," Shane said. "It's right up there with mom and apple pie when it comes to cultural icons."

"You forgot Chevrolets," Eve said.

"Never been a Chevy man, myself."

"Heretic." Eve broke off to give Claire a fierce look. "Eat. I'm not kidding."

Claire managed to choke down the rest of her chili dog, but one was all she could manage. Despite Shane and Eve's bantering, there was a sadness that hung around Michael like a second skin. He didn't say much, except, "My parents are here. They flew in to El Paso and drove from there."

Wow. Claire had never heard much about Michael's parents, except that they'd moved away, and he'd never expected to see them back in town again. She finally said tentatively, "I guess that's good . . . ?"

"Sure," he said, and got up from the table. "I'm going to get ready." He walked out, and the rest of them watched him leave. Eve looked very sad, suddenly. And very adult.

"His mom had cancer, you know," she said. "That's why they got to leave Morganville. Because she needed serious treatments. Sam made sure she got them. This is the first time they've been back."

"Oh," Claire said. "Is Michael okay?"

"He just won't let it out," she said. "Guys. What is it with you and emotions, anyway?"

"They're like Kryptonite," Shane said. "He'll deal. Just give him time."

Claire wasn't too sure about that.

Michael drove, and nobody had much to say, really. It felt sad and uncomfortable.

As soon as the car stopped at the church, vampire escorts were at the doors to open them. The undead valet service. Under normal circumstances that might have been creepy, but there was something almost comforting about it tonight. Claire looked up and realized that the vampire offering a hand to her was, of all people, Oliver. She froze, and his eyebrows tilted sharply upward.

"Today, if you please," he said. "I'm here as a courtesy. Don't take it personally."

"Oh, I don't," she promised, and accepted his strong, ice-cold touch to help her out of the car. Shane quickly took her arm, giving Oliver a go-away glare, which was a little funny, and then they fell in behind Michael and Eve.

It was bizarre, Claire thought. The church was full, standing room only to the back, but the crowd parted as they walked in, led by Oliver. And every head turned to follow them.

"Okay, this is weird," Claire whispered. She felt like she had a target painted on her back at first, but then she realized that most of the people looking at them weren't angry—they were interested. Or sympathetic. Or even proud.

"Very weird," Shane whispered back.

The front row held Amelie, sitting alone, dressed in a white suit so cold and perfect that it made her look like an ice sculpture, head to toe. Behind her sat a man and woman in their late forties, and as soon as she saw them, Claire saw the family resemblance. The woman must have been really beautiful when she was younger; she was now very handsome, the way older women got, and her hair was a faded shade of gold with red highlights. They both stood up as Michael let go of Eve and came toward them.

"Honey," Michael's mother said, and Michael fell into a three-way embrace with both of his parents. "Oh, honey—"

"Mom, I'm so sorry, I couldn't—I couldn't do anything . . ." Michael's voice failed, and Claire saw his shoulders shake. His mother smoothed his hair gently, and the smile she offered him was kind and full of understanding.

"Just like him," she said. "Just like your grandfather. Don't you apologize, Michael. Don't you dare. I know you did everything you could. He'd never blame you, not for a second."

Claire hadn't realized that Michael felt guilty, but looking back on it now, she couldn't imagine he wouldn't. His mom was right—he was just like Sam, really.

He'd feel responsible.

Mrs. Glass looked past Michael, and her eyes focused on the rest of them. Claire first, then Shane, then Eve. She took a deep breath, moved toward them, and held out her hands to Eve for a hug. "I haven't seen you in years, Eve. You look wonderful. And Shane . . ." She moved on to him. Shane wasn't a hugger, not like Eve, but he tried his best. "I'm so glad you're here for Michael."

He looked down. Claire knew he was thinking about how angry he'd been with Michael over the past few months—too angry, sometimes. "He's my best friend," Shane said, and finally met Michael's eyes. "Vampire or not. He always will be."

Michael nodded.

Mrs. Glass hugged Claire, too. "And you're Claire. I've heard so much about you. Thank you for all you've done for my son."

Claire blinked. All *she'd* done? "I think it's the other way around," she said softly. "Michael's a hero. He's always been there for me."

"Then you've been there for each other," Mrs. Glass said. "True friends."

The crowd was parting again, letting more people pass, and as Claire looked around, she saw her own mother and father. "Oh no," she whispered. "I didn't know they were back yet."

"Your parents?" Michael's mom asked, and Claire nodded. Mrs. Glass quickly moved to greet them, gracious and sad, and then they closed in on Claire.

And Shane.

She winced at the icy stares her parents gave Shane, but they knew better than to start that here, now. They took seats to Claire's right, with Shane, Eve, Michael and his parents stretching out to her left.

And directly ahead, Amelie.

At the front of the church, surrounded by a blizzard of flowers of all colors, was a shiny black coffin with silver trim. The lid was closed. The discreet sound of organ music got louder, and the whispering buzz of the crowd in the church quieted as the door opened off to the side, and Father Joe came out, dressed in a blinding white cassock and a purple stole. He mounted the steps and looked out at the crowd with quiet authority. For a young priest, he had a lot of presence, but then Claire expected he'd have to, to serve a Morganville congregation that was composed equally of vampires and humans.

"We come to celebrate a life," he said. "The life of Samuel Glass, a son of Morganville."

Claire's eyes blurred under a wash of tears. She couldn't imagine Sam would have wanted to be remembered any other way, really. She barely heard the rest of what Father Joe said about Sam—she found that she was watching Amelie, or at least the very still back of Amelie's head. Not a hair out of place, not a whisper of motion.

So quiet.

And then, suddenly, Amelie was getting up, in absolute silence, and walking up the steps. She stopped not at the podium, but at the coffin, and opened the hinged cover. It clicked into place, and Amelie stayed there for a moment, staring down at Sam's face.

Then she turned and faced the hundreds of people gathered in the church.

"I met Samuel Glass here in this church," Amelie said. Her tone was soft, but it carried. No one moved. No one coughed. As far as Claire could tell, no one breathed. "He came here to demand—*demand*—that I right some wrong he imagined I had done. He was like an angel with a flaming sword, full of fury and righteousness, with absolutely no fear of the consequences. No fear of me." She smiled, but there was something broken in it. "I think I fell in love with him in that moment, when he was so angry with me. I fell in love with his fearlessness first, and then I realized that it was more than mere courage. It was a conviction that life must be made fair. That *we* must be better. And for a time ... for a time I think we were."

She paused, and looked again at Sam's pale, still face.

"But I was weak," she said. "Weak and afraid. And I let him slip away from me, because I didn't have his courage, or his conviction. This moment, this loss, is my fault. Sam gave himself, again, to save lives. To save *me*. And I have never deserved it."

There were tears running down her cheeks now, and her voice was trembling. Claire couldn't breathe because of the weight of emotion in her chest.

"Someone else recently demanded that I change the rules of Morganville," Amelie continued. "Just as Sam demanded it fifty years ago, and continued to demand it of me at every opportunity."

Claire realized, with a shock, that Amelie was talking about *her*. As if what she'd said was somehow brave.

Amelie reached up and pulled pins from her hair, one after another. Her icy crown of pale hair began to unravel and fall loose around her shoulders.

"I have decided," she said, "that changes must be made. Changes will be made. Sam earned the right for humans to stand as equals in this town, and it will be done. It will be painful, it will be dangerous for us all, but it *will* be done. In Sam's memory, I make it so."

She leaned over, and very gently, placed a kiss on Sam's lips, then closed the coffin. No one spoke as she walked away, down the steps and out through the side door. Oliver and a few of the other vampires exchanged silent looks, then moved to follow her.

Father Joe spoke over the rising tide of whispers. "Let us pray."

Claire clasped her hands and looked down. Next to her, Shane was doing the same, but he whispered, "Am I crazy, or did we just win?"

"No," Claire whispered back. "But I think we just got a chance to."

Four weeks later.

"Chaos, disorder, mayhem," Shane said. "Situation normal in Morganville." He took a drink of his coffee and pushed the other one across to Claire.

Common Grounds was holding a grand reopening, with half-priced coffee, and the place was packed. Everybody loved a bargain. It wasn't exactly normal for the two of them to be sitting in Oliver's territory like this; Claire never thought Shane would do it voluntarily, but the lure of cheap caffeine proved powerful.

He'd further surprised her by exchanging some semi-civil words with Oliver himself as he'd claimed the coffee. Speaking of which . . . "What did Oliver say to you?" Claire asked.

Shane shrugged.

"I asked Oliver if they'd found my father, but he was his usual douchey self. Told me to forget about my dad. I don't know if that means they found him, they killed him, or they just don't care. Dammit, I just want someone to tell me."

Claire looked up at him, struck into silence. *I need to tell him,* she thought. *I really do.*

She just couldn't quite think of the words.

Life was getting back to normal in Morganville. Amelie had declared an absolute ban on hunting. The blood banks had reopened, and the people of Morganville had been given a choice—start over, or start running. Plenty had taken the second option. Claire figured that half the town had decided to seize the chance to leave . . . but she also knew that some of them would come back. After all, some of their families had never been out of town at all. It was a whole new world out there. For some, it would be too much.

Common Grounds had renovated in record time, and was open to students once more. Oliver was behind the bar, wearing his nice-guy face and pulling espresso shots like nothing had ever changed.

The bronze statue of Bishop was gone from the university. In fact, all traces of Bishop were gone. Claire didn't know where François and Ysandre had ended up, but Myrnin assured her, with a perfectly straight face, that she didn't *want* to know. Sometimes, she was content to be ignorant. Not often, true. But sometimes.

Shane, however, needed to know about his father. Frank Collins, as far as Claire knew, had just vanished into thin air. If Amelie knew, she wasn't saying.

This was a moment that Claire actually had wanted to avoid, in a way. She'd put it off as long as she could, but Shane was getting more aggressive about asking people if there was any sign of Frank Collins in Morganville, and she really couldn't put it off any longer.

"I have something to tell you about that," she said, and cleared her throat. "Your dad—I . . . I saw him."

He froze, coffee cup halfway to his lips. "When?"

"A while ago." She didn't want to be too specific. She hated that she'd hidden it from him for so long. "He . . . ah . . . he could have killed me, but he didn't. He said to tell you that . . . that he loved you. And he was sorry."

Shane blinked at her, as if he couldn't quite believe what she was saying. "Where did you see him?"

"In the cells where the sick vampires were being kept. He's not there anymore. I looked. He's just . . . gone." She swallowed hard. "I didn't want to tell you, but I think . . . I think he was going to kill himself, Shane."

Something changed inside of Shane for a long second— she didn't recognize the look in his eyes or on his face. And then she did. It was his dad's look, the one that came before he lashed out at someone.

Shane closed his eyes, took a deep breath, and bowed his head. She didn't dare move for a few seconds, then carefully reached out and put her hand on the table, just a few inches from his.

His fingers twined with hers.

"Dammit," he whispered. "No, I'm not mad. I just feel . . . I guess I feel relieved. I wanted to know. Nobody would talk to me."

"I should have said something," she said. "I know. I'm so sorry. I just didn't know how. But I didn't want you to hear it from Oliver or something, because that would just . . . bite."

"No kidding." He took another deep breath, then raised his head. His dark eyes were glittering with unshed tears, but he blinked them back. "He wouldn't have wanted to go on like that. He made a choice. I guess that's something."

She nodded. "That's something."

She'd ripped off the bandage, and now at least he could start healing.

It was the same everywhere. Healing. All over Morganville, burned buildings were being demolished and rebuilt. City Hall, destroyed by a tornado, was getting a municipal makeover, with plenty of marble and fancy new furniture. All of the surviving Founder Houses—even the Glass House—were getting repaired and repainted. The ones that hadn't survived were being rebuilt from the ground up.

In an amazingly short time, Morganville life had gone back to normal. As normal as it ever was, anyway. And if the vampires weren't happy about things changing, well, they were—so far—keeping their objections on their side of the fence.

Shane sipped his coffee—plain coffee, not the fancy milky stuff she liked—and watched people go by outside the front windows. She let him sit in silence and come to terms with what she'd said; he was still holding her hand, and she figured that had to be a good sign.

"Oh, great," Shane said, and nodded to the door. "Trouble, twelve o'clock. Just what we needed."

Monica Morrell posed in the doorway, making sure the light caught her best side. She'd returned to town, along with her BFFs, and slipped right back into her role as Morganville's queen bitch without a pause. It helped that Richard Morrell was still mayor, of course, and that Monica's family had always been rich.

Monica surveyed the busy room disdainfully, snapped her fingers, and sent Gina to stand in the coffee line. Then she and Jennifer made a beeline for the table where Claire and Shane sat.

Nobody spoke. It was a war of stares.

"Bitch, please," Shane said finally. "You can't be serious. Out of all the people in here, you pick us to evict? Really not in the mood today."

"I'm not evicting you," Monica said, and slid into the chair next to him. Jennifer looked deeply shocked, then put out, but she bullied some poor freshman out of his chair at the next table, and yanked it over to plop down as well. "I thought since you had extra chairs, you wouldn't be a complete dick about it. Should have known you'd be a bad winner or something."

He blinked.

"Not that you *won*," she said quickly. "Just that you're, you know, still here. Which is a form of winning. Not the best one."

Shane and Claire exchanged looks. Claire shrugged. "Oliver take you back?" she asked. Monica traced some old carving on the tabletop with a perfectly manicured fingernail, and then flipped her still-dark hair over her shoulders.

"Of course," she said. "What would Morganville be without the Morrell family?"

"Wouldn't I like to know?" Shane muttered. Monica sent him a freezing glare. "Kidding." Not.

"I heard you're working," she said. "Wow. Good for you. Shane Collins, actually earning a paycheck. Somebody should alert the press."

He flipped her off, then checked his watch. "Speaking of the job, damn," he said. "Claire—"

"I know. Time to go."

He leaned over and kissed her. He made it extra-special good, with Monica watching, which made Claire warm all the way down to her toes; he took his time, to the extent that people at other tables started clapping and hooting.

"Watch your back," he murmured, his lips still against hers. "Love you."

"Watch yours," she said. "Love you, too."

She watched him walk away with an expression she was sure made her look like a total fool, and she didn't care. Other girls watched him go, too—they always did, and he rarely noticed these days.

Monica made a retching noise into the coffee that Gina thumped down in front of her. "God, you two are disgusting. You know it's not going to last, right?"

"Why, because you're going to take him away?" Claire asked, and smiled slowly. "Too much car for you, rich girl."

"Is that a challenge?"

"Sure. Knock yourself out. No, really. Hammer to the head, works every time." Claire drained the rest of her mocha as Gina settled into Shane's vacated chair. "Hey, kid. Here." Claire scooted her chair back over to the bewildered freshman Jennifer had bullied out of a seat; he settled gratefully into it, nodded, and put his headphones back on. Studying.

Claire had a stack of that to do, too. She'd aced the semester, but that was just the beginning of her challenges. Ada had a lot to teach her, although the computer still hated her and probably always would. Myrnin ... Myrnin had absorbed so much of Bishop's blood that he was a walking serum factory, to Dr. Mills's delight; the vampires of Morganville were being cured, one by one.

All except Sam. Sam's absence was a hole in everyone's life. Amelie hadn't left her home except for official appearances; she'd become a hermit again, dressed in formal white, back to being the ice queen Claire had first met. If she grieved, she didn't show it to the unwashed public.

But Claire knew she did.

She knew Amelie always would.

As Claire headed for the door, someone caught the strap on her backpack. "Hey, Claire!" The voice wasn't familiar, but it seemed cheerful and happy to see her. She turned. It took her a few seconds to place the face barely visible over a pile of books.

It was the awkward boy with the emo haircut—the one she and Eve had met at the University Center before everything had blown up in Morganville. The one who'd once been friends with Shane.

"It's Dean, remember? Do you have a minute?"

She wasn't too sure it was a good idea. There was something odd about him, something she'd filed away in her memory . . . Oh yeah. "Before we get into that, how do you know Jason Rosser?" she asked.

Dean froze in the act of clearing his backpack from the chair next to him. "Oh. Uh . . . busted, I guess. When I moved here, me and Jason hung out when he got out of jail. I mean, my theory was his sister was living in the house with Shane, so he'd be a way to keep track. Only he was kind of nuts, you know?"

Claire kept watching him. He seemed honest enough. "He must have shown you some things. Secrets, I mean. About the town."

Dean's ears turned red. "You mean—yeah. The short-cuts? The ones that take you from one place to another? Honestly, I never used them except that once. Scared the holy crap out of me."

He sounded ashamed of himself, but Claire could fully get behind the concept of finding Morganville terrifying. Granted she thought it was kind of fascinating, but then, she was a freak of nature.

Dean looked pathetic. "Let me guess. I blew it, right? You'll never talk to me again."

"No, it's okay." She sighed and slid into the chair. "It's just that Jason's not what I would call a great character reference."

"I hear you. But then, I was working for Frank Collins, and my brother was a crazy biker dude, so it really wasn't that much of a stretch." He shrugged. "Thanks for cutting me some slack, Claire."

"Everybody deserves a second chance. Hey, did you see Shane? I thought you wanted to talk to him."

"I did. Where is he?"

"Gone to work. He just left."

"I missed him?" Dean looked around, as if Shane would just materialize out of thin air. He looked disappointed when that didn't happen. "Damn."

"Well, it's pretty busy in here. If you didn't see him, he probably didn't see you, either. It's not like he's avoiding you or anything."

"Yeah, probably. So. You're, ah, staying on? In Morganville?"

"Yes." She left it at that. Between her new, completely amazing relationship with Shane, and the fact that Myrnin was teaching her physics so advanced that most Nobel Prize–winners would weep, no way was she leaving now. "You?"

He shrugged. "Got no place else to be. You still living at the Glass House?"

"Uh, no. I made a deal with my parents. I have to live at home with them until I'm eighteen, and then I can move back. Eve promised that they'd keep my room for me, though." The truth was, she pretty much still lived there, and she looked forward to the time she spent with her friends—shared dinners, board games, zombie-smashing video games, and Wii tennis . . . And Eve doing dramatic readings from her favorite vampire books as Michael squirmed in embarrassment.

She looked forward to everything.

Morganville wasn't perfect. It would never be perfect. But Amelie had kept her promise, and humans were starting to feel like equal citizens, not possessions. Not walking blood banks.

It was a start. Claire had plans for more, in time.

"Hey," she said. "Maybe you could come over tonight, to the Glass House? Have dinner with us? I'm sure Shane would love to see you. It'd be a great surprise."

"It would," Dean said, and gave her a matching grin. "Yeah, okay. Seven o'clock?"

"Fine," she said. "Listen, I have to get to work. See you then!"

He hastily stood up and shoveled his books and papers into his backpack. "I'm going too," he said. "Just a sec."

Is he hitting on me? Claire wondered. She knew what Eve would say, but she couldn't quite believe it. Dean seemed like a nice guy—but there was a glint in his eye when he looked at her.

She wondered if she should just take off, but that seemed rude.

Oliver was watching her from his place at the bar. She nodded to him, and he gave her a cool look that told her just what he thought of her. No, they were never going to be friends. And that was fine with Claire. She still thought he was a creep.

Dean stumbled over his own feet getting up, jostled the arm of a jock at the next table, and had to apologize his way out of trouble, backing into Claire as he did so. She sighed, grabbed his backpack, and towed him toward the door.

She was surprised he didn't fall over the cracks in the sidewalk, but once he was out of public view, he seemed to straighten up and be a little more coordinated. Huh. He was taller than she'd thought. Broader, too. Not Shane-broad, but solid, after all. It was the hair that fooled her—emo hair always made guys look kind of wimpy.

"Where are you heading?" she asked Dean. He adjusted the weight of his backpack on his shoulder.

"Oh, you know," he said vaguely, and pointed down the street. She was starting to think that he really was trying to hit on her. The going-my-way routine must have been old when Rome was still building roads. "You all done with classes and stuff?"

"Mostly. I have a couple of labs still to finish out, extra credit stuff, really. You looked like you were studying hard."

"Not really," Dean said. "I mostly carry the books around just to make stupid girls like you think I'm safe to be around."

She blinked, not sure she'd heard that right. He'd said it exactly the same way he'd said everything else. Like a nice, normal guy.

They were just passing an alley between the buildings. Nobody in sight.

"What—"

She turned her head toward him, and the last thing she saw was his backpack, full of books, heading at full speed toward her head.

Claire woke up not really sure she was waking up at all—everything seemed weird, smeared, dreamlike. She couldn't move, and her head hurt so bad she started to cry.

She heard voices.

"... can't believe you brought her here," one said—she knew the voice, but she couldn't place it; the headache was too huge to think around. "Are you mental? That's not just *anybody*. She's going to be missed, Dean!"

"That's the point." Dean. That was Dean's voice. "I want them to miss her. I want them to look all over. They won't find her until I want them to. Come on, Jason. Man up, already."

"Dude, I knew you were crazy. I didn't know you were stupid, too. We have to let her go."

Sound of scuffling. Feet on wood. Grunts. Two men fighting.

One went down.

"Shut up," Dean snapped. "You're always whining. All you ever had to do was carry the bodies. I'm not even asking you to get your hands dirty."

"No! Look, I *know* her. You can't—"

"That's why she's perfect. *Everybody* knows her. C'mon, man, get it together. She's just a girl. Worse, she's a vamp lover. We're making the world a better place, and having fun while we do it." Dean laughed. It was the worst sound she'd ever heard from a human—and a good match for the worst sound she'd ever heard, period.

Jason must be Jason Rosser, Eve's brother. The one Dean said he barely knew. Maybe this was some horrible dream. It made sense that she'd put Jason's brother in a dream about being abducted and tied up, right? Because Jason had been accused of those murders . . .

Claire opened her eyes and stared at the ceiling of what looked like an old, abandoned house. Spackle was peeling off in sad sheets, hanging down, waving in a slight breeze through a broken window.

Jason had been accused of those murders. But he'd told Amelie, straight up, that he hadn't killed anybody.

He'd just seen it happen. He'd never said who was behind it. *Dean.*

Claire felt short of breath. *This is bad; this is really, really bad. . . .* Her head felt like it had been smashed with a brick. She felt sick enough to barf, and when she tried to move, the pain got worse. She couldn't do much, anyway. She was tied up, ankles and wrists.

There was sunlight coming in the window, but it was at a low angle. She'd been out for hours, and there was a bitter, nasty taste in her mouth. They'd given her something, on top of knocking her in the head. Maybe chloroform.

By twisting her wrist, she could see her watch.

Five o'clock.

The sun would be down soon. Nobody would have missed her yet; it wasn't dinnertime, and she'd been casually intending to drop in at Myrnin's lab to see how far he'd gotten with setting it back up. But he hadn't been expecting her.

Nobody had been expecting her. Shane had gone to work, and wouldn't be home until dark.

Phone.

It wasn't in her pocket. They'd taken it.

She blinked, and she must have lost time, because when she opened her eyes again, Dean Simms was sitting next to her, staring down. In the doorway of the decaying room stood Jason Rosser, looking sick and ill at ease.

Dean was smiling like he owned the world.

"Hey," he said. "So, you're up and around, right? Good. I thought you'd be tougher. I mean, they all talk about you like you're something special, but you went down just like the others. No problem at all."

"I . . . " Nausea boiled up inside when she tried to talk, and she stopped and swallowed helplessly until she could talk again. "My friends will look for me."

"Yeah, that's what I figured. So when they find you drained like some sad little vamp quickie outside of Oliver's back door . . . well. They won't be real happy, will they?" Dean's eyes practically glowed. "Man, you were so *easy.* Frank thought you had backbone. Guess not."

"Why?" she whispered. "Why are you doing this?" She really wanted to know. Somehow, if she had to die, she felt like she wanted to understand. She wanted it to make sense.

"Look, it's not personal." Dean dragged a fingernail down her cheek, scratching her. "Well, maybe a little personal, because, you know, fun. But this is about setting this town free. Fighting evil. It's what Frank Collins wanted. It's what I want. It's what you want, right, Claire? I know it's what Shane wants, too. So you're doing everybody a favor by dying."

Dean hadn't come to Morganville just to have Shane's back; he'd come to have his fun. If he even knew Frank Collins at all, he'd just been using Frank. Once he'd come to Morganville, he'd realized it was open season, and he could do whatever he wanted.

Still could, Claire realized sickly. Nobody suspected him at all.

She certainly hadn't.

"What?" he asked her. "You're not going to tell me I'm making a mistake? Beg me not to do it?"

"Why bother?" she whispered. "You'll do what you want, right?"

"Always do." Dean leaned back. "Jase. Hold her feet. I don't want her kicking me."

"It's not right. This isn't right, man."

"Shut up or I'll make it two bodies tonight. It just makes my point better."

Claire kicked out, but it was no use; Jason leaned on her ankles and held them down. Dean forced her arm down and opened up a rusting medical kit. He took out one of those hollow needles doctors used to draw blood, but instead of connecting it to a sample tube, he stuck on some rubber tubing.

The rubber tubing ended in a big empty gallon jug that had once held milk.

"Little stick." He smirked and slid the needle into her vein.

Claire screamed. Jason looked away, guilt written all over his face, but Dean just kept on smiling. Red flooded out into the tube, ran along the coils, and began pumping out into the milk jug.

"How's it feel?" he asked her. "You like vampires. How's it feel to have your life drained out of you, just like they do it? I hate vampires. I really, really do. And if I can get this town to rise up and kill even one more by doing you, it's a bargain."

She squeezed her eyes shut and tried to think of something she could do.

Blood.

A black-and-white ghost flickered into view at the far end of the room. Ada's image looked quiet and composed, and just a little bit pleased. She'd come to watch Claire die.

"Get help," Claire whispered. "Please, go get help!"

Jason and Dean, at least, had no idea who she was talking to, since Ada had manifested behind them. "Who are you talking to, idiot? Jason's not on your side. Jesus, Jason, hold her feet! Come on, man! I'm not asking you for much, here!"

Ada raised thin eyebrows. Her image flickered. Claire didn't want to look at the red line rising in the milk jug; she could feel herself getting weaker, her heart pounding harder to keep up.

"Myrnin," Claire panted. "I need Myrnin."

Ada flickered out. Claire had no idea whether or not she'd even make the effort.

Outside, the sun settled below the window.

Twilight.

Jason jumped up at a sound from outside. "What the hell is that?"

"Nothing," Dean said. He was watching Claire's face. She was breathing too fast, and she tried to slow down; her heart was racing, and she was losing too much blood. *Ada, please. Please.* "Don't worry about it. It's the wind."

Jason let go of Claire's feet. She was too weak to move much, anyway. "No, it's not. There's somebody out there. Dude, leave her. Let's go!"

"No frickin' way. We're almost done here. Five more minutes. Keep it together, bro."

"I'm not your bro!" Jason snarled. "You're on your own, asshole!"

He took off. *No—please wait.* Claire tried not to cry, but she was losing track of why she ought to be strong. Was somebody coming? No, she had to save herself. Nobody was coming to save her.

"Dean," she said. "You know about the portals, don't you?"

That got his attention. Full on.

"I can tell you something about them you don't know. If you stop this."

His dark eyes took on a strangely stubborn look; he didn't like being robbed of his pleasure. "What kind of something? Because it'd have to be really good."

"Oh, it is," she said. "I can tell you how to make your own portals. How to go anywhere. Do anything. Imagine what you could do with that, Dean."

He was imagining it, all right, and she could see color rising in his cheeks. He liked it.

He liked it a *lot.*

Dean glanced over at the milk jug, which was shimmering with her blood. A steady stream flowed out of the tube to patter down inside. "Start talking," he said. "If I like what you say, I'll turn it off."

He was lying to her; she could feel it. "You can stop pretending you're killing me for a cause. You're not. You're killing me because you like it, Dean. You're not a vampire; you're worse. They're like tigers. You're a cannibal."

His eyes flickered, and he leaned forward. "Maybe I'll try that, too," he said. "Maybe I'll start on you."

She blinked, light-headed. The world seemed to shift in front of her. She had a vision, and it was so *real*.

She was looking past him into the living room at home, just like through a tunnel. The TV was on. Eve was singing along to some obnoxious commercial, shimmying her hips as she put a plate full of hot dogs on the table. It was Eve's night to cook. Michael was tuning his guitar, intent on frets and strings and sounds.

Shane walked in from the front hall, dropped his keys on the table, and said, "Where's Claire?"

"Not here yet," Eve said. "Probably on her way."

I'm not. I'm not coming. I'm sorry.

Shane dug his cell phone out and dialed.

Somewhere in another part of the abandoned house, Claire heard her ring tone echoing. The odd thing was, Shane seemed to hear it, too. He looked around, raised his eyebrows at Eve, and Eve shrugged. "Maybe she left it."

They could hear the phone. But the phone was here.

Claire pulled in a breath to scream, but she didn't have to.

Shane looked right at her, and for a second, she realized what that tunnel was, that silvery shimmer at the edges.

She realized that Ada hadn't let her down, after all. It was a portal, and Shane was going to save her.

He saw her.

His eyes widened.

"Claire!" he screamed, and lunged at the portal.

It closed right before he got there.

"Oh, man," Dean breathed. "Close. You can do that thing, too? The portal thing? Comes in handy; am I right?" He waved his arm, and the portal shimmered back into existence—but in place of the tunnel that had led to the Glass House, there was one leading into darkness. No—not quite darkness. It was the old prison, the one where the sick vampires had been kept. "Ada locked me out for a while, and man, I was starting to sweat. But I promised her some fresh blood if she'd just let me have it for a couple more days."

He'd been using the network to kill, and Jason had helped him—probably just because Jason was a joiner, and lonely, and Dean knew how to make people feel wanted. Even Claire had felt it, and she should have known better.

Her heart was racing so fast now.

"See?" he said. "I can do it from anywhere. Just like you. Guess that makes us special."

He was smart, she realized. Clever and cold. Like Myrnin.

Only Myrnin had a conscience.

Something moved on the other side of the portal. A ghost. Ada?

No, although Claire saw the flicker of her black-and-white image for a second standing in the portal, facing away from her. Beckoning to someone else on the other side.

Then misting out of the way.

Ada had brought help, after all, but it wasn't Myrnin. It was Frank Collins.

Shane's dad stood on the other side of the portal, staring through at them, looking more like a ghost than Ada had. Claire must have made some sound, because Dean turned to look, and his face went completely slack with surprise. "Frank?" he asked. "Frank, wait—let me explain . . ."

Frank Collins reached through, grabbed Dean, and dragged him through the portal.

Dean screamed, once, and then there was silence. Just . . . nothing.

Claire felt herself getting cold. *This is how it feels*, she thought. *Becoming a vampire. Except I won't wake up.*

Frank stepped through the portal.

"Keep breathing," he told her, and crouched next to her as he took the tube out of her arm and tossed it away. He wadded up a piece of bandage and stuck it in the bend of her arm, then bent it back to add pressure. "Sorry about Dean. I always knew he wasn't good in the head, but I never thought he'd go this crazy."

He looked at her for a few seconds, then pushed to his feet and headed for the portal.

Along the way, he grabbed the milk jug, and then he was gone.

Ada's ghost misted back into view, staring at Claire. She was smiling.

"Help," Claire whispered.

"I did." Ada's prim voice came out of the distant, tinny speaker of the cell phone. "He promised me blood, but I don't want *yours*. I don't like it."

Ada disappeared.

She was alone, and cold. For a little while, that was all there was.

Then hands were lifting her, and she felt a tiny sting in her numb arm, and there were voices.

Light.

Then a different kind of nothing.

The hospital room was dark in the middle of the day, out of courtesy to the visitors. The overhead fluorescent lights bleached everybody, but at least nobody burst into flame.

That was Morganville in a nutshell. Compromise.

"I'm told that you're doing well," Amelie said, and pulled up a chair at Claire's bedside. Her bodyguards had taken up posts at the door. One of them winked at Claire, and she smiled back. "I feel I must apologize for my lack of care for your safety."

"You couldn't have known I was in trouble," Claire said.

"You wear my mark on your bracelet, and that makes you my dependent." That seemed to settle everything for Amelie. "That does not reflect well upon my stewardship. Luckily, Dr. Mills believes you will make a complete recovery. You may thank your friends for being so quick to act on your behalf."

Claire felt pleasantly warm, safe, and a little drugged. "Yeah, about the rescue," she said. "What happened?"

"Several things. First, Eve called me and demanded my help." Amelie nodded to Eve, who managed to look simultaneously smug and embarrassed as she leaned against the wall. "Although Eve presumed a great deal about my willingness to help, I decided to speak with Ada." Claire bet that had been an interesting, scary conversation. "She admitted that she knew where you were. From there, it was a simple enough matter to open a portal to you and bring you help."

"Who was it?" she asked. Her eyelids felt heavy. "Shane?"

"In fact, no," Oliver said, from the darkest corner of the room. "I carried you. Don't get sentimental; the doctors saved you, not me. I simply moved you from one place to another." He sounded as if he deeply wished to be out of the round of thanks at all costs. Claire was happy to oblige him.

"The blood bank came in handy," Dr. Mills said cheerfully, leaning over her to check her tubes and wires. "About time it did humans some good, too." He didn't seem shy about saying it in front of Amelie and Oliver, either. "You owe us about four pints, kiddo. But later, I promise. No rush at all."

"Thanks," she said, and gave him a drowsy thumbs-up.

"Just doing my job," he said. "Of course, some days it's a pleasure. Rest. You're going to be here for a few days. Oh, and I hope you enjoy off-brand flavors of Jell-O."

She thought he was kidding about that last part, but she absolutely couldn't be sure. Before she could ask, he scribbled something on her chart and hurried off to the next patient. Jell-O victim.

Amelie's cool fingers adjusted the covers minutely—for Amelie, that was positively fussy. "I am pleased you'll be working with us a while longer, Claire," she said. "Sleep now."

Claire badly wanted to, but she had another question. "Did you get him?" Claire asked, and opened her eyes again. "Did you find Dean?"

"Yes," Amelie said. Her expression was absolutely unreadable. "We found Dean." She rose, nodded to her bodyguards, and left without an explanation or a backward glance. Oliver pushed off and followed, but he made it look like it was his own idea.

Oh, that was going to be trouble, if Oliver kept up with the attitude. But it was trouble that Claire didn't have to worry about. The only thing she had to worry about, in fact, was choking down horrible, weird flavors of gelatin.

About a minute after the departure of the vampires, the door opened again, and Shane came in juggling a handful of drinks. Coffee, it smelled like. The sight of him made Claire feel like a sun had exploded inside her—so much happiness she was surprised it wasn't leaking out of her skin, like light.

His smile was *amazing*.

"Hope you brought some for me," Claire said, as he handed Eve and Michael their cups. There was one left over.

"You're kidding, right?" Shane asked. "You don't need caffeine. You need sleep." He held out the last cup, and Claire realized she'd been wrong; there was someone else in the shadows. Deeper in the shadows even than Oliver had been.

Myrnin.

He looked completely different to her now, and not just because he wasn't crazy anymore. He'd remembered how to dress himself, for one thing; gone were the costume coats and Mardi Gras beads and flip-flops. He had on a gray knit shirt, black pants, and a jacket that looked a bit out of period, but not as much as before.

All clean. He even had shoes on.

"Yes, you must sleep," he agreed, as he accepted the cup and tried the coffee. "I've gone to far too much trouble to train up another apprentice at this late date. We have work to do, Claire. Good, hard work. Some of it may even earn you accolades, once you leave Morganville."

She smiled slowly. "You'll never let me leave."

Myrnin's dark eyes fixed on hers. "Maybe I will," he said. "But you must give me at least a few more years, my friend. I have a great deal to learn from you, and I am a *very* slow learner."

Claire laughed at that, because it was just silly. At least, she thought she did. She felt pleasantly floaty, and so very tired.

Her parents dropped in and evicted everyone, for a while. Even Myrnin. She supposed that was all right, in her dreamy haze. It was nice, being loved like that.

When she opened her eyes again, it was night. Her

parents were gone, and Eve was asleep in one of those uncomfortable hospital chairs, curled up with her head on her arms and a hospital blanket covering up her pink Goth bowling shirt. Michael had his guitar, and he was playing very quietly—something slow and sweet and peaceful. When he saw Claire's eyes flutter open, he stopped, looking guilty.

"No, go on," she murmured. "It's really beautiful."

"I'm supposed to play at Common Grounds later," he said. "I can blow it off if you need me to stay, though."

"No, you go. Don't rob Morganville of the amazing Michael Glass comeback tour."

"Yeah, like anybody will care," Michael said, but he smiled in that way that meant he was kind of embarrassed about it. And delighted. "I wouldn't leave, but it looks like you've got a permanent bodyguard already."

Shane was asleep, too, head down on the edge of her bed. She longed to run her fingers through his hair, but she didn't want to wake him up.

She didn't have to. Shane's breathing changed, and he sat up, blinking, as if he'd gotten some invisible signal. He focused on her instantly. "Hey," he said, and she saw him relax as relief rolled through him. "Sleepyhead." He reached out and took her hand in his, then leaned forward and kissed her. It felt warm and drowsy and sweet, like a promise. "Welcome back."

She felt like she'd never take her life for granted again. "Did you talk to my parents?"

"I did. Man, my ears are still burning. It's all my fault, apparently." Shane smiled, but she could see he really did feel that way, about his guilt. "I can't believe I wasn't there for you, Claire. I can't believe I couldn't get to you—"

She put a finger on his lips. "You've always been there when I needed you," she said. "You're here now, right?"

"You know what I mean."

She thought about telling him about Frank, about

how he'd saved her. But she wasn't sure, really sure, that she hadn't just imagined it.

And if Frank Collins was around, he could show up and tell his son himself.

"I know," she said. Something Monica said back at Common Grounds haunted her, especially in this weakened state: *You know it's not going to last, right?* Things changed. People changed. Even Morganville changed. "Don't go." She hadn't meant to say it out loud. *Needy much, Claire?*

Shane took her hand and raised it to his lips in an old-fashioned kiss worthy of Myrnin at his best. "I'm not going anywhere," he said. "Not even to take a shower. And you're really going to regret that, by the way."

"Dude," Michael said. "I already regret it."

"Shut up, man."

Michael threw a box of tissues at him. Shane fielded it and fired it back, which wasn't much of a challenge to Michael's vampire reflexes.

Eve woke up, wiped drool from her chin, and yawned. "You jerks want to take the Super Bowl outside? Some of us need our beauty rest—*don't say it, Collins.*"

Shane caught the tissue box. "Say what?" he asked, and tossed the box underhanded in Eve's direction. "Fetch!"

She came out of the chair, picked up the tissue box, and whacked him over the head with it. Several times.

Claire couldn't stop laughing. Tears burned in her eyes, and she loved them so much.

She loved them all so much.

Michael rescued Eve from a tissue paper war and towed her toward the door with his guitar case in the other hand. "I'm calling a truce," he said, and looked back at Claire from the door. "We'll come back after the show."

None of them were letting her stay the night alone; she got that. She supposed later, that might annoy her, but tonight, it just felt . . . great. She loved being looked after.

Then the door shut, and it was just her and Shane.

"So," she said. "What's on TV tonight?"

"Hockey."

"I'm pretty sure there's something other than hockey."

"Nope. Just hockey. It's on every channel. Better complain to the cable company." He kicked back in the chair and settled in with the remote.

"Jerk." She sighed. "I'm the one with low blood pressure, here. Shouldn't I get the remote?"

"I'm thoughtful. Look, I brought you a present." He pulled a wooden stake out of his pocket and put it next to her hand, on top of the blankets.

"What's this for?"

"Emergencies," he said. "Morganville emergencies."

She examined the stake. It looked like it might have been one of Eve's, at least originally. "I hate to break it to you, but Dean wasn't a vampire."

"Bet it would have worked good on him, too."

She spotted some writing on the side. "You put my name on it!" Hand-carved. That must have taken a while.

"I had time, sitting around here waiting for you to wake up. Anyway, Amelie just issued a new law. All humans are allowed to carry stakes for self-defense. See? Progress."

"Or mutually assured destruction."

"Well, whatever works."

Claire held up the stake. "Some girls get jewelry. But they're such losers."

He reached in his pocket, came out with a small velvet box, and set it next to her pillow. She took a deep, sudden breath, and felt her whole body go a little bit woozy around the edges.

"What is it?" she asked softly.

"It's . . . kind of for later," he said. "I just didn't want you to think I'm not well-rounded or anything."

He kissed her, and she felt everything melt away. All

the pain, the fear, the worry. It was all just going to be . . . okay.

Somewhere, Michael Glass was playing to a packed house at Common Grounds.

Amelie was sitting alone in her study.

Myrnin was writing down secrets in a leather-bound book.

Monica Morrell was sneering at a blushing freshman girl.

And Claire Danvers was . . . happy.

At least for tonight.

TRACK LIST

In celebration of reaching book six, I'd like to share with you a list of some songs that have kept me going through the writing process! As always, if you've got suggestions, I'd love to hear them (rachel@rachelcaine.com).

"Bridge to Better Days"	*Joe Bonamassa*
"Believe"	*The Bravery*
"Danger Is Here"	*Elliot Scott*
"The Geeks Were Right"	*The Faint*
"Sister Self Doubt"	*Get Shakes*
"Caravan" (DJ Smash's Smashish Remix)	*Dizzy Gillespie*
"Video"	*India.Arie*
"Hole in the Middle"	*Emily Jane White*
"Black Is the Color of My True Love's Hair" (Jaffa Remix)	*Nina Simone*
"Hell Yeah"	*Rev Theory*
"Count to Ten"	*Tina Dico*
"Silence" (DJ Tiesto's In Search of Sunrise Edit)	*Delerium and Sarah McLachlan*
"Let It Die"	*Foo Fighters*
"Get Free"	*The Vines*
"Violet Hill"	*Coldplay*
"Could've Had Me"	*Lex Land*
"Mercy"	*Duffy*
"Feeling Good"	*Nina Simone*
"Not Dead Yet"	*Ralph Covert and The Bad Examples*
"Burnin' Up"	*Jonas Brothers*
"Let It Rock"	*Kevin Rudolf and Lil Wayne*

"Disturbia" *Rihanna*
"Hot N Cold" *Katy Perry*
"Heavy on My Mind" *Back Door Slam*
"Guess Who" *Nekta*
"Now You Know" *We Are The Fury*
"What You Want" *Neva Dinova*
"Get Back" *Demi Lovato*
"Sacre Couer" (Live) *Tina Dico*
"Ghost Town" *Shiny Toy Guns*

Look for me on MySpace, Facebook, LiveJournal, and Twitter!
www.rachelcaine.com

About the Author

In addition to the Morganville Vampires series, **Rachel Caine** is the author of the popular Weather Warden series, which includes *Ill Wind*, *Heat Stroke*, *Chill Factor*, *Windfall*, *Firestorm*, *Thin Air*, and *Gale Force*. Her eighth Weather Warden novel, *Cape Storm*, will be released in August 2009. Rachel and her husband, fantasy artist R. Cat Conrad, live in Texas with their iguanas, Popeye and Darwin; a *mali uromastyx* named (appropriately) O'Malley; and a leopard tortoise named Shelley (for the poet, of course).

Please visit her Web site at www.rachelcaine.com and her MySpace, www.myspace.com/rachelcaine.

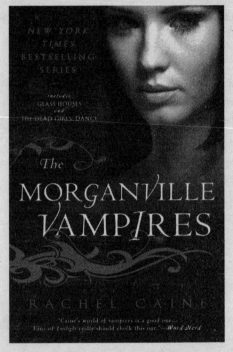